Murder in the Haunted House

A murder mystery and party play

by

Carolee Russell

Order this book online at www.trafford.com
or email orders@trafford.com

Most Trafford titles are also available at major online book retailers.

Illustrations by Carolee Russell

Printed in the United States of America.

ISBN: 978-1-4669-7521-7 (sc)
ISBN: 978-1-4669-7520-0 (e)

Trafford rev. 06/02/2014

 www.trafford.com

North America & international
toll-free: 1 888 232 4444 (USA & Canada)
fax: 812 355 4082

I dedicate this book
to my friends and neighbors in

Woodhaven Oaks, Wexford, Pa.,
who were the first brave souls
to experience my first play.

They gave splendid
performances.

PART ONE

THE STORY

CAST OF CHARACTERS

PHYLLIS STEIN. . . . . Widow of Frank N. Stein
DOMINIQUE DUMBELLI BALDWIN . . . . Phyllis' daughter from first marriage
RALPH BALDWIN . . . . Dominique's husband
RUBEN STEIN . . . . Phyllis and Frank's son
HELENE STEIN . . . . Ruben's wife
FRANCINE STEIN . . . . Phyllis and Frank's daughter
PRISCILLA PENNILESS . . . . Phyllis' next youngest sister
PAUL PENNILESS. . . . . Priscilla's only son
PRUDENCE PIREET. . . . . Phyllis & Priscilla's youngest sister
PRENTICE PIREET . . . . Prudence's new husband
CARLTON BRENNER . . . . Frank N. Stein's business partner
LILY BRENNER. . . . . Carlton's second wife
CHRISTIAN BRENNER. . . . . Carlton's son by his first wife
CASSANDRA BRENNER. . . . . Christian's twin sister
CHARITY BRENNER SVENSON . . . . Carlton's daughter by his first wife
PROFESSOR SVEN SVENSON. . . . . Charity's brand new husband
CALVIN BOOKER. . . . . Business Accountant
BONNIE BOOKER . . . . Calvin's wife
LANCE KNIGHT. . . . . Business and Personal Lawyer
HOLLY KNIGHT. . . . . Lance's wife
DR. ARTHUR HART . . . . Family Doctor
AMANDA HART . . . . Arthur's wife and Phyllis' dear friend
FLORENCE CURTAIN. . . . . Phyllis's nurse
WILLARD HEMLOCK. . . . . Frank and Carlton's college friend
MADAM ANGELICA . . . . Séance Conductor and Medium
HUGO HANDY . . . . Madam Angelica's Bodyguard and Chauffeur
CONRAD DIDDIT. . . . . Family Butler
CAMILLE LEON . . . . Network News Reporter or Maid (Hostess)
JOE PHOENIX . . . . Bartender
FRANK'S SPIRIT . . . . Séance Spirit
INSPECTOR CLOQUE JOUSEAU . . . . Police Inspector (Host)

TABLE OF CONTENTS

"ONE YEAR AGO TODAY, CHEMICAL MANUFACTURER FRANK N. STEIN TRAGICALLY PERISHED IN AN EXPLOSION AND INTENSE FIRE WHICH DESTROYED THE RESEARCH WING OF THE STEIN-BRENNER CHEMICAL PLANT"

Such was the headline of the *Lightning Gazette*. Phyllis Stein did not need to be reminded of the gruesome, painful details of her husband's death. A year had not been enough time for her to recover from the horrifying shock and devastating loss of her dear husband. Unable to cope, she sank deeper into depression, alienating herself from family and friends, and becoming emotionally and physically drained to a point of threatening her health. The only people she could turn to for consolation and understanding, it seemed, were her youngest daughter, Francine, who was a soothing comfort to her during this tragic time, and Madam Angelica, a mystic of some note, whom Phyllis met shortly after her husband's demise. It was Madam Angelica who had given Phyllis hope . . . hope of making contact with Frank's spirit in the Other World . . . hope of speaking with him and hearing his comforting words . . . hope of sorting out the confusion of her life . . . HOPE in the form of a SEANCE!

*

Frank had not been her only husband nor she his only wife. Her first husband was billionaire Arnold Dumbelli of the Madison Avenue Dumbelli's Training Pants fortune, who had died suddenly in a yachting accident less than a year after they were married. Since his body was never recovered, a Memorial Service was held at the spot where Arnold's boat capsized in Long Island Sound. That marriage had made Phyllis a rich widow and had produced a healthy baby girl, Dominique. But because of Phyllis' immaturity and insecurity, neither brought her any joy.

Her second marriage to Bruce Brassiere, heir to the Itty Bitty Titty Brassiere fortune, was equally disconcerting and ended in a "hushed" annulment due to irreconcilable "likenesses" . . . both preferred the company of women in the afternoons and men in the evenings. The family managed to keep the scandal from the newspapers and made it monetarily worth her while to cooperate in this. Bruce was too wrapped up in the family business to put up much resistance. It comes as no surprise that there were no children from this marriage.

Then she met Frank! He was tall and handsome and full of enthusiasm about his future plans in the chemical research/manufacturing field. His easy charm and flashing smile just melted her heart. His first marriage to his college sweetheart had ended in a bitter, ugly divorce only a year before he met Phyllis. The legal entanglements had left him penniless, without a job and worse . . . without his young son to whom he had been devoted. His ex-wife had disappeared after the divorce taking the boy with her and all efforts to find them had failed. Frank was just getting his life together after the divorce and contemplating starting a chemical company with his college buddy, Carlton Brenner, when he met Phyllis. It was love at first "site" . . . since they both were in the Fairwinds Real Estate Office looking over property. They merged. With Phyllis' financial backing, Frank was able to join Carl in building a chemical research/manufacturing empire. Frank and Phyllis' long marriage had seemed all peaks and few valleys and produced a son, Ruben, and a daughter, Francine. It was a blissful union with staggering financial and social success.

And then the fire . . .

CHAPTER I—PHYLLIS STEIN

"Lan' sakes, Mizz Phyllis! Dem guests gon' be here any minute and here you is not a bit presentable. Dis be yo' big night. You should be real 'cited, not lyin' there lookin' so glum. You get up from there this minute and sit here at the mirror whilst I comb yo' hair. Dat'll make yo' feel better."

"Oh, Camille, I know you're right. But I'm just so very tired and, quite frankly, very afraid this evening will not be successful. If it isn't, I think I shall give up entirely," said Phyllis as she closed the manila folder holding many news articles about the fire all frayed and thin from constant reading.

"Now, don' yo' go sayin' such nonsense. I cain't say as I knows much 'bout séances an' such, but I do know yo' is a good lady an' yo' deserves good to be don' 'er. Yo' jus' have to have faith an' hope. Now set yo' here whilst I do up yo' hair."

Phyllis rose from the large four-poster, absently brushing the wrinkles from her slip as she slowly made her way across the rich brocade carpet to the ornate dressing table. Camille was busy arranging the combs and brushes and assortment of hairpin decorations which Phyllis was fond of wearing in her long coiled hair. The once burnished gold crown of scrupulously tidy thick hair was now dull with gray, shockingly thin and often unkempt. Once a person of meticulous personal hygiene, Phyllis now had to be pushed and coaxed through this daily routine.

As she glanced around at the rich and elaborate furnishings adorning her bedroom, her thoughts rocketed back to her meager childhood. Her uneducated and unskilled parents worked hard at any thankless job they were lucky to get—sometimes two—just to make ends meet. Her mother had worked at the local diner in town. It was a long walk home on cold nights. Her father did odd jobs around town, sometimes pumping gas at Danny's Garage or delivering groceries from Harper's Hometown Market. His longest continuous job was as janitor for Township Elementary School until his drinking got bad. Phyllis remembered he had had a paper route about that same time, which she often had to do for him. She had gotten quite used to covering for him just so he wouldn't lose the job.

As Phyllis was the oldest, it was her job to take care of her younger sisters, Priscilla and Prudence. She was sure they resented it as much as she had. They saw their parents so little it was almost like not having parents at all. And when they were around they were either too tired or, in her father's case, too intoxicated. And when he was in that state, it was best to be out of the house.

Her school mates thought she was a bit shy but actually she didn't talk much because she really didn't have much to say that she thought anyone wanted to hear. Inviting a friend home was out of the question. However, her ready smile and complacent nature made her a comfortable person to be around, which meant she had a lot of friends. But because of her home chores and family responsibilities, she had few chances to socialize with her friends outside of school. Some thought her quietness meant she was smart but that couldn't be further from the truth. She considered herself to be of average intelligence but her social skills had never developed because of a severe inferiority complex. Add that to the fact that she was born under the sign of Libra, which meant she could never make a decisive decision.

That warm spring Saturday night was now vivid in her memory. The night her mother was off work because of a deep cut in her hand, her dad was setting pins at White's Bowling Alley, Priscilla was sleeping over with a friend and Prudence was working on one of her school projects, so Phyllis was free to go out with her friends to the community dance held once a month in the Empress Hotel Ballroom. That's when she met Arnold Dumbelli and her life changed forever.

Arnold was in town on business and was staying at the Empress Hotel. He told her he had passed the ballroom doors and was *mesmerized by a heavenly vision gliding on the dance floor*. She didn't realize at first that he meant her. That thought provoked a slight grimace at her relentless naiveté. He was handsome, lively and adored her and she was completely swept off her feet.

The day she graduated high school, she and Arnold married at his parents' estate on Long Island. She was 17 and he was 30. His mother had planned the whole affair without asking Phyllis even one question. Phyllis thought, therefore, that was the reason she neglected to invite her family to the wedding. On her cloud nothing mattered . . . she was free . . . and now very rich.

As happy as the marriage had begun, most of that year was lost in a fog. The joy of having her first child, a daughter she named Dominique, certainly stood out, but Arnold's tragic and mysterious death in a boating accident left her dazed and defeated. Yes, but not as devastating as Frank's death had been to her.

The thought of Frank, as well as Camille's voice, broke her reverie. "Yo' be lollygaggin' again, Mizz Phyllis. Hurry, now, ever'thin' be ready."

Her bubble of memories broken, Phyllis hurried her step. As she seated herself at the dressing table, the door burst open causing Phyllis to jump so violently she knocked all the hair implements off the dressing table where Camille had so neatly arranged them.

CHAPTER II—PRISCILLA PENNILESS

"What's this! Phyllis! You haven't begun to get ready and you know your guests will be here any minute. Why, the doc and his wife are here already and here you are putzzin' around. What *are* you thinking? Isn't this the night you've been waiting for and talking about for so long? Where's all that enthusiasm you displayed yesterday?" stormed Priscilla.

"Here . . . Camille . . . give me those things and you go downstairs and see that everything is ready down there. I'll take care of getting Phyllis dressed. Go . . . GO, girl!"

Camille obediently left the room muttering under her breath, "What I have to do downstair? She done did ever'thin' herself ten time since breakfuss!"

As Camille quietly closed the door, still muttering under her breath, Phyllis' sister Priscilla was already brushing out Phyllis' hair with a tirade of expletives. Although a rather large woman, Priscilla has complete control of her space like thunder and lightning.

She is several years younger than Phyllis but a hundred times less fortunate in life's fateful choices. She is all things that Phyllis is not: strong-willed, domineering, organized, quick-minded, stern, calculating and POOR.

Priscilla and her sisters—Phyllis the oldest and Prudence the youngest—came from a lower class family who struggled for their existence, facing many hard challenges. Phyllis managed to cross paths with husbands of fortune, except Frank had needed a little of Phyllis' money to become successful, but successful nonetheless. Priscilla started out lower class and managed to marry beneath her.

Priscilla was only thirteen when her sister, Phyllis, made her first rich conquest and married Arnold Dumbelli, of the Madison Avenue Dumbelli's Training Pants fortune, but she was not too young for the envy to begin.

Arnold's sudden death, barely a year into the marriage, did stir sympathy in Priscilla but she never could understand why Phyllis could be so unhappy with all that money and a beautiful baby daughter too.

She remembered vividly the day Phyllis left for her wedding on Long Island. The shiny black car, nearly as long as the width of their house, had pulled up in front and a man in uniform got out and helped Phyllis disappear into its inky depths. She would never forget the heartache she felt at Phyllis leaving her. She had stared in its wake long after it had disappeared around a corner several blocks down the street. And when she finally turned to go back into the house she called home, she had felt the deepest fear she would ever know. It was then that she discovered courage.

She remembered, too, the day not even six months after Arnold died that Phyllis had married Bruce Brassiere heir to the Itty Bitty Titty Brassiere fortune and thought how unfair that such happiness had not blessed her. Of course, when that marriage turned out such a mess, although it made Phyllis even richer, she couldn't help being a bit gratified. But, how could Phyllis not know Bruce was gay? That's when Priscilla stopped envying Phyllis and started pitying her, realizing she couldn't possibly take care of herself properly and was totally at the mercy of life's pitfalls.

Although Phyllis' first two marriages made her rich, they did not make her happy. The marriages did one thing for Phyllis that Priscilla admired most . . . allowed her to escape from an even more unhappy life with her family. And that is the excuse Priscilla used when she ran off at age sixteen and married a sailor she barely knew. As it turned out, she jumped from the frying pan into the fire, so to speak. But she never once complained about the beatings, the drunken rages, the verbal abuses and her having to be the breadwinner because he gave her the pride of her life—her son, Paul. Soon after Paul's birth, her husband beat her one last time, shouted words only sailors knew, and then went after the infant. That was unacceptable. She reacted instantly like a tiger protecting her cubs and nearly killed him. That night, he took all the money and anything of any value and left never to come back. She shed no tears, but that's when her life began.

Phyllis' marriage to Frank was the match Priscilla had hoped her sister would be fortunate to find and she did envy her for that bit of luck. No longer would Priscilla have to worry about her weaker sister because she knew Frank would take care of her forever. And so it was for all these many years until forever ended last year in a blaze of fire.

Priscilla wasted no time in packing up everything she owned and moving into Phyllis' mansion taking on the unsolicited full time job of caretaker of both the house and her sister. Although everyone else was aghast and not happy with the arrangement, Phyllis could hardly object and was very generous financially. Naturally, Paul moved in as well.

Priscilla earned her keep. She was not a slacker but ran the household with an iron fist, much to the chagrin of the servants. Phyllis' children also felt her domineering attempts. Francine tolerated her aunt's interference because she realized her mother needed Priscilla, but the other children couldn't complain enough.

Priscilla was never deterred because she not only wanted desperately to experience some of the opulent life her sister had enjoyed for so long, but also because she truly loved Phyllis and wanted to care for her as she had cared for Priscilla from infancy.

"There, now, that's a masterpiece, if I must say so myself," Priscilla said as she gave Phyllis' elegant coiffure a few last pats. "Makeup looks passable although you are still so pale, my dear sister. You need some color." Priscilla added some light pink rouge with little resistance from her sister. "Now for the dress."

"Over there," Phyllis said, as she pointed toward the huge walk-in closet. "Camille has already pulled out the black satin suit."

"Black!" exclaimed Priscilla, "Heavens no! No more black. It has been a year since Frank died. When are you going to put that business behind you?"

"Sister, please, I can't . . . not just yet. Maybe if the séance . . ."

"Right. The séance," Priscilla said with a slight edge in her voice as she turned away so her face would not betray her true feelings. "But you are NOT wearing black! Let's compromise," she said, condescendingly, "with the navy silk Armani. Wasn't that Frank's favorite?" she added in a conciliatory effort.

Before Phyllis could object, Priscilla had the dress in hand and was helping her into it. Minutes later the diamond and sapphire necklace and earrings were in place, shoes on, and Priscilla was coaxing her forcefully out the door onto the landing.

CHAPTER III—FLORENCE CURTAIN

Florence was halfway up the wide carpeted staircase, the focal point of the huge entrance hall, when she saw Priscilla guiding Phyllis along the top hallway to the stairs.

"Thank heavens, there you are. You had Arthur and me sick with worry that something had happened to you. Are you all right? Arthur wants to see you immediately," Florence said practically in one breath. She hurried up the remainder of the stairs to give the impression she intended to assist, knowing full well any efforts along those lines would be thwarted by Priscilla.

Phyllis had sunk into such a deep depression after Frank was consumed in the chemical plant fire a year ago that her doctor, Arthur Hart, had insisted she retain a live-in nurse. Ten months ago, nurse Florence Curtain was hired to fill that position. From the very first day, she regretted accepting the job. How is she expected to do her job and hold onto her respectability with that *animal* Priscilla constantly sparring with her and countering her every move? If Phyllis' daughter, Francine, hadn't been there every evening to smooth her feathers and commiserate with her, she would have left long ago and would now be in a more rewarding position, albeit less financially attractive. Her only hope now is that the men in white coats will come soon and take Phyllis away to a place people can do her some good. This séance tonight might just turn out to be a *moving* experience.

By the time Florence reached Phyllis, who gave her a weak salutation, Priscilla had positioned herself to parry any helpful attempt, so Florence gritted her teeth and followed them down the stairs where Dr. Arthur Hart was waiting anxiously.

CHAPTER IV—ARTHUR HART

"My dear Phyllis . . . I fear I have worn a path in your carpet anticipating this moment. I am an old man. Would it not have been kinder to me and your rug had you sent word of your situation?" said Arthur Hart in a clearly affected stern voice. He knew Phyllis too long to be seriously angry with her but such a friendship could not deny serious concern for her welfare.

"Please, Arthur, forgive me for worrying you. I am fine. Really I am. Priscilla has taken good care of me as usual. But you are right, I should have sent word to you that I was detained," Phyllis said, apologetically.

"Arthur!" Priscilla interjected, "After all these months, surely I have earned your trust and confidence in my ability to care for my sister. You worry yourself needlessly."

"Not needlessly," rebutted Arthur, "as I acknowledge the competence of nurse Florence as well as yourself. But, I am also aware of the additional stress that Phyllis must be under in anticipation of this séance. Come into the library, Phyllis, to humor an old doctor and let me check your vitals. Florence would you mind joining us? Priscilla, isn't there something that needs tending to?" With that, the three of them disappeared into the library and closed the door on Priscilla whose mouth was open with an argument caught in her throat. Pausing in stunned disbelief, she finally snapped her mouth closed, grimaced angrily, raised her head haughtily, gave a sniff, turned and stomped off in a huff looking for some poor soul to harangue.

Arthur has been the friend and family doctor of both the Stein and Brenner families since Frank and Phyllis needed a blood test in order to marry. He not only delivered both son Ruben and daughter Francine but he and his wife, Amanda, stood as Godparents for both children. Amanda is her closest friend and both served on many charity boards together over the years and joined nearly every women's club in the area. Doctor, yes, but their friendship was more dear.

He took Frank's death especially hard, mostly because of the nature of the incident. No one knew how the fire began, but because the plant was full of highly flammable chemicals the fire was so intense that everything was reduced to ashes. Not even a bone fragment could be recovered for burial.

Frank's horrible death was so devastating to Phyllis that Arthur was seriously concerned about her health . . . mental as well as physical. A year had done nothing to alleviate her depression. He had to admit that Priscilla's presence was a godsend despite her abrasive dominant nature. She certainly took all the day-to-day stress of running the household and making decisions off Phyllis' shoulders; well, off everyone's shoulders, actually. And he conceded she was good to her sister . . . almost gentle for Priscilla. Even so, he could never like her.

He had hoped that by sending Florence to take care of Phyllis' health needs, her sister would have less influence on her. Regretfully, what he inadvertently created was a competitive battleground. Thank goodness for Francine who had an inherent knack for diffusing most potentially explosive situations.

What he fears most is Phyllis' obsession with that Madam Angelica person who has somehow mesmerized her with some sort of spell. Silly thinking, of course, but Phyllis is completely susceptible to most any suggestion, especially in her state of mind.

Arthur does not believe in spirits . . . unless they are the liquid kind . . . and he certainly has no doubts this séance is a complete phony. But Phyllis would not be deterred. So, like it or not, everyone has gone along with this *dangerous* show.

He knows Phyllis is not very quick-minded, especially now in her delicate mental state, but, still, he thought, Angelica would surely have to pull off the biggest miracle of the century to sell this act. He shuddered to think what Phyllis would do if she saw through the ruse. All he can do is be here for her and prepare her medically the best he knows how.

As Florence escorted Phyllis to a nearby chair, Arthur set his bag on a table and rummaged through it for his stethoscope.

"Dear Arthur! I told you I am fine. A bit tired, perhaps, as I have been having trouble sleeping and that is because I am so anxious to see and talk to my dear Frank tonight," Phyllis said, breathing hard. "I know you are concerned, but really, there is nothing wrong with me."

"Let me be the judge of that," he said, with the utmost softness in his eyes. "The anxiousness you speak of is *stress*. I have warned you before that stress is a silent devil. Let me take a listen to see what there is to hear."

After some minutes, Arthur seemed satisfied with the exam, removed the stethoscope from his ears and returned to rummage again in his bag while directing Florence to take Phyllis' blood pressure.

Arthur turned to face Phyllis and settled his frame against the table for support. "The results of this cursory exam are not as alarming as I had expected, but they do concern me. Your blood pressure is higher than I would like and your heart is working too hard." He paused, stood and approached her holding out his hand. He took her hand and placed two small pills on her palm. "I want you to avoid all stress but I understand that would be impossible tonight," he said as he gave a signal to Florence, who turned and retrieved a glass of water from the sideboard. "So, my only choice is to try to diffuse the stress a bit."

Phyllis looked down at the pills and understood the plan. Accepting the glass from Florence, she downed the pills without question. She raised her head seeking Arthur's eyes which were smiling gently and compassionately down at her. "Thank you, Arthur." She turned, "Thank you, Florence." She turned back and smiled up at Arthur, "I'm certain, now, to get through this ordeal calmly. That is your plan is it not, my dear friend?"

Arthur nodded and returned her smile as he offered his hand as Phyllis rose to her feet and the three of them left the room.

CHAPTER V—BUTLER CONRAD DIDDIT

Phyllis no sooner stepped out of the room and into the downstairs hall when Conrad was at her side with concerns of his own.

"Madam, if you please," he said, nearly out of breath, "If you don't do something about her, the entire staff will walk out. I'm certain of it this time."

"Conrad, whatever are you talking about. You aren't making sense," Phyllis retorted, bewildered.

"It's your sister, Madam. She is criticizing the staff and trying to change all the preparations the staff has worked on all day. And guests are already arriving. Won't you speak to her?" he pleaded.

"Allow me, Phyllis," Arthur interrupted, as he handed his medical bag to Conrad for safe-keeping. "I believe I can handle this . . . or die trying. If you notice people stepping over my prone body, please call the paramedics," he joked. No one of the three found him amusing but gratefully allowed him to proceed to his doom.

Conrad turned to Phyllis and assured her as convincingly as he could manage that he was certain that the doc could handle Priscilla and that the evening would be saved. If it weren't for two little pills, Phyllis would not have missed detecting the anxious doubt in the butler's strained eyes. On the other hand, Florence missed nothing. With a wink to Conrad, she slipped her arm through Phyllis' and guided her into the grand salon leaving Conrad alone with a desperate expression on his face.

Conrad had been butler to the Steins since they moved into this magnificent mansion many years ago. Francine was still in diapers then. He remembered how very fortunate he had felt when Frank had offered him the position and proceeded to celebrate the appointment by offering him a brandy. From that day on he was not only the best butler he knew how to be, and the most loyal, but he and Frank had become great friends. He was Frank's greatest confidante which was, as propriety would require, not evident to anyone outside their society of two.

Conrad had learned his trade in England under the tutelage of his maternal grandfather who was once butler to the Duke of Gloucester. Conrad's English mother had fallen in love with an American flyer assigned to the RAF. Months after their relationship began, he was killed in action over Germany and his body never recovered. She was left with an infant on the way and no marriage license. The circumstances being what they were in England at the time, her parents were very sympathetic to her situation and could not turn her away. When Conrad came along, he gave their lives a new purpose and when his mother was killed in a bombing raid only months after he was born, his grandparents took solace in the child. Three decades later when illness took their lives, Conrad came to the United States and fortunately crossed paths with Frank and Phyllis.

Life had been good to him . . . until he lost his best friend in a most bizarre and horrifying fire so intense that there was nothing left to identify. He understood what his mother must have gone through when his father had died because he had had a difficult time coming to terms with the death of his best friend with nothing physical to grieve over.

This year had been hell for Conrad. Every day was a challenge to keep himself together for the family he cared for as if they were his own. But so much has happened this year that he feels his sanity is in serious jeopardy. How is he ever going to manage to get through this evening, he thought, as his forehead sprouted new and deeper lines.

"I must! And I will!," he said aloud without realizing he had done so.

The doorbell rang.

CHAPTER VI—DOMINIQUE . . . BALDWIN

The sound of the doorbell released Conrad's transfixed body and mind causing him to blink several times and slowly focus on the reality of his surroundings. The bell had rung several times before Conrad had composed himself enough to reach the door.

"Dear Conrad! It's so good to see you again. How's mother? Is she still going through with this charade of a séance? I must see her. Where is she?"

Conrad's back stiffened as he recognized the familiar voice. "Good evening Miss Dominique . . . Mr. Ralph. It is good of you to come and show your support. This séance means quite a bit to your mother, madam. I hope I am not out of line in suggesting a bit of caution in conversing on such a subject with Miss Phyllis. Dr. Hart is very concerned about her health already and the evening is quite young," interjected Conrad. He fully expected her not to take his advice but he didn't expect what happened next.

"Conrad!" she exclaimed in a loud angry voice. "How *dare* you insinuate I do not have my mother's best interests at heart or that I would ever put her in harms way. I am her first born daughter . . . her flesh and blood. How could you think I could possibly do or say anything to upset her?" Her voice was rising with each declaration and her face was turning deeper shades of red with each inhalation. "You are just a hired butler! You have no business advising *me* on how I should relate to *my own mother!*"

Conrad had taken several steps backward in response to Dominique's advance toward him as she continued her tirade. He hit the wall with Dominique mere feet from him when Ralph Baldwin, Dominique's husband, caught up with her. Hooking his arm around her waist, he gently spun her off course as he calmly spoke, "My sweet! The wind has mussed your hair a bit. I know you'll want to repair the damage before you see your mother. I'll help you up to the lounge." As quickly as the attack had begun, it was over, forgotten by Dominique and replaced by a new all-consuming quest.

"How does he do that with her?" Conrad murmured under his breath, as he shook his head peering after them in astonishment as Ralph guided Dominique up the staircase continuing to speak softly to her. Conrad could not hear the conversation but it was obvious he was in control and had her complete attention.

Dominique was perhaps ten, Conrad recalled, when she and her family had moved into this house. Conrad, himself, had been hired on shortly after. Although he did not know much about her life before that event, he was an excellent witness to her actions within his environment in years that followed.

He was no psychologist, but that woman needed help. That didn't mean he had no compassion for her situation. He believed he understood the basic conflicts that were ruining her life. Frank had known, too. In fact, they had discussed Dominique on many occasions. However, despite Frank's seemingly complete control over Phyllis, he could never seem to convince her that she was responsible for Dominique's desperately unstable mental condition.

Neither Conrad nor Frank, nor anyone else for that matter as far as he knew, really had any idea what Phyllis had experienced before she met Frank. Of course, it was common knowledge who her parents were and her marriages and divorces were public record, but she never shared with anyone how she handled those years emotionally. Conrad honestly believed she had long ago sealed those years away in a separate unattainable place in her memories. They were forever dark to her so it was impossible for her to realize that she had in fact shut Dominique out of her heart or even understand why. Frank called this her only flaw.

The tragedy in the relationship between Dominique and her mother was that Dominique believed that her mother was perfect, totally flawless and faultless. So the fault had to be hers and the burden to find salvation in her mother's eyes totally consumed her. Her life had little room for anything else except ultimately achieving the specific comportment to deserve her mother's love. It was apparent to Conrad that Phyllis was completely unaware of her daughter's emptiness and obsession let alone that she, herself, could in any way, past or present, be responsible for it.

Dominique reviewed her reflection in the mirror, tucked a few more stray hairs into their proper places and sighed at the results. The scene from downstairs only moments ago wasn't even a wisp of a memory. The frustration that had prompted such behavior had melted into the despair with which she was most familiar. The huge emptiness within her was accompanied by an equal amount of desire for something unidentifiable and, subsequently, unattainable.

There was a time, shortly after her mother had met and married Frank, when all the unnamed demons overloaded her fragile psyche. Even now, so many years later, she would have flashback memories of those summer months she spent in the *special home* where Doctor Dorothy helped her find her way back. Of course, the doctors all tried to convince her that her mother's neglect during her younger years was the root of her miseries. They wanted her to believe that so she let them think they had done their job; but she could never believe that. Dominique could accept nothing else except that *she* had failed her mother in some way. She just needed to find that one special thing that would make her mother approve of her and then the emptiness would disappear and her mother would *love her.*

Her life was a quest to find that one elusive thing.

All her life, she had never truly experienced *love,* therefore, Dominique had never learned to recognize love in any form. Even the love she purported to have for her mother was not love at all, but a mixture of jealousy, obsession and irrational focus with a compelling desire to share in normal relationships.

Her marriages, too, were acts of desperation to love and be loved. On the outside, Dominique was not an unattractive woman. Believing her mother held all things beautiful in high regard, personal appearance was number one on her list of necessary achievements. Anything less than *best* risked displeasing her mother. With her own considerable fortune inherited from her father, money was no object in achieving such perfection.

It was not difficult for men to fall in love with her. She had beauty as well as a hint of a schoolgirl's innocence mixed with curiosity. However, usually after just a few short months in a marriage, the ugliness within would show and erode the relationship quickly. Since Dominique did not really understand love, a broken relationship did not affect her heart . . . but it did affect her head. It meant another failure . . . another rejection.

Then a miracle happened. Ralph came into her life.

CHAPTER VII—RALPH BALDWIN

Ralph Baldwin is just an ordinary, unremarkable looking man who could easily have been the inspiration for the song "Mr. Cellophane". People often walk right into him and are astonished to find him in their way. Ralph is very comfortable in his skin and takes life as he finds it, always with an abundance of humor and patience.

He has acquaintances but no real close friends. Before he met Dominique, his social life consisted of going to the Moose Club every Friday night for a couple of beers. On the other nights of the week he stayed home with his parents and watched TV or read a book. He could easily be mistaken for a rather dull and stupid man as he rarely makes conversation. Although he is unimposing and content with a *sideline* life, he is well educated, well read and intuitive. He is always watching and learning; not much gets past his observing eyes.

He isn't especially ambitious, either, for he is quite happy with the modest life. His parents had started their own local furniture moving business which brought in a comfortable living. As is normal with father and sons in small business, Ralph's father brought him into the business so that someday he could retire and hand over the reins to his son. Soon after the partnership, Ralph noticed there was a need for specialized moving of critical and sensitive pieces, like, valuable antiques and pianos. Since the Baldwin Family Furniture Movers were just about the only movers that could offer such specialized care, their services were in demand. As is Ralph's way, he can't help seeing the irony in being a mover of pianos when he can't even carry a tune.

So that's how Ralph came to be the one who delivered the new baby grand piano to the home of recently divorced Dominique Dumbelli Johansson O'Reilly Schwartz Gonzales Wellington Subaru Gundermann Chang Polanski Jones. It was fortunate that the family lawyer, Lance Knight, had been present to advise her to demand a prenuptial agreement before each marriage.

Ralph was in the moving business but rarely was he ever moved himself. There was something about Dominique that touched his heart and cleared his mind. Yes, she was attractive to look at but he had seen many beautiful woman. Her dizzy, frantic behavior when the piano arrived and she had to make a decision as to where to put it would have turned off most ordinary men. But Ralph was not the ordinary man people mistook him for. There was something fragile about her; fragile and innocent but somehow desperate and helpless. Those qualities touched him in such a way that he was overcome by some kind of an epiphany. He realized his purpose in life was to rescue this soul, love her and care for her, and ease her pain. His life had purpose stronger than any drug addiction.

It took five months of slow but persistent pursuit in such an off-handed style that the erosion of Dominique's defenses was totally complete and her awareness of his plan was never suspected. For the first time in her life she felt completely relaxed and comfortable with another human being. It was like taking a "feel good" tonic just being near him. Oh, she still had her tantrums but he was always able to calm her and make her forget. It was remarkable, she thought, how this plain, unassuming man had such power over her. Could this feeling she had for him be . . . *love?*

Dominique heard a soft knock, and through the mirror she saw a familiar smiling face peering at her from the doorway.

"Are you ready now to go down and see your mother and her guests? You are beautiful. I feel I must defend your honor with every man here tonight," Ralph declared with all the romantic flourish of King Arthur's era.

Dominique blushed, an ability she hadn't know she possessed until Ralph unlocked her spirit. "I suspect it is not my honor you must defend but me from myself," she countered, worriedly. "Shall we face the throng?"

CHAPTER VIII—FRANCINE STEIN

"There you are, dear sister. Conrad informed me you were here. Where have you been? I expected you long ago," said Francine as she rushed toward them and gave each a quick hug and peck on the cheek. Francine felt the familiar stiffness in her sister but ignored it and went on with her generic chattering.

"Has mother asked about me, then?" Dominique interrupted with a challenging edge in her voice.

"What? Oh, yes, mother. Of course, she's been asking about you," she said. Well, she hadn't actually *heard* her mother ask about Dominique but surely she had thought about it, Francine thought. "Everyone is wondering where you are. Come in and greet everyone. Naturally, Ruben's not here yet."

Francine, Frank and Phyllis' youngest child, is the most well adjusted of Phyllis' three children and no question her favorite. Dominique was naturally insanely jealous of her because Francine got all her mother's attention . . . all the attention Dominique thought she, herself, deserved. Ruben, on the other hand, had no issues with Francine where his mother was concerned. But he had had a problem with the attention his father had given her.

Anyone would be jealous of Francine because she was smart, extremely attractive, young, stylish and full of self-confidence. Fresh out of college, she started immediately taking over her father's management duties at the plant. The new research wing was still under construction but there was much to learn about the business to keep her busy. But she was certainly every bit up to the task.

For the past five months, with the guidance and assistance of their family lawyer, Lance Knight, Francine has been going over the financial ledgers, patents, contracts and other legal papers to learn all she could about the business so she could serve the Stein family interests in the business her father built with his college friend, Carlton Brenner.

Frank's expertise had been strictly in research and development, while Carl handled the manufacturing and marketing. That arrangement had worked well for twenty-five years and was financially very successful. Her father's Will as well as a Partnership Agreement had provided a stipulation that on the death of Frank, Francine would become his replacement and sole caretaker of the family's interests in the half of the partnership that once belonged to Frank. And Francine was certainly up for the challenge and fully capable of handling whatever she encountered.

As it has turned out, the business part was not a problem. The problems arose from the people around her, starting with her own family.

Obviously, Dominique and Ruben had issues with her purely out of jealousy and envy. Her mother was an entirely different story. She loved her mother intensely but without her father's kindly care and management, her mother now relied on her for her major support and consolation. Besides her mother claiming her attention, there was Aunt Priscilla trying to run everything and everybody, and nurse Florence who was in constant conflict with Priscilla over jurisdiction over her mother. And the servants were threatening to quit every day. Francine was getting very good at smoothing ruffled feathers but with trying to learn the business, she had little time or energy for anything else a young healthy woman might enjoy. Which reminded her of her jerk of a cousin, Paul, who hound-dogged her at every opportunity.

Despite all the confusion and petty bickering, there was only two things that really concerned her . . . her mother's health, especially as it related to her obsession with Madam Angelica and this Séance . . . and *uncle* Carl, her father's partner.

The only one she could talk to about such concerns was Lance Knight. Lance had been their personal lawyer and the company's lawyer since he graduated law school ten years ago. He understood the territory and would listen and give her excellent advice.

One gift she thought she possessed was an innate sense of *bad vibes*. She could tell, for instance, that Dr. and Mrs. Hart were excellent people who were incapable of doing harm to anyone or anything. And her sister's husband, Ralph, did not have an unkind bone in his body and was a miracle find for her sister. Lance, of course, regardless of what people say about lawyers, could be trusted, explicitly.

Her sister, bless her heart, was not inherently a bad person but circumstances while growing up had made her resentful and envious but she couldn't imagine her doing anything *bad*. Francine believed her brother was a product of bad parenting as well. Although her father was a wonderfully kind and honest man who could be trusted with one's life, he was overly demanding when it came to his only son, Ruben. That was natural, she supposed, since her father had such high expectations for Ruben to be like himself. Ruben, however, was nothing like his father and the pressure to perform at a level so much higher than Ruben was capable, broke his spirit and turned him into an angry, hateful drunk. Regardless, she didn't see him as an *evil* person but she could imagine him making bad choices.

Conrad had generally given off good vibes all the years she had known him, which was nearly all her life. She knew he had been her father's closest confidant and friend although the appearance was one of employee and employer. But there were times recently she had sensed that Conrad was not totally truthful with her. Not that he blatantly lied but she felt sometimes that he didn't tell her the entire truth. She rationalized it was probably because, in his position, he had the confidentiality of the other servants to protect.

She admitted to herself that she didn't like her cousin, Paul, not only because he was an unwanted nuisance, but she didn't feel he was the innocent sort. She felt he could be capable of more than petty crimes, which were evil enough, actually.

Her sister-in-law, Helene, was certainly someone to watch closely. Her father had told her that when she married Ruben. Her ambitions made her capable of anything, if she thought she could get away with it.

Madam Angelica had a frightfully troublesome aura about her from the moment they were introduced. She remembered shaking the proffered hand in introduction and the cold, clammy hand sent chills down her spine. She had heard the bells and whistles going off but her mother had not. Instead, her mother had given her heart and her hopes completely and irrevocably to this woman. Francine had hired a private detective hoping to find some evidence of illegal activities, but there was very little information to be found before Angelica had entered their lives, which was, in itself, a *red flag*. Outwardly, Angelica was sweet and most convincing in her craft. Francine was just waiting for the hammer to drop. Could it be tonight?

She could honestly say that Calvin Booker, the company controller, known also as the *bookkeeper*, had no discernable evil vibes about him. But she could sense there was something wrong in his life. No doubt he regretted his choice of an ex-showgirl as a wife. Bonnie wasn't a bad person, really, but she was proof that one couldn't make a silk purse out of a sow's ear. She was an embarrassment at any gathering but Francine always enjoyed the show.

Willard Hemlock was a . . . well, there was no other word for him but *creep!* Francine could never understand why her father and Carl ever allowed him to be a part of the company. Thank God he had quit after the fire which seemed kind of suspicious to her. There was absolutely nothing honest and decent in the man. He made her skin crawl and here he was trying to date her mother . . . for her money, no doubt. As long as she was alive, there was no chance in hell he would ever be her step-father.

Uncle Carl was the hard case. The Brenners were like part of her own family. Her father and Carl were best of friends from college days. He must have had complete trust in him to go into business with him . . . a business that lasted nearly three decades. But to her there was just something off kilter with the man. The vibes were unclear but she had to conclude there was something dark and sinister about Carl. She never could discover the real truth of what happened to his first wife, Elizabeth. And Lily's make-up didn't quite cover the bruises it was meant to hide. Yes, he must be a bad man but to what extent his evil could go, she couldn't offer a guess.

So . . . the gauntlet was waiting. She felt as though she were going into battle, and perhaps in some ways she was. She certainly didn't believe in ghosts so this séance was certainly a sham. But her mother was completely rooted in the belief that she would be able to contact Frank and actually speak to him. Oh, how she wished it *was* possible because she would dearly love to have such a conversation with her father right about now. But, there was no way to deter her mother from going through with this séance, so she had stopped trying and turned simply to cautioning her to accept the possibility of an outcome that wasn't as predicted by Madam Angelica. Francine had decided earlier that day to ignore all the petty squabbles and devote all her efforts in protecting and comforting her mother. Just how she was going to accomplish that she didn't know.

Francine, in an effort to demonstrate sisterly love and respect, linked her arm with Dominique's and with Ralph following behind, they literally *marched* into the salon.

CHAPTER IX—WILLARD HEMLOCK

The first person they encountered was Willard Hemlock who seemed to be agitated, looking around for someone in particular. As soon as he saw them, he threw up his hands in relief.

"Francine! I've been looking all over for you. Your mother is in a panic without you. I can't seem to console her at all so I promised I would come find you," said Willard, desperately. "Oh, Dominique, Ralph, good evening. Err . . . Phyllis will be delighted to know you are here too," he added, conciliatorily.

"How nice of you to say so, Willard," Dominique retorted with unmistaken contempt.

"Yes, yes, of course," added Willard, uncomfortably. "Follow me." He casually pointed to the opposite side of the room and started leading the way. Francine had taken off as soon as Willard had opened his mouth and was already at her mother's side.

Dominique was boiling and immediately felt Ralph's strong but gentle hand take hers. She turned to gaze at him with eyes now absent of flames and said, "My dear husband and friend . . . where had you been all my life?"

Willard detesteds children . . . even the adult kind. He had been around Phyllis' children most of their lives only because of his connection with Frank and Carl. When Dominique was in her mother's presence, she was constantly trying to command Phyllis' complete attention hoping for just one nod of approval. But mostly she ended up complaining about everyone and anything. However, since she had married Ralph, her obnoxious tirades were considerably less abrasive to him. He could just be getting used to them but he didn't think that was likely. He was curious just how Ralph manages her so well, as he needs some of what it is that Ralph has, hoping it will work for him equally as well on Dominique's mother.

Willard goes way back in his relationship with Frank and Carl . . . to their college days at Hemlock College, a small private college serving the Appalachian corridor. Willard belongs to the family who established Hemlock College which was the only means he had to acquire a college degree, although not necessarily an academic education.

As the last male in the Hemlock line, the family was very tolerant of his meager scholastic abilities, but that's not to say he wasn't smart in other ways . . . smart like a fox. His *inventive ideas* have not always been of a legitimate nature and over the years he has become a successful con-man and manipulator.

Considering his family situation and successfully *creative mind,* Willard can be an obnoxious, slimy weasel. Over the years, most people, fearing his tactics and subtle threats, tolerate him, taking care not to rile him, or simply avoid him.

Willard had the acuity to perceive great potential in associating himself with and insinuating himself onto his former college roommates, Frank and Carl. So, when he heard that Frank and Carl were forming their own business, he wheedled himself onto the payroll as a marketing representative, for which his talents were well suited. His efforts were very successful for the company but the contacts he made in pursuit of company sales provided a much larger nefarious side-business with Carl in the illegal drug trade of which Frank was unaware.

The drug trade had been his idea and he had put it in motion. Carl, it seemed, had similar ideas and discovered his set-up early in its development. Willard might be an unsavory character, but Carl was downright dangerous and soon pressured Willard into a subordinate position. Resentment lay smoldering in his stomach waiting for just the right opportunity to even the score.

When the fire alarm blared at the plant a year ago, Willard knew in an instant that the time was ripe for retribution.

The entire facility was composed of several large buildings: a large warehouse at one end connected by a wide passageway to the huge main factory which was divided up into areas of connected clean rooms; a secondary smaller building abutted the main factory which housed the packaging area; a two story office building connected the main factory to the four story box-shaped building fartherest from the warehouse which was the research hub and which Frank spent 99% of his time. The public and employee parking area began in front of the small office building and extended around the research building to the back of the office building. The warehouse had a separate entrance driveway and parking for the trucks at the opposite end of the property so the noise of the big trucks would not interfere with the office staff or the research center. Frank had insisted on as few distractions as possible around his work area and Carl approved the design of the plant as highly efficient.

On the night of the fire, Willard had been in his office in the connecting building between the research lab and the manufacturing plant having a relaxing drink, as he often did well into the evening, when he heard the alarm and saw the flames through his office window. He rushed down the hall, through the connecting corridor and into the burning building. He could feel the heat intensifying but the object of his pursuit was in a safe in the first office in the part of the building which was not yet consumed with flame but filling up quickly with smoke. As luck would have it, the safe was already open and it took no time to find the particular chemical formula file he intended to pilfer.

As the smoke was already filling the vestibule and seeping under the office door, Willard wasted no time in exiting the building through the far outside door nearest the back parking lot. He drove off, lights doused, and headed to his mountain hunting cabin forty miles away.

Willard saw no one and felt confident that no one had seen him. He had no idea what had caused the fire but with the extent of dangerous chemicals in the building, he gave it no further thought. Still, he didn't relax until he had reached the cabin and started creating a plausible alibi as well as a plan for the purloined papers. It wasn't until early in the morning while watching the news, that he learned the fire had apparently claimed one victim . . . Frank!

Willard's first reaction after hearing the news of Frank's demise in the fire was that of surprise . . . which quickly gave way to fear. Suppose someone had seen him leaving the scene. How could he explain? He was guilty of many vile and illegal acts in his life and never had to pay the price to society. Now he had visions of being called to task for something he was innocent of.

The fear of retribution enveloped him and ultimately turned into panic. Others might find it disturbingly curious, had they been aware of Willard's dilemma, that Willard never once gave way to any emotional loss for his friend, Frank. Willard mourned no loss but his own.

Managing to overcome his panic, Willard had immediately gone into protection mode. His exceptionally adaptive mind automatically entered overdrive and, for the next twenty-four hours, he formed a plan.

Always cautious and suspicious, Willard began by making discrete phone calls from the cabin. He was setting the stage for an alibi while at the same time attempting to learn just how far his foot was stuck in the mud.

After a number of calls, Willard was convinced there was no evidence to tie him to the scene nor any fingers pointing in his direction. He cautiously relaxed, knowing full well he was not out of the woods yet as there was always the chance lucky eyes would make themselves known and apply their own annoyingly dangerous pressure. Experience had taught him he would not have to wait long if there was something to wait for. Every hour that passed unmolested was encouraging.

By the next morning, Willard's confidence had taken him to another level . . . how could he capitalize on the situation. He wasn't thinking of the stolen formulas because, for obvious reasons, that plan would have to move to the back burner until the timing was right. He did not wish to have to explain their present domicile. He did see the possibility of an even better score. Phyllis was now an *available* widow . . . an available *extradinarily RICH* widow!

Naturally, this was a complicated plan that would need delicacy, resolve and patience. Willard never had any doubts about his ability to succeed in any endeavor for the prosperity and financial advancement of *Willard!* But, having never been married or having even some social experience with women, he would need a detailed plan of attack and a whole new mind-set for this caper.

First, he picked up the phone and called Phyllis with his *outstandingly believable, emotionally riveting condolence speech.* He had been one of the first, outside family, to call and comfort her and she was obviously hungering for an understanding, equally compassionate supporter. He performed admirably.

For the next several days he persistently made himself indispensable to Phyllis by being with her as much as he dared, offering her attentiveness and a sympathetic ear. Progress was slow but he definitely had his foot in the door, he thought.

At the same time, he was clearing up loose ends at the plant in preparation of turning in his notice and leaving the company. He used the obvious excuse that he was overcome by Frank's death and had to disassociate himself from the plant. He certainly didn't fool anyone with that story since his attentions were now focused on Frank's widow.

At the end of the first week his elation took a severe hit. He had just entered the mansion to take tea with Phyllis, a custom then early in development, when his way seemed blocked by Paul, Phyllis' smarmy nephew whose mother, Phyllis' sister Priscilla, had recently moved into the house and had taken over the care of her sister and the running of the household. Paul, despite his youth, was already a seasoned opportunist. He skillfully laid his cards on the table, never relinquishing an irritating smile, and highlighted all the possible ways he could blow Willard's obvious plan *or* how an association with him could be beneficial in any of Willard's future endeavors.

Willard's initial resentment in Paul's haughty encounter faded into admiration as his memories of himself at that age neatly overlapped the present. Willard sensed how dangerous it would be to have Paul as an enemy. So, reluctantly but equally enticed, he shook Paul's hand and agreed to meet later that day to discuss details of their alliance.

During the next several hours, Willard weighed the pros and cons of Paul's "offer". He saw only disaster if he did not accept Paul's conditions but on the other hand, having an apprentice had enormous appeal. Right now he did need an ally against Carl. Willard had never really put his trust in anyone completely, but his back was against the wall so he took the leap. So far, he had no cause to regret that decision . . . well, not much.

CHAPTER X—PAUL PENNILESS

A slap on the back brought Willard back into focus. He turned and stared face to face with the smiling, glassy-eyed Paul himself.

"Hey, daddy-o, how's it hangin'?" Paul chirped, bouncing slightly on the balls of his feet brandishing that same irritating grin.

"My God! You're high already. You might want to wipe the white stuff off you nose before others spot it. I believe the police inspector is here tonight," Willard said as he handed Paul a handkerchief. "Didn't I tell you *no drugs tonight!*"

"Oh, chill out, pops, it's cool," Paul said, almost *sang*, in a lilting voice. "I'm in control. No worries."

"No worries? You better worry, young man. I thought you wanted to learn from me. I'm trying to teach you what I know, what I have experienced . . . like father to son. It's the only thing I have to bequeath. And, if you haven't noticed, I am still on this side of cell bars. At the rate you're going, you'll be in San Quentin before the year's up."

Paul's smile vanished and his eyes tightened, "I *said* it's cool, old man, so *it's COOL,*" he said with a low, threatening tone. He grabbed Willard by the shoulders and gave him a soft shake and then brushed some imaginary speck off his shoulder. Willard stiffened. Paul's face broke out into that huge grin again as he patted Willard's cheek several times with his fingers and hissing, "Coooool," he turned and swaggered off laughing loudly.

"Willard is such a jerk . . . past his prime," Paul thought. But he had to concede he had made the right move a year ago when he hooked that fish. Lot of water ran through that dam, he was certain. He felt, however, he had gleaned everything he could possibly learn from Willard in just three months. He really didn't need him, but it wouldn't hurt to hang around just in case something better turned up. It always did.

Paul's mother might have come from a poor family and she might have had a hard time with his father, but Paul had had a pretty good life growing up. Sure, they didn't live in the best neighborhood, but his mom showered him with everything he ever wanted. Just about every cent she could earn went to benefit him and him alone. He learned early on that he was the total center of his mother's life and the only reason she existed. He never really knew his father so didn't miss him a bit.

When he was a youngster, her clinginess was sometimes a drag but now it was nearly intolerable. But if he wanted the money to keep coming, he had to put up with it. He knew expertly well how to work her and never gave it a thought about the hardships she endured just to provide Paul with anything his heart desired. He grew up learning that mother's are the piggy banks of society. So, when he needs money . . . or merely wants some . . . tap the piggy bank. He made a mental note to do that very thing tonight as he needs some "stash" from Ruben for his Mulberry Street clients tomorrow.

College? Work? Nah, not for him. It was easier to bleed his mom or *work the angles* which he had developed a propensity for. There were always angles that returned big dividends.

The real bump forward in his life's prospects came last year when his uncle died and his mother announced they were moving in with his aunt . . . his *rich* aunt. Opportunity lay ahead of him and he wasted no time in capitalizing on it when he cornered Willard only a few days after they moved in.

Life was good. Then Willard introduced him to Carl. Life got better.

CHAPTER XI—CARLTON BRENNER

Paul found himself at the bar. "Hey, barkeep! Joe, isn't it? How 'bout a scotch and soda, my man." Paul pulled out a cigarette as Joe came over and proffered a lighter. Their eyes met through a cloud of smoke. Paul's eyes widened ever so slightly and he choked on his next inhale. "Who is this guy that stared him down so calmly but intently?" he thought.

Suddenly, a slap on the back nearly knocked him off the bar stool and Carl's booming voice said, "Careful, kid, those sticks can kill ya." He chuckled as he offered his hand for a welcoming shake, which Paul afforded him absently, as he watched Joe turn away to fix his drink.

"And you, Mr. Brenner? What will you have? Cognac, with a twist of lime, right? Joe said without turning around.

"R-i-g-h-t. How did you know?" quizzed Carl.

"I recognize the remnants of the drink you're holding. I made it earlier. Do you not remember?"

"Yes, of course. You're not the usual bartender hired for these occasions, are you?" Carl asked.

"No sir. I needed a job and Conrad hired me for this gig," Joe answered as he set their drinks in front of them on the bar. "Name's Joe Phoenix," he added. Paul noticed Joe kept his head down and didn't look *Carl* in the eye.

"Nice job," Carl said as he took his fresh drink in one hand and Paul's elbow in the other and steered him away from the bar toward an unoccupied corner of the room taking one last look at Joe over his shoulder. He was a bit older than his usual recruits, but he could do well in his *organization*. Joe did say he needed a job. Must ask him about that scar, though, he thought.

Carl and Frank grew up together although on opposite sides of the railroad tracks. Carl's family owned a successful perfume manufacturing business and Frank's father was a simple shoemaker. Carl was the youngest of seven boys; Frank was an only child. Regardless of their social status Carl and Frank were soul brothers and were nearly inseparable all through school so it was only natural that they chose to go to the same college. And that college was Hemlock College because it had an excellent chemistry department.

They both had strong characters and absorbent minds; both were tall and muscular in physique; both had handsome facial features; Frank had Caribbean blue eyes one could lose themselves in; Carl's eyes were black and fathomless; Frank's smile could melt bones; Carl's smile could shrink skin.

Frank's dream was to find a formula that would save hundreds of thousands of lives. Carl's dream was for a quick trip to the top of the heap becoming the richest and most powerful man alive. Both were consumed with their dreams. Although they couldn't be closer in their friendship, they never fully shared the total capacity of those dreams.

As close as they were, they weren't completely reclusive. They had other friends. One such friend was Willard Hemlock who they enjoyed having around more as a mascot and servant. Willard, on the other hand, was overwhelmed at being included in their inner circle but had no idea how lightly they thought of him. He became their "step-and-fetch-it" side-kick and he gladly and willingly did whatever they demanded. Frank's commands were simple requests, like, "Fetch me a beer, Willie." Carl, however, had more dirty deeds to do, like, spying on people or stealing exam papers. Willard found he liked the latter tasks and had a rather unique talent for it.

In their senior year, they both met girls that would become their wives days after graduation and their lives took separate directions. Frank went to work in a local research laboratory earning a modest salary. He and Angel moved into an equally modest apartment and soon welcomed a handsome baby boy they named Frank N. Stein, Jr. Carl's family pressured him to join the business, but with six other brothers to compete with, he quickly left to seek his fortune elsewhere. His father retaliated for Carl's rebellion by burning every possession Carl had left behind in the family estate including the Harley he had given Carl for his high school graduation. Carl never looked back.

Carl's obsession with money and, more importantly, power, sent him in lots of directions at once, hunting for the perfect *avenue* which would lead him in the direction he favored. Hunger for money and power grew like a malignancy and nothing was ever enough.

On the night his wife, Elizabeth, gave birth to twins, Christian and Cassandra, Carl went out and got drunk. Always one who could hold his liqueur, this was unusual. He seemed like a man on a mission. By the time he ricocheted through the front door jam of "Lobo's", the fifth nightclub he had frequented that night, he was in high form and his presence could not be ignored. Despite the influence of alcohol, he still possessed clarity of mind. He swore he would never lose control of *that!* It was here he met Louis Botalinni who was better known throughout the *back streets* as Lobo the Wolf.

As a young boy, Lobo came to the States from Sicily twenty years earlier. Through family connections, and wolf-like instincts, he quickly made a name for himself and a substantial place in the crime organization. His specialty was drugs. He had no tolerance for "don't have" or "can't do". He *could* and he *did*. His six foot four frame was powerful and muscular in those days so it was only natural that he started his unsavory career as a hit man. He was very very good at it.

He and Carl hit it off right away and before Carl left the club he was a member of the *organization*. His assignment: find a better and safer way to import, store and move the drugs. Carl immediately thought of Frank.

He found him easily but it took a week of trailing Frank's every move before the optimum opportunity presented itself. Frank had hailed a cab and Carl pretended to do likewise and both entered the cab at roughly the same time. Frank was happily surprised at what he thought was a chance meeting and Carl's expert acting portrayed equal delight and astonishment. They agreed to stop at "Wet Your Whistle" to have a drink and get caught up.

Frank, it turned out, did most of the talking. He had just gone through a rather nasty divorce and he was broke and out of a job. Worse than that, his wife had taken their year old son and disappeared. He had tried to find them but there seemed to be no trace. Frank had just come from a job interview, which hadn't panned out, and he was delighted to see Carl as he was about as low as he could go and really needed the lift.

Carl couldn't have been more pleased to hear of his friend's situation for it led in nicely to his plan. He proposed to Frank that they combine efforts and start a chemical business. Frank brightened immediately but then his face dropped, "Where is the money coming from?" he had said.

"We'll worry about that later. Let's look at some property and check out the legal stuff," Carl had answered.

So that's how they came to be in the Fairwinds Real Estate Office where Frank literally bumped into Phyllis who was looking for property suitable for a new medical clinic she was sponsoring. Before both of them had concluded their business, they had fallen in love and had become business partners as well. Phyllis, intrigued by their story of opening a chemical manufacturing business, had agreed to finance the endeavor.

By the time they had finally broken ground for the plant, Phyllis and Frank were married and a year later welcomed a rather thin, colicky baby boy they named Ruben.

Carl and Elizabeth had also added another daughter to the family and named her Charity.

Carl again visited Lobo's bar to celebrate, as he had done nearly every night since the twins were born and where he had first met Lobo and joined his organization. Lobo now welcomed him with open arms with a salutation one normally extends only to brothers.

Lobo was very happy and impressed with this young man. It seemed apparent that he was well on his way to solving the problems that had plagued him for years—safer import, storage and distribution of the myriad of illegal drugs that made up the bulk of his business. The plant would take time to build but he was a patient man. He'd spend the time counting his projected future profits.

Carl was also good at recruiting people. As a matter of fact, Lobo mused that Carl might just be too good at everything sooner or later. He would have to keep his eye on him and treat him with kid gloves. He didn't want to snuff the goose that laid the golden egg . . . at least not before finding another goose. This Hemlock fella Carl brought in with him the last time, had the disposition for the organization but he was second rate and clearly unlikable and untrustworthy. Lobo had a guy he trusted on the construction crew to keep him informed. And he was already preparing a dozen others to work in the plant once the business was up and running.

He escorted Carl to a secluded back table and eased his large frame, carrying many extra "pasta" pounds, into an amply padded captain's chair. Carl took the less comfortable chair beside him. A waiter brought them a bottle of Cognac and a bottle of Chianti chilled.

"Any snags?" Lobo inquired.

"Lobo, my man!" Carl said incredulously, while leaning back, arms wide, palms up, "Haven't I earned your confidence after all this time? Everything is running like clockwork. Plant is finished and being stocked as we speak. Your men arrived on schedule as I left. Offices and research building should be finished next month. Once the research lab is ready, Frank will be totally out of my hair."

"Ah, I like all this good news," Lobo beamed. "No chance to turn Frank to our objective? His contributions could be invaluable."

"Nah, too squeaky clean. Always has been and I've known him since we were small kids. His value lies in giving the business legitimacy. We couldn't ask for a better setup," said Carl. "He won't be a problem, I can assure you. Willard, on the other hand, could be a problem unless we bring him on board. He would be an asset on all accounts."

"I'm counting on you, Carl. I've not only sunk two mil in this project but I have given you my trust and I don't give either lightly . . . or for free!" Lobo downed his drink, never breaking eye contact. His eyes were silent words that Carl fully understood, and he returned Lobo's gaze unblinkingly with a smile on his face that had not reached his eyes.

"Shall we drink to a new era?" Carl cooed, and refilled both glasses.

For the next twenty years the business . . . rather, businesses . . . ran so smoothly Carl was no longer worried about discovery and often took careless chances. But still his covert operation remained under cover. This was, in large part, because of the successes from Frank's research and development in medical pharmaceuticals and in industrial compounds. Not a day went by that Carl didn't congratulate himself on his aforethought to partner with Frank.

And the money kept coming in, starting with the two million he pocketed from Lobo for start-up money, although he did pay him back with hefty interest by way of a separate off-shore investment which had tripled over the years. Naturally, Lobo was not aware of that deal. And, because Phyllis financed the chemical plant, he saw no need to mention to Frank he had the money. So, he had money coming in from the illegal drug racket and also shared in the profits from the income Frank was responsible for generating. How sweet it was . . . but his sweet tooth was never satisfied. His eyes had always been on the next step in the ladder and fate presented the ideal scenario.

It seemed Lobo had a roving eye. Despite his advancing years and hefty size, he still could attract the ladies and knew how to appreciate the fair sex. Apparently, he finally strayed in the wrong pasture and was having an affair with the young wife of the area's King Pin. For weeks, the network news carried the story of a freak explosion on the mega yacht of a suspected underworld mafia leader. All hands, including Lobo and his mistress, went down with the ship in the Bermuda triangle. Carl had gotten the call before the news even broke. The next time he walked through "Lobo's" doors it was as its owner *and operator.* Life is good.

Now he had found an ideal new apprentice in Paul. Carl's own son, Christian, was such a disappointment to him. He had all the dash, good looks and affected charm like his father, but had absolutely no backbone or inspiration for real work let alone *dirty work*. He sure could spend his father's money, however, and had a penchant for fast cars and drove in the race car circuit. Surprisingly, he was good at it, which was the only reason Carl continued to finance this lifestyle. Paul was the son he had hoped for. He had the *killer instinct* while a morale conscience was absent. He wasn't the brightest bulb in the pack but that was actually an asset in this business. He would do what he was told.

As Carl and Paul settled in chairs away from the milling guests, Carl said, "Willard giving you any problems? I couldn't help noticing the tongue lashing. But he's right, by the way. Carelessness will not be tolerated in my organization." Carl's voice had gotten lower but stronger and his eyes burned through Paul's. "Are we clear?"

Carl did not miss the flicker of fear in Paul's eyes. When Paul spoke, his voice and attitude attempted to deny this. "Crystal. Whatever you say, my man. Willard's old news but he thinks I'm loyal to him."

"It is my wish you do nothing to disturb that illusion. There is much more you can learn from Willard. He's a true artist in his field, so don't be forgetting that. More important, you need to be my eyes and ears." With that said, Carl casually stood, adjusted his clothing and added, as he looked around the room, "We should not be seen too often enjoying each other's company, especially tonight. Gotta keep my wits about me during this séance. You should too."

"I'll do my job, sir," said Paul.

"See that you do," Carl said, as he walk off toward his wife, Lily, who was greeting his daughter, Cassandra, who had just arrived.

CHAPTER XII—LILY & CASSANDRA BRENNER

Cassandra did not want to be here. It wasn't just being around all these people; she was petrified of ghosts and she honestly believed she was going to see one tonight. If her brother hadn't forced her to come with him, she would have risked defying her father and stayed away. She knew the consequences of defying her father was painful and humiliating; but she would have taken that misery over this one.

No one knew about the terrible things her father had done to her since she was very small. No one except her mother who had died many years ago and taken her secret with her to the grave. Her mother took her own secrets to the grave as well. Her father didn't discriminate when it came to beatings.

Her sister, Charity, was the fortunate one. She was a young infant when her mother died and her father allowed her maternal grandparents to raise her. Cassandra had prayed every night since her mother died that her father would let her and Christian go with granny as well. But her prayers were never answered. Well, that's not true; "NO" is an answer.

Then her father married Lily, one of the secretaries in the office and she had someone who would hug her again. It didn't take long for both of them to share hugs for the same reasons . . . Oh, how she hated her father but feared him more.

She and her brother had entered the hall and were welcomed by Conrad, whereupon Christian spied Francine and he was gone. Conrad had kindly pointed out Lily fidgeting in a corner all by herself. She couldn't get to her fast enough.

Lily was as happy to see her as she was to see Lily. They were kindred spirits living under the same dark cloud. Lily, however, was a very attractive woman, whereas, Cassandra was painfully plain. Years of abuse had taught her she could not be anything else but plain. But Lily had not been introduced to Carl's abuse until after they were married. If she weren't beautiful, Carl would never have married her. And if she didn't *stay* beautiful, she felt his dissatisfaction.

Lily was beautiful but very timid and insecure. She may not have been physically abused as a youngster, but her parents had never said an encouraging word to her but rather criticized everything she did.

Carl knew how to turn on the charm when he wanted to. Lily had attracted his eye and he knew immediately she could be *owned*. He wined and dined her until stars filled her eyes. She thought him so handsome, strong, smart and powerful. She couldn't understand why he would court *her* but he *was* courting her and she felt more wonderful than she ever thought possible. It was like a fairytale.

When he proposed, she was in shock. So when he pronounced they would fly to Las Vegas to be married, she discarded her lifelong dream of a big wedding, and agreed . . . did she really have a choice? A fairytale romance quickly dissolved into a night of hell. Carl, it seemed, was a violent and cruel lover. When he wasn't having sex with her, he was down in the casino with pals. She came back from Vegas a terrified and broken Mrs. Carlton Brenner.

Lily saw Cassandra coming from the hall and hurried to greet her. They grabbed hands and hugged like they had just been drowning and suddenly found a life preserver. Carl approached from the opposite side of the room and wrapped his arms around both of them, giving them a group squeeze. They were shocked and terrified at the same time.

"So, the Brenner ladies are together again," Carl said as he released his hold on them. "Now get your sweet little asses out of the corner and mix with the other guests. My family shouldn't be in corners. Shake your head if you understand." Both ladies looked up at him wide-eyed and shook their heads in unison. He turned on his heel and headed for the hall, leaving the women frozen to the spot.

CHAPTER XIII—CHARITY & SVEN

Carl spied through the doorway to the hall two newcomers being welcomed by Conrad and rushed to meet them. His youngest daughter, Charity, had just recently married some Swedish religious nut and was stopping by on the way home from Sweden to meet her family. He was very anxious to check out his credentials. Although Charity had not lived with him since her infancy, he was still miffed that she had not consulted him about her choice of a husband. She is still family, he thought, and her actions certainly reflect upon the family.

When Carl's wife, Elizabeth, died so many years ago, Charity was still a small infant and Carl had no use for helpless beings. His other two children were older and could communicate which he could handle. After all, nannies had them most of the time until they were old enough to start getting in his way. Sometimes they amused him.

Elizabeth's parents were overwhelmed when he asked them if they would be interested in raising the infant. Having just lost a daughter, it was their salvation. They were so delighted that when Carl offered support financially, they refused. They were so grateful that they made certain Charity grew up knowing her father through letters. She had only seen her father a handful of times since her grandparents brought her to their home in California.

So Carl recognized her immediately from pictures that were sent over the years but this was the first time she had come to visit him . . . and she brought a *stranger!*

"Hullo father!" exclaimed Charity, as she opened her arms to greet him. After a cursory embrace, she continued in her *valley girl* affected speech, "It's so peachy to finally get here. The last weeks have been top drawer with the wedding and honeymoon to Sweden. Oh, what a *marvelous* place, Sweden. Oh, the wedding! Forgive me, father, I haven't introduced you to my wonderful super scrumptious husband." She turned a half turn and linked her arm with the rather dapper gentleman there and gently steered him to a position facing her father. "Father," she beamed, "this is my husband, Professor Sven Svenson. Sven, my sweet, this is my father."

Carl was impressed at the firm handshake he received, but there was more he needed to learn. "Professor?" he said inquisitively.

"Yes, sir. I am a professor of theological studies at Berkley. Charity took one of my classes last semester before graduation. She is an excellent student with an interest in many things. Rest assured, sir, for I know you must be concerned for your daughter, I have committed my life and my love to Charity and will do my very best to sustain her happiness and comfort," he pronounced with a slight Swedish accent.

"Yes . . . I'm certain you will," Carl said softly with an ever so slightly threatening undertone, which did not escape Sven. "The wedding was quite . . . sudden shall I say," Carl continued.

"Now, father, reeeeally," Charity said saucily. "We knew right away we were meant for each other and we wanted to go to Sweden and come here. I couldn't do that without being married, could I?" she said with a pout.

"Sweden, you say. Where may I ask?" said Carl.

"My family keeps a place in Stockholm to be near our shipping business. But most of the family have houses in our compound on Lake Limmaren which is just off Highway E18 not far from the town of Norrtalje which is north of Stockholm. Beautiful country around Norrtalje. I extend an invitation to visit any time that is convenient." answered Sven.

"Oh, father, do lets go soon. It is just too marvey," gushed Charity. "And Sven's parents are top drawer. You would just love them to pieces."

"Yes, I'm sure I would. Thank you young man for the kind invitation. Perhaps after things settle down. I'm sure Charity has told you about the tragedy we had last year and the death of my partner," Carl probed.

"Yes, yes, very upsetting. I understand this particular gathering tonight intends to make contact with the . . . afterlife?" Sven questioned delicately. "I, personally, don't believe in such things."

"Well, I assure you not all here have such high expectations. But our hostess deserves our support all the same." Carl said with a hint of an apology as well as sneer at the ridiculous. "Out of curiosity, what is your take on this séance?"

"The mind is a mystery. And so too is faith. A weaker mind gripped by faith can believe so fervently as to create their own reality. You would call this an hallucination. I believe this strength of faith has been responsible for many of the impossible stories in the Bible," Sven said, philosophically. He looked Carl straight in the face and smiled. "As for me? I don't expect to see any ghosts tonight."

Carl matched his smile and added "You don't take into account some trick behind this séance?"

"As I said, the mind will play its tricks. But you refer to some sort of *magic* trick? In this situation, highly probable but exceptionally risky, don't you think?"

"With this assembly of id . . . er . . . gentry, I think half of them want to see a show and the other half are scared sh . . . er . . . to death," Carl declared.

They had lost Charity from this conversation long ago and she was now in conversation with Lily and Cassandra. Carl had steered Sven towards the bar during their discussion and Carl inquired of Sven what his liquid pleasure would be. A merlot was requested and promptly delivered by Joe, who's services had become more in demand since Carl had been there last.

As Carl lead the way to his ladies for introductions, he asked, "You will, I suppose, settle near Berkley? I assume you will continue to teach there."

"Yes indeed. Young minds in a classroom are just waiting to be molded, wouldn't you say? Teaching is the most fulfilling employment I have ever experienced. My family are very supportive and overjoyed at my success. You really must meet my parents. They are quite worth knowing, I think. Not many can boast having the ear of a monarch."

"Indeed!" Carl said, astonished.

As they approached the ladies, their conversations stopped instantly and they turned toward them, Lily and Cassandra eager for introductions.

CHAPTER XIV—CALVIN & BONNIE BOOKER

Carl allowed his daughter, Charity, to handle the introductions and continue the conversation because he noticed, out of the corner of his eye, the arrival of the bookkeeper of his company, Calvin Booker, and his wife, Bonnie, and that was worth watching.

He took one look at Bonnie and just shook his head. Fortunately, his little group were too busy making small talk to notice his reaction. There was no mistaking it, Bonnie was a trip! He knew Bonnie long before Calvin met her. She had been a headline stripper at the "Cheek2Cheek" nightclub just down the street from "Lobo's". And she deserved the title *headliner*.

Bonnie was born on the wrong side of the tracks and was promptly left on the doorstep of the local Catholic church and orphanage. At age eleven, she ran away and never looked back. She never blamed her parents for her lot in life; in fact, she never thought of them at all. She was a survivor. About the only thing she learned at the orphanage school, besides reading, writing and 'rithmatic, was to depend on no one but herself. By age eleven, she was mature emotionally as well as physically. A prime piece of meat for the body sellers. So her education continued in back streets and hotel rooms.

Eventually, she used her connections to land a job as a stripper and, through her ingenuity, developed an appealing act that quickly earned her a fan club of sorts which catapulted her to headliner in short order. She was so excited to BE somebody at the top . . . even if it was the top of a dung heap. What she wanted more than anything was respectability.

One Friday there happened to be a bachelor party for one of the men in the office and Carl offered to plan the evening. It took some begging to get Calvin to come along but he finally agreed to go for one drink. Eventually, they ended up at "Cheek2Cheek". Calvin was deeply under the influence by then so when he set eyes on Bonnie all decked out in red feathers, he was hypnotized. His heart and mind fused together and before the night was done, had offered them to Bonnie forever and ever. She thought he was touched in the head, which was actually the truth, but she found he had touched her respectability button and she quickly started thinking seriously.

One week of wining and dining and baskets of flowers, Bonnie rushed Calvin to the alter before he could have a chance to come to his senses. She needn't have worried for Calvin was completely smitten and thought himself the luckiest man alive.

Calvin was not a worldly man. In fact, he had never had a date . . . well, unless you call taking his cousin to the senior prom on threat of death by his mother and his aunt, a date. He had always been a rather small, skinny kid growing up; the target of all the bullies. He learned quickly all the evasive moves to avoid confrontations. He considered himself extremely lucky to have gotten out of high school alive but college didn't improve his situation. But by then he had managed to get used to all the taunts and ridicule because he knew deep inside that he was smart and worth something, if only to himself. He actually liked his own company.

He felt fortunate to be hired right out of college by the Stein-Brenner Plant in their accounting department. The plant had just opened and was a fresh slate for a smart, innovative accountant. Calvin was instrumental in setting up the entire accounting system and within the year was head of the department and eventually become Controller. It was then he met Bonnie and life became a *real* challenge.

Bonnie had totally swept him off his feet and awakened that feral part of him he never knew existed. He affectionately called her his little witch because of the spell she had cast upon him. He had offered her the moon if she would marry him. But the moon came with a heavy price tag.

Bonnie did not care where the money came from. She just spent it. Only the priciest clothes would do, which wouldn't have been so bad if she had any taste. And, of course, she had to keep her body beautiful so there were hair dressers, nail salons, makeup and massage parlors. Only the high end establishments would do. All the best restaurants knew who they were and several had standing reservations for them on the weekends. Calvin wanted Bonnie to have anything she wanted because he feared if *he* couldn't provide those things she would look for someone who could. In little more than two years he had gone through his entire savings and the reasonably large inheritance his parents had left him.

In his desperation, he saw only one choice . . . to creatively *borrow* from the Company. His *system* seemed to be working beautifully until the evening Carl called him into his office at closing time. He was so petrified he knocked over his coffee, tripped over the file cabinet nearly breaking an arm and barely made it to the bathroom in time.

His worst fears were correct. Carl had found him out. It was all he could do to keep from passing out right there in the office. But then Carl did the unimaginable . . . he agreed not to prosecute if Calvin would agree to do some creative accounting for *him* and not divulge to *anyone* the nature of the job. And if Calvin was especially talented in this regard, he would provide adequate bonuses to keep Bonnie in style. This offer he couldn't refuse.

Being a nervous and high-strung person to begin with, Calvin was now on the verge of a breakdown. He jumped at every squeak and sunbeam. He should have felt a huge amount of relief but he only felt he had dug his hole deeper than ever and the day of reckoning would come eventually.

Yes, he believed in ghosts and he was certain Frank would show up tonight and point the finger right at HIM! But here he was in the Lion's Den and he couldn't stop shaking. When he talked, his voice sounded like he was sliding down a washboard. But who looked at him? All eyes were on Bonnie, and not in an admiring way.

Bonnie was fond of red and nearly every outfit she owned had at least some red in it. Tonight she wore a strapless sequined mini-dress at a barely decent length. There were black sequins down the front forming the shape of a dragon. Red ostrich feathers adorned her curly bleached blond hair as well as her red sequined four inch open toed shoes. The black fishnet stockings also displayed a dragon down the full length of each side. A red ostrich feather boa hung just off her shoulders. A ruby necklace and dangly ruby earrings completed the outfit but was over-shadowed by the heavy black eyebrow and eyeliner pencil, purple shadow, long false eyelashes with heavy mascara, and ruby red lipstick over collagen-filled lips. All had the desired affect—people stared.

She stopped to talk to everyone, trying hard to achieve the objective of her diction class, but she was sadly in need of Professor Higgins. The whispers and forced politeness had no affect on her. Attention was attention.

Poor Calvin tottered after her, stuttering answers to questions from time to time. As he passed the table set up for the séance, his eyes nearly popped out of their sockets and he bumped headlong into Bonnie who had stopped to talk to Phyllis. Phyllis genuinely greeted Bonnie and Calvin with affection and thanked them wholeheartedly for sharing this evening with her.

"Calvin, my dear," said Phyllis, "Frank was so very fond of you and Bonnie. I have set up chairs for the séance right behind Carl and Willard. They should be grand seats for when Frank shows himself"

If Calvin hadn't stiffened at that very moment, his knees would have buckled and sent him to the floor at her feet. But a quick arm around Bonnie steadied him. "I . . . ah . . . I th-think I ne-need a dr-drink. Ladies wo-would you ca-care for an-anything?" he stammered.

CHAPTER XV—HELENE STEIN

As Calvin was downing his Dewer's scotch, everyone's attention turned to a loud commotion coming from the hall. Along with loud expletives, there were sounds of breaking glass, then an unmistaken thud. More scrambling sounds came from the hall and still no one moved but all stared toward the entrance to the hall. Shortly a body came staggering into the room and fell with a now familiar thud at the feet of Phyllis.

"Hi, Mumsey. Your shun hass arrived," Ruben slurred as he looked up from the floor with a silly grin.

"And what a spectacle you have made of yourself, Ruben. You know how important this evening is to me. How could you embarrass me so? You disrespect your father as well," Phyllis whispered, angrily. "Not get up and try to get sober before Madam Angelica gets here. Helene, come help your husband."

Helene was tall and thin with black hair and eyes so light blue there seemed to be no color at all which gave her a very eerie appearance. The look of frailness belied the strength within for she reached down, grabbed the collar of Ruben's coat and pulled him to his feet in quick order. No one offered assistance, as they were still frozen to their individual spots. No one except Carl who came from nowhere and guided Ruben to the bar where he asked Joe to brew some coffee.

"I do apologize, Phyllis darling," purred Helene. "I simply couldn't control Ruben. You know how headstrong he is. I believe his father had a strong will as well, am I not right?"

"My husband was *not* a drunkard, Helene. Surely you have more influence over your husband than I ever had as his mother. Frank had none of those weaknesses that Ruben displays. I don't know where he gets it from," Phyllis said on the verge of tears.

Angry at the obvious implication, Helene couldn't help herself and retorted, "Don't you, Phyllis? Indeed!" Then joined her husband at the bar.

Helene was a "climber." She came from a low middle class family, the oldest of ten children. Naturally it fell to her to take care of the younger siblings as they came along with regularity. With so many children, her mother often shopped at Goodwill or other second hand clothing stores. This was such an embarrassment to her with her friends at school that she managed to get a job delivering groceries to make enough money to buy a brand new outfit all her own. She has never been prouder than that day she wore her new outfit to school for the first time. From that moment on, she vowed to greatly improve her station in life.

One Saturday in the Fall of her senior year of high school, her girlfriend paired her up with Ruben on a blind date. She knew who Ruben was as he was also a senior and was actually in her science class but she had never seriously spoken to him. Observations of his classroom behavior indicated he was a loud, boisterous bully but not a hurtful one; he just liked to have his own way. Considering the wealthy family roots, she would have expected no less.

On their date, Helene was surprised to learn just how troubled Ruben was. What the outside world saw was a rich man's kid who had everything just waiting for him to inherit. But in fact, Frank apparently was a hard task master, demanding Ruben *earn* his place in the company before the reins were turned over to him. Ruben was nothing like Frank, and in his mind, Ruben believed he could never achieve what his father expected of him. Defeated before he began, Ruben cowered at home but created a false-confident persona when away from home and away from his father. As long as no one called his bluff, he was safe.

As far as Helene could tell, Ruben's father began putting pressure on Ruben to perform at a higher standard than he was capable as early as infancy. Helene actually felt a measure of compassion for this teenager; but she managed to squash that *weakness* in her. In her plan, she couldn't afford to have such *baggage*.

Her plan took shape on that first date with Ruben. She would marry Ruben and mold and manipulate him into something his father would approve. She had enough strength, intelligence and confidence for both of them. Her future would be assured. Ruben seemed to like her or he wouldn't have opened up so quickly and freely, so she had no doubt she could snare him. He was tall and nice looking which was a plus. He was a little clumsy in bed but correcting that would be her first assignment.

No, she had thought, Ruben would not be a problem to secure. His parents, no doubt, would be her first test for they may not be so easy to sway. It took her two weeks, longer than she had expected, to convince Phyllis and Frank she and Ruben were in love and that she could make a difference in Ruben they would be pleased with. If they married right out of high school, they could attend college together and her influence on Ruben would delight them both. They had bought it . . . they wanted to believe it.

All through their senior year of high school, she worked hard tutoring Ruben so that he was able to get passing SAT scores. Still, it took Frank's influence to get them both into the Wharton School of Business at the University of Pennsylvania.

By the end of their sophomore year, Helene realized she had nearly bit off more than she could chew. The more she pushed Ruben, although gently, the more he resisted and became increasingly frustrated as his limitations became more obvious. He started partying and drinking too much. By graduation, she had given up nagging in favor of more hard nosed threats and a heavy hand. It pained her to finally accept failure to make Ruben into the object of her, and Frank's, desired imagination. She would have to be a *puppeteer*.

Over the succeeding years, the position of puppeteer has been an enormous challenge but her efforts were generally rewarded . . . just not to the degree she had envisioned. Every year her ambitions grew and she worked harder doing whatever it took to assist Ruben in doing his job.

Frank, on the other hand, had been bitterly disappointed at the outcome of the promises Helene had made; although, if he were honest with himself, he had not been surprised. He should have been impressed that Helene continued to put forth such outstanding effort in support of Ruben, but he could not forgive her for building up his hopes only to have them dashed. She had convinced him to believe in her, and that kind of trust was sacred. He did not make her efforts any easier.

Helene understood the obstacle Frank presented. When he died, she was elated because she fully expected Phyllis would be more of an ally. Wrong.

CHAPTER XVI—RUBEN STEIN

Ruben sat propped up on the bar stool at the end of the bar downing his third cup of strong coffee and second roast beef sandwich. His eyes were beginning to focus. As the fog cleared, he found his eyes locked onto angry, bitter, disgusted eyes. He blinked to clear his head and when he opened his eyes again he saw Joe bringing him another cup of coffee. He tried to convince himself it was just an hallucination, but he couldn't get the image of those eyes out of his head. Fear is a most sobering emotion.

His father had those eyes. From as early as he could remember, he couldn't do anything to please his father. The more he tried to be what his father wanted him to be, the more he failed. Those eyes terrified him, although why they terrified him he could not pinpoint. His father had never been rough with him or physically punished him when he failed at each and every activity his father tried to teach him. Those eyes of disappointment was enough punishment. They had haunted him all his life.

Amazingly, when he was away from his father, he found the courage to be bold and fake confidence. He knew it was an act but it felt good just the same.

He had noticed Helene in class on the first day of his senior year. Those pale blue eyes crowded out those others he lived with daily. He wanted those eyes so he contrived to be asked to be Helene's blind date one Saturday. He was lost in the comfort of those eyes and for the first time in his life all his fears and memories came tumbling out. Helene just seemed to gather them all up and sort them out for him.

He couldn't believe his good fortune when Helene suggested they marry and she would be his crutch, his support, his salvation. She even took it upon herself to run interference with his parents and was impressively shocked when she persuaded them to consent to their marriage. She even managed to get Frank to help them get into college, a feat he thought was impossible.

So, when he got to college, the pressure to perform, despite Helene's constant tutelage, was too enormous to bear. By his junior year, he could do it no more so lost himself in partying and drinking. He allowed Helene to drag him through the basics enough to graduate but not with the illustrious record his father had counted on. But Helene never failed him. She was always there to push, drag and threaten him to keep going . . . keep trying. But her eyes no longer kept those others at bay.

Thank God for bourbon. And thank God for Uncle Carl. Carl had been his savior the day he drove his car over the cliff, but not before his father had driven him off a similar cliff in his mind. That was also the day his father finally realized Ruben could never be the man he had tried to force him to be. In some ways Frank also went over a cliff but he would never quite recover from that disappointing fall.

Ruben spent six months in the hospital healing all his numerous broken bones. It was a miracle he was alive but he hadn't wanted a miracle. His mind and spirit seemed just as shattered as his body but he saw no chance in their recovery. But at his lowest point right after the accident, with pity tears streaming down his cheeks, there, through a layer of tears, was the unmistakable figure of Carl standing in the doorway of his hospital room smiling at him.

"Your nightmare's over, son," he said to Ruben as he pulled up a chair beside the bed. "I've had a nice long talk with your dad and he has agreed to let me take charge of your education. But . . . and this is a big *but* . . . you have to give your heart and soul to me in total loyalty and confidentiality . . . and in return, I will give you a new life. No expectations. No condemnations. No recriminations. Just a goal you can set at a level you can feel comfortable achieving." He sat back in his chair to let that sink in, and then continued, "How does that sound to you?"

"Wha . . . what do you mean? Dad agreed to . . . what? What are you saying? I don't understand?" stammered Ruben somewhat in a daze by being caught off guard.

"I mean . . . you are coming to work for *me* . . . and your father is okay with that," Carl answered, and then added as an afterthought, "In fact he was delighted and couldn't believe he hadn't thought of it himself years ago."

"So, what you're saying is he's given up on me. He doesn't want anything more to do with me," Ruben said wistfully.

With more compassion than even Carl knew he had, and certainly more empathy than he had ever shown his own children, Carl looked Ruben square in the eye and said, "Son, I've known your father since both of us were in diapers, and one thing your father is not is a quitter and he hasn't given up on you."

Carl stood up and paced the room and continued, "You're father and I have been friends for a long long time but we are not alike. Your father has ideals even I couldn't stand up to but he expects even more from himself than from anyone else."

"But Uncle Carl, you don't know how hard . . ." but Carl cut him off.

"Of course I do. You just don't understand what a perfectionist your father is and he doesn't understand that you are not him." Carl continued, "As I said, your father and I have had a talk. This little stunt of yours has really opened his eyes. He was terrified he had lost you forever and he feels damned guilty about it."

"He . . . he's not angry with me?" Ruben said incredulously.

"No," he lied. It was true Carl had talked with Frank but Frank would never understand why he had failed with his son because he would always believe his son had failed him. He expected Frank would always harbor some anger.

"I'm not like your father, Ruben. I can take you at face value and I'll only ask of you what I think you can deliver. If you trust me and do what I say, I promise you a new life, but on my terms," Carl said seriously. Putting both hands on Ruben's shoulders, he said, "Are you willing to take this step?"

"Do I have a choice?"

Carl released his hands and laughed, "Sure, kid. There are always more cliffs to drive over. But how did that work out for you?"

"Right. Point taken. Okay, when do I start?" Ruben said gesturing to his broken body.

"Right now. Start working on your attitude. And listen to Helene. Now get some rest." He was out the door before Ruben could sputter a thank you.

CHAPTER XVII—CHRISTIAN BRENNER

Ruben finished up his fifth cup of coffee as the memory of Carl's visit years ago faded and his eyes focused on the faintly familiar smiling face of Christian Brenner sitting next to him at the bar accompanied by Paul.

"Welcome back, Cuz. I would say it was nice seeing you but you look awful." Christian poured another cup of coffee for Ruben and one for himself. Clicking cups he said, "Here's to better days."

Ruben blinked a couple times and made an effort at a weak smile. Then he promptly threw up in the bucket someone had propitiously set in his lap.

Unfazed by this behavior they had seen before, and done themselves on past occasions, Christian and Paul took one arm each and escorted Ruben out of the salon and upstairs to the bath lounge to get him cleaned up.

The three men, cousins of blood or friendship, had created a special bond between them growing up together. Each one so different in personality and consequence, one would wonder how such a pact had been possible yet each one's uniqueness added special mortar to the connection. In actuality, the common thread was their fathers.

Paul never knew his father and never cared to know him. He considered himself lucky to have avoided the conflicts the others seemed to have. The irony was that Ruben and Christian were nothing like their fathers, consequently their relationships were like oil to water, while Paul, who never knew his father, had turned out exactly like him in nature and probably would have had a great relationship with him had he still been a presence in his life. Not knowing this was his conflict.

Christian was nothing like his father but he was not without strength of character, intelligence and abilities, the lack of which was Ruben's undoing. Christian was capable of defying his father's wishes because he had the talent and confidence to excel in other ways that earned enough of his father's respect to sustain a truce, although arguments inevitably arose to unnerve him for good measure. It wasn't that he didn't love his father, because he realized he did possess that innate love, but he didn't like him at all.

To keep the peace, Carl kept the greenbacks coming and Christian stayed away from home as much as possible. But that was easy to do when you follow the race car circuit as he did. He was making a name for himself in his own right, had a great many interesting friends, traveled to breathtaking places, and lived the high life . . . so why was there so much inner unrest within him? He knew the answer . . . Cassandra. The guilt of leaving her unprotected sometimes overwhelmed him for he knew what his father was and what he was capable of.

Cassandra was his weakness; after all, they were twins and had shared the same womb. That kind of closeness never fades. If it weren't for that invisible connection, he would never come home. So he called her his weakness . . . the weakness that made him return just for her.

At least that was the case until on a recent visit he noticed Francine who had just graduated from university. He had not seen her since high school but it was like seeing her for the first time. He couldn't believe this was the same girl he had spent much of his childhood riding bicycles with and climbing trees with. He had been around many women all over the world, but the day he saw Francine . . . truly saw her for the first time . . . that day he lost his heart.

CHAPTER XVIII—PRUDENCE & PRENTICE

Paul, Christian and Ruben, now under his own power, were coming down the stairs when they noticed newcomers had entered the hall where Conrad had collected their outer wear upon welcoming them.

"Aunt Prudence! Is that really you?" Paul exclaimed with sincere joy. "We didn't expect you until next week."

"Paul, dear, how nice to see you. You look quite well. Christian! Ruben! How have all of you been? It has been much too long between visits," replied Prudence. "Please," she said with enthusiasm, as she pulled forward a quite attractive and handsomely dressed gentleman that was obviously her escort. "I wish you all to meet Prentice Pireet . . . my husband."

All three of the young men in unison turned their eyes to meet the stranger's while their mouths fell open identical margins. Again in unison, their right arms slowly rose in automatic response to shake the introducee's hand but no words could escape their lips.

Unfazed by the men's shock, Prentice smiled broadly and shook each hand in turn saying, "Good to meet you Paul . . . Christian . . . Ruben. So sorry we sprung this on you but we were married aboard ship and had no time to forward the news."

His words seemed to prove the reality of the scene, and the boys quickly recovered with rounds of handshakes repeated along with hugs and best wishes for Prudence.

"You must tell us the story if we are to believe this is happening," Paul laughed.

The third degree had started, Prudence thought, but that would be expected since she had been an *old maid* for so many years. Who would imagine she would ever get married at such a late stage in her life. "Do you believe in *fate*?" she asked them, but continued without an answer. "Well, you know how I have never wanted to travel or do much of anything with my fellow teachers or church friends . . . well, several of the other teachers planned a cruise to the Bahamas and bought a ticket for me as a surprise birthday present. They literally hijacked me to get me on the boat. Oh, what a state I was in. But the very first day I bumped into Prentice . . ." She paused as Prentice shook his finger at her. "Oh well, okay then . . . actually Prentice tripped over my shoe that had fallen off and when I bent down to see if he was all right, well, our eyes met and, well, there you have it."

"That's it?" the boys said as one.

"Yes, that is pretty much how it happened," affirmed Prentice. "I was there on the cruise as part of a family reunion trip my parents had planned. They are getting on in years a bit and wanted to enjoy the family together again. I had been campaigning for a Senate seat and welcomed the break. Your aunt here must have performed some spell on me, I think, because from that first moment I wanted to know everything about her. By midnight it seemed we had known each other forever. We were married the next evening and I am pleased my whole family was there to welcome her into the family."

"If that don't beat all," spoke up Ruben, now sober enough to stand without assistance. "I sure want to see mother's face when you tell her. And Aunt Priscilla's too. Well, congratulations to both of you. I'm really very happy for you both." There were handshakes and hugs all around again.

While Ruben was making more small talk, Christian disappeared into the salon and when the newlyweds entered the room the chamber music group played their best rendition of *Here Comes the Bride*. Everyone stopped what they were doing and focused their eyes on Prudence and Prentice. Paul and Ruben scurried around them to see everyone's face while Conrad, in a most noble voice, presented "Mr. and Mrs. Prentice Pireet."

Realization dawned on Priscilla almost immediately causing her to hoop and howl and throw up her hands while running through bodies to embrace her married sister. By that time, Francine had leaned over and said to her mother, "It's Prudence! Why . . . she must be married! How is that possible?"

For the next twenty minutes, there wasn't a bit of conversation involving the séance. Everyone had to hear the *whats, wheres, whens* and *hows* involving the newlyweds. Prudence handled the questions extremely well which caused everyone more astonishment as they knew her only as a painfully shy middle aged school teacher. She was radiant with happiness and no one was prouder than Phyllis . . . unless it was Prentice. For a brief pleasant time, Phyllis did not think of Frank or the séance even once.

Poor Prentice was battered with questions too, in turn. It seems his family came from "old" money giving Prentice, and his two brothers and one sister, all the advantages in life. That was his good fortune indeed but he would say that his family's modesty was the real treasure. They were all properly schooled in manners and academics in equal measure with love and attention from his parents. He had followed his father in business, as did his brothers after him, and between them, had tripled the size of his holdings, employing well over 300,000 workers throughout the country.

He had married young, but like all young executives trying to make his own name in business, he seemed more married to his work than his wife so the marriage failed in short order. He had not remarried but threw himself into work. Despite his position, and perhaps because of it, he developed compassion for the trials and tribulations of the working class and became a champion of their grievances beginning with city councilman, then mayor and now he was running for a senate seat. With such a life it seemed hard to believe this man remained untouched by greed and power but he was a true jewel in the dessert, or, in this case, on the high seas.

Prudence was a perfect match for Prentice . . . well, not in family or station in life, but in intellect and disposition. As a child, her refuge was school and books and she grew up well informed but lacking in societal experience. But put her in a classroom full of students and she was eloquent. She had a rare gift for teaching young minds and her students adored her. All the teachers tried to emulate her. But they, too, noticed what little life she had outside of the school room and thus perpetrated a ruse to get her out of her element even for a short time. Little did they know what a life-changing experience it would ultimately become for her.

Prudence, more than anyone, was still having trouble believing the change in her life. She hadn't even attempted to embrace her new circumstances. Her modest life would need to become a thing of the past. If she should become a senator's wife, she must learn quickly to be an asset by her husband's side. But then again, learning was her life.

CHAPTER XIX—LANCE & HOLLY KNIGHT

Lance and Holly stepped through the front door into the front hall and their ears were greeted by what appeared to be many voices talking and laughing through festive music coming from the salon at the end of the hall. It was decidedly not what either had expected to be a prelude to a séance. But there was no mistaking it.

With no Conrad in sight, they removed their coats and laid them on the hall chair and anxiously headed for the salon to have their curiosity enlightened. Conrad immerged from the room as they reached the doorway.

"Conrad!" exclaimed Lance, "What the devil is going on in there? I expected a séance to be more sober than that."

"Ah, Mr. Knight . . . Mrs. Knight . . ." Conrad began with a joyful face, "It is Miss Prudence . . . or I should say Mrs. for she is now Mrs. Prentice Pireet just off her trip to the Bahamas. It seems her teacher friends coerced her into going with them on a cruise and she met a mighty fine gentleman who took a rather quick shine to her and she to him. They married on the ship and here they are—a surprise to beat all surprises."

"Well, I'll be . . . That is the last thing I would have guessed. Pireet you say? Hmmm. Isn't he the man running for senator of Connecticut or Rhode Island or one of those northern states?" said Lance.

"Yes indeed he is. Can you believe our dear Prudence a Senator's wife?" Conrad added in happy astonishment.

"Lance, dear," interjected Holly. "Shouldn't we go in and extend our happy best wishes?"

"Of course, yes, of course we shall," Lance agreed, and they both hurried into the salon just as the exuberant noise level was returning to a normal hum and the music had returned to more classical faire.

Francine saw them first and came rushing to greet them. "Have you heard the news about Aunt Prudence? She's a married lady now. How splendid is that!"

"Yes, we were just informed by Conrad," said Lance as their eyes met briefly. "We thought we should add out best wishes as well. It is obvious from the noise when we arrived that everyone was delighted with the news."

"Oh, it couldn't have come at a better time. The conversation was getting exceedingly dull and morbid and mother's nerves were escalating. This news certainly took everyone's mind off the séance even if only for awhile. Now she has someone new to indoctrinate with the occult . . . Prentice."

"Well, confidentially, I'm not too comfortable with this séance," Holly surprised them by saying. "You don't really believe in . . . well, in spirits . . . spirits showing themselves and speaking to us mortals, do you?"

"I'll go along with anything if it placates mother," Francine answered, "but, truthfully . . . I can't see it happening. But that poses a worrisome problem . . . if a spirit doesn't show, mother will sink even lower and maybe so low she won't recover. So, what I think is Madam Angelica better have some magic up her sleeve or I will be real pissed." She looked to Lance for support, which did not go unnoticed by Holly.

"Come on, I'll introduce you." said Francine as she slide between them, linking their arms with hers, and escorted them to the newlyweds.

Holly was uncomfortable tonight but it wasn't wholly because of the séance. She was worried about her marriage. Lance had been her high school sweetheart and they had married right after graduation, as many of her friends were doing, but in her case it was more urgent and necessary. Shortly after their wedding, she had a miscarriage and the ensuing complications rendered her sterile. To hold onto Lance, the love of her life, she offered to work in order to put Lance through college and law school. It was a tremendous sacrifice but she was certain it would be worth it. What she hadn't anticipated was the metamorphosis that occurred in Lance as a result of an education. It hurt to admit, but she no longer fitted into Lance's life. She had stayed the sweet little high school girl but Lance was a long way down another path, almost a continent away from her. She had won a battle but was losing the war.

She had always been a religious person but lately more than ever. She prayed but God had turned away and she felt anger which gave way to guilt. Fear of God's wrath made her nervous about the spirit world . . . the séance.

Lance had loved Holly, but it was high school love and his hormones had gotten the better of him. The last thing he wanted then was to get married and have the responsibility of a family. He had such high dreams of getting a good education and maybe becoming a high priced lawyer and really make a name for himself. He had great respect for his parents who eked out a living running a neighborhood grocery store, but he wanted more.

His parents were disappointed when he told them about Holly's condition but pressured him into doing the right thing and marrying her. So he hid his disappointment, married Holly and went to work for his father. He thought those months were the most depressing months of his life until Holly lost the baby . . . and more than that, could never have another child. The world seemed to crash down around him. He had given up his dream for nothing. Why couldn't this have happened sooner, he thought. More than anything he wanted to leave Holly and resume his dream but his parents again shamed him into staying with Holly. He had to admit she was probably going through as much torture as he was, if not more. So he vowed to make the best of it.

Holly couldn't help but notice Lance's unhappiness no matter how hard he tried to dismiss it. So one night at dinner she announced that she had been offered a job as secretary at the General Electric offices downtown. "Why don't you see if that scholarship you were offered is still available," she mentioned casually. "I've been doing some figuring and I think we can manage on my salary if we are careful, and maybe your father can use you on weekends."

He couldn't believe his ears so she had to assure him several times that it was her wish that he go back to school. The next day he inquired about the scholarship and was delighted to learn it was still his. He immediately enrolled at State College and just made it into the Fall term. His dream was going to come true. But as much as he appreciated the sacrifices he knew Holly was making, he could no longer recapture the love of innocent youth.

It may have been different had Holly tried to improve herself by reading or at least keeping up with current events, but she was a homebody and content to be just a homemaker and take care of him. But an education is a powerful amplifier and soon Lance could no longer carry on a stimulating conversation with his wife and she seemed to have no interest in what he wished to discuss. He began finding reasons to go out with school friends at night or stayed longer on campus. Although they lived under the same roof, they had their separate lives. He would have guilty moods and bring her flowers or candy now and then but mostly he was content with the arrangement. Holly knew what was happening but had run out of ideas to keep him home. The fault was all hers and she carried it well but her lonely nights were full of tears.

Although their marriage was far from ideal for her, *he* had seemed content with the arrangement and always came home at night to sleep with *her*. Mostly it was to sleep; any intimacy was minimal and banal. As unfulfilling as the relationship was, her heart was a prisoner forever and would cling to any fabric, any scrap, of Lance.

Nearly a year ago Holly noticed changes in Lances routine. He spent more and more time at the Stein-Brenner Plant or at the big house visiting Phyllis *because she was having vapors or needed assurance or legal advice or . . . something!* Then there were nights he didn't come home. She had discreetly checked with some of his friends and colleagues who had wondered about him too as he had stopped his society with them as well.

One evening about three months ago, she could stand it no longer and went cruising the usual spots looking for him. She spotted his car in the back lot of the plant, nearly hidden in a dark corner. She had missed it at first but the white tags picked up her headlights as she turned. There was a low light on in one of the offices and the blinds were not quite shut tight. She peered in through a narrow crack and saw them . . . Lance and Francine.

Why had she gone hunting him? She should have known she would see this. It would have been better to have been ignorant but the deed was done. She would never be able to wipe that brief vision out of her memory no matter how hard she squeezed her eyes and washed them with tears.

How she got home she couldn't say but she laid awake all night fearing Lance's return. It was a relief he didn't. The tears had dried up long before the sun came up but still she lay in bed, fully clothed, staring into space. By noon she had made up her mind. Last night never happened; she erased it from her mind. Then she showered, dressed in her brightest outfit, and headed off to the library where she checked out an arm load of books: *The Republic* by Plato, *The Rise and Fall of the Third Reich* by William L. Shirer, *The Communist Manifesto* by Karl Marx, *The Prince* by Niccolo Machiavelli, *Atlas Shrugged* by Ayn Rand, and *Common Sense* by Thomas Paine. The gloves were on.

CHAPTER XX—AMANDA HART

The salon had become quite full and most of the guests were still on their feet milling around after the mini-celebration and congratulations to the bride and groom. It took Lance, Holly and Francine a while to weave through the crowd of people, each stopping to greet the newcomers. At last they reached the group of sisters still chattering away with Prentice the object of their dialogue.

"What is this? Has the Séance already begun and are these spirits before us here to haunt us for certainly they are a vision to behold," taunted Lance. "Phyllis, can this lovely lady be you sister, Prudence?" Lance closed his eyes and laid his fingertips to his brow pretending to be in a mock trance. "Wait . . . I'm getting a message. This gentleman is Prentice Pireet . . . soon to be Senator Pireet. But no . . . we are celebrating another event . . . could it be a wedding? Yes, yes . . . Congratulations to Mr. and Mrs. Pireet," he said as he opened his eyes and arms to give Prudence a big hug and kiss on the cheek and then turned to shake hands with Prentice. Holly followed his lead.

With the amenities concluded, the little group broke up into two groups: Lance and Francine held Prudence and Prentice in conversation, and Phyllis, Priscilla, and Holly were joined by Amanda Hart.

"Dear ladies, wasn't it nice to have a bit of an uplifting spell to the party," Amanda said exuberantly. "The scene was getting rather dull, don't you think? I believe it has brought some color back to your cheeks, Phyllis. How wonderful."

"Yes, Amanda. It is the best of news to know my little sister is happy and well cared for. You know how I worry," Phyllis responded.

"You are right about this party being dull," Priscilla repeated. "You would think this was Frank's funeral all over again."

"Oh! Priscilla how could you say such a thing," Phyllis exclaimed.

"Madam, I don't think she meant any disrespect," cut in Holly. "I've only been here a few minutes and think it an excellent gathering. I think you should entertain more often in the future as I observe this one seems a success."

"Exactly!" cut in Amanda. "I've been saying the exact thing for months, dear, and still she is unmoved. Perhaps now you will listen to me, Phyllis. You need to get out. The charity groups we used to administer are in great need of your kind services."

"I told you before, Amanda. I'm just not ready for social commitments."

"Sister, charity work sounds like the ideal work to take your mind off the past," Priscilla added. "I would love to get involved myself. We could do this together . . . with Amanda, of course. And Holly too."

"Me? You would want *me* to join you?" Holly said incredulously.

"Wonderful idea," said Amanda. "The charities always need volunteers and it is most satisfying work. I'm sure Lance would approve. No doubt he will be as proud of you as Arthur is of me for doing such needy work."

Hearing Lance mentioned spurred Holly to respond, "I would be honored to join your group. Phyllis, please, you really must do this. It sounds so . . . so . . . satisfying."

"You're outnumbered, Phyllis, what do you say?" Amanda said pointedly.

Amanda had been hounding Phyllis for nearly a year to come back into her social circle. Naturally she waited a descent period of time after Frank's death but after that she ought to have put it behind her and gotten on with her life.

Amanda had met Phyllis the first day the Steins moved into the *mansion on the hill*, as Amanda liked to call it. Amanda was active in the Welcome Wagon organization, which was very active in the area. She came bearing a gift basket of food and drink items, flowers, and, more important, a Directory with names and addresses of most everyone in and around the town as well as service providers, emergency numbers and general community information. It was a new neighbor's bible. It also included a calendar of events which Amanda specifically pointed out and, before ten minutes had passed, Amanda had signed Phyllis up for the Ladies Book Club, the marathon bridge league, the church picnic committee, the Women's Club, Hospital Helpers Anonymous, and, of course, Welcome Wagon. More would come later. They quickly became the best of friends, almost like sisters. Naturally the husbands became close as well.

In those early days, Phyllis and Frank were quite the socialites. They were always having dinner parties and Phyllis would have the ladies for tea. Consequently, every week there would be an invitation or two to attend other soirées around town. They even joined the Chamber Music Group; Phyllis had learned the piano and Frank played a pretty decent flute, which he learned in college. Phyllis' calendar was always booked full.

When Frank died, she stopped going anywhere and would not be swayed by her best friend or even her beloved daughter. But even though a year had passed, they never gave up trying.

"Amanda, you are my dearest friend. If I can say no to you, you must understand how seriously unable I am to continue that life . . . without Frank." Phyllis started to tear up and retrieved her handkerchief from her cuff while the other ladies murmured their apologies.

"Don't apologize. There is no fault in what you are trying to do. In fact, I am so very fortunate to have friends like you who are looking out for me and care so much. I really do appreciate you efforts, but . . ." she said as her lower lip began to tremble. "Perhaps after the séance. After I talk to Frank. Perhaps then I will have my mind settled and want to do other things. Just have patience with me."

"The séance. If that is what it must be, then it must," said Amanda with the others nodding agreement. "Exactly when are you expecting Madam Angelica? Shouldn't she be here by now?"

"Very soon, I believe," interrupted Francine, as their little group had ended their discussions and Francine had overheard Amanda's queries. "She wanted everyone to have had a chance to arrive and get settled. Actually, I believe she truthfully wants a *grand entrance*," she whispered conspiratorially.

"Francine! How can you say . . . she's not at all . . ." Phyllis defended.

"I'm just kidding, mother. Don't be upset. Just having a little fun."

"Well, all right, but this isn't funny at all. As I have just stated, the rest of my life will be determined by Madam Angelica's success tonight. I *need* to talk to your father. I must have him tell me what to do. He's the only one who can. He always advised me well, and I always did what he told me. Can't you all understand. That's why I'm like this . . . I'm helpless without him." The confession was too taxing on Phyllis so she sat down in her plump chair exhausted.

"Don't despair, Phyllis," interjected Lance, "you simple must learn to trust others to advise you. Which reminds me, do you think you are up to signing those papers we talked about? I'd like to get that concluded before Madam Angelica's arrival stirs everything up."

"Of course, Lance, I best take care of that," Phyllis agreed. "Let's go into the library."

"Amanda. Would you and Arthur be kind enough to accompany us and sign as witnesses?" asked Lance. To the rest he said, "Please excuse us for a moment. This really won't take long."

With Lance in the lead, escorting Phyllis toward the library door at the end of the room, Amanda picked Arthur from the crowd as they proceeded past him and disappeared through the door.

CHAPTER XXI—THE WILL

Lance lead Phyllis to the desk and held the chair as she seated herself. He then motioned for Amanda and Arthur to be seated in the armchairs nearby. He then proceeded to reach into his inside jacket pocket and retrieved several folded groups of parchment paper and laid them out on the desk in front of Phyllis.

"Here are the papers we discussed earlier this week. Please read them over and make sure you agree with the disposition of your property as laid out in the Will." Then Lance continued, "If you have questions or wish to make changes, please don't hesitate to make your wishes known now."

Phyllis was having difficulty reading and said, "You realize this is so hard for me to update my Will as you suggested. You are right that it should be done, after all it has been a year since Frank . . . She turned back to the paper in her hand and began again to read. The best she could do was glance at the important points. When she had satisfied herself that all parties were listed with the agreed distributions, she asked for a pen.

After she had signed all necessary copies, Lance turned to Amanda and Arthur and asked them if they would please sign as witnesses. They signed the papers in turn and Lance collected the papers, folded them and placed them back in his inside pocket.

"Now that didn't take long and now you won't have to think about it for many long years." Lance finished by thanking Amanda and Arthur for being witnesses. "Let's all return to the main room and have a glass of champagne to commemorate the signing and wait the arrival of Madam Angelica."

All were in agreement, and joined the others.

CHAPTER XXII—MADAM ANGELICA
and HUGO HANDY

Lance, Phyllis, Amanda and Arthur had no sooner toasted and downed their champagne when Conrad announced the arrival of Madam Angelica . . . and Hugo Handy. All conversation stopped and all eyes turned to assess the much anticipated and mysterious Seer. Even Joe the bartender stopped in mid pour and narrowed his eyes.

The Madam stood for many moments in the doorway in a regal pose and let the effect wash over her subjects. She was dressed in a many layered tiered skirt of black lace with a low cut black lace bodice. The sleeves were long and came to a point over the back of her hand. A red lace shawl was draped over jet black hair which was pulled severely back from her face and coiled into a bun on top of her head. The shawl was long and ran down her back nearly to her thighs. Her pale hands had taken the corners of the shawl and held them crossed at her shoulders as in a hug. There were many rings of precious stones adorning her fingers and a ruby tied at her throat. Four diamond studs ran up each ear and a collection of golden discs dangled from her earlobes and made soft tinny sounds when she moved her head.

Her pale face wore an expression that demanded respect and commanded compliance. Her eyelids were heavily shadowed in a purple hue and long thick black lashes hooded her eyes. But it was her full red lips that held everyone mesmerized. They parted and she spoke in a clear earthy European accent, "Good evening. I hope I have not kept everyone waiting."

It was Phyllis who broke the spell and rushed to Madam Angelica and gushed with breathless enthusiasm, "No indeed. We are all at your disposal. Please, won't you come have a libation and meet everyone."

Phyllis, and others who discovered they could move, escorted The Madam to the bar where she nonchalantly glanced at Joe and ordered, "I would have a Sherry."

By the time she took her first sip of sherry, most of the guests had gone back to their respective conversations and a buzz hung over the room once more. Madam had moved some steps away from the bar to sip her sherry and meet each guest curious enough to present themselves. Phyllis was in her element now and couldn't stop chattering with everyone especially Madam Angelica. Madam noticed the ones whose fears prevented even eye contact and those that were falsely brave. Her eyes seemed focused on the scene in front of her but expertly scanned the entire room undetected. She had done this on every visit she had made with Phyllis over a good part of the past year. This was going to be so easy, she thought.

Madam Angelica had honed her trade for over twenty five years and she is good at what she does . . . very good . . . perhaps the best. She had her start in college by choosing psychology as her major and used that knowledge to influence and manipulate her subject's mind. She practiced the art of deception and misdirection and fine-tuned her manual dexterity skills. In the early days, she had practiced picking people's pockets with nary a hint of exposure.

The eyes were very import. If one can capture a subject's eyes with their own, one can do most anything with their hands and the subject will not see it. Voice was also a special tool. Certain modulations had a hypnotic effect. And one must choose one's words wisely to build a picture and strengthen confidence and faith in impossible possibilities.

Sometimes she used special effects and other props. For this séance, she had brought with her a special crystal ball she had had made to her own specifications. The orb was crystal clear, set atop a special stand with a tiny electronic receiver hidden inside. Between the stand and the globe were tiny holes, some allowed colored smoke to flow into the interior of the ball and other holes allowed light to shine up through the globe, not only lighting the inside of the ball but also projecting figures on the ceiling and walls. Also inside was a small microphone which could receive and transmit sounds and voices. All these functions were wirelessly controlled by tiny buttons on one especially prominent ring she wore which she could activate with her thumb unobserved. She had spent many years developing this instrument and was very proud of her handiwork.

She was also very adept at telling fortunes with the use of the Crystal Ball, Tarot cards, Rune stones or even a regular deck of cards impromptu. She had a gift for storytelling earning her a high percentage of **believers** with an equally high percentage of return customers. She had studied her craft well and was expert in all applications.

Her son, whom she referred to as *Hugo Handy*, who served as her driver and bodyguard, was a constant presence whenever she was with a client, either at the client's residence or other chosen site. Hugo was a big man in his early thirties; tall and muscular. His head was shaved and he had a tattoo of Celtic knots running from one ear across the top of his head to the other ear. His face displayed no expression and he rarely talked unless it was to whisper to Madam Angelica. He wore black trousers and a black jacket over a black turtleneck. As big as he was, he was able to make himself invisible in the shadows and most people were not aware of his presence. Hugo has his uses.

Her given name at birth was Angina Pectoris; but when she made the decision to pursue a career in the mystic arts, she became Madam Angelica Austin. She chose Angelica because it sounded so . . . well . . . angelic, but mostly she felt it added an additional mental connection to the afterlife.

She not only changed her name but changed her way of life from the way she dressed, wore her hair (she was really a redhead), chose her makeup and the type community she lived in, which was a sort of commune of nearly one hundred other seers. Most of them had *specialties* that earmarked them; i.e., one might be especially adept at reading palms, another might read Tarot Cards and a third may simply create crafts. Many had written books which were for sale and every client had to have one. Angelica had not written a book nor did she intend to. Why give away her secrets for a pittance.

The Madam, as she sometimes liked to be called, has her own system of finding ripe pigeons. She looks in the obituaries. She and Hugo live in a modest but quaint house decorated with *expensive things*, some of which were stored in hidden rooms, but she was still a gypsy at heart. All of the clients she picks from the obits survivors, or those who answer her ads, are domiciled outside a thirty mile range from her dwelling. She never sees clients in her home for that is her secret refuge.

A year ago, her search through the columns turned up a "Frank N. Stein" and she immediately stopped looking any further. Being a relatively important man in his town, the obituary was a rather extensive, informative one. Using a yellow highlighter, she marked the interesting parts and then went to the internet in search of more information about the deceased and his family and acquaintances. By the time she finally contacted Phyllis, she knew more about the whole family than they knew about themselves. She tried to leave nothing to chance. And, of course, Hugo has his uses.

It was exceptionally easy to win Phyllis' trust and support. In fact, she hung on every word Angelica spoke and hungered for more. The other family members were not so easy to fool, but it came down to the fact that they would go along with whatever made Phyllis feel a little better or gave her hope and guidance that she actually heeded, was fine with them. And it was fine with her, as long as the money kept rolling in. Angelica would visit Phyllis at least three times a week; sometimes more. The money added up, for her fees were not cheap, but she had her eye on a bigger score. Willard altered that plan.

With both Willard and Angelica taking up much of Phyllis's time, it was inevitable they would cross paths. She had not counted on anyone recognizing her from the early days. She had gone to great lengths to alter her appearance and presentation and felt confident no one from her past would ever see through the veneer . . . but weasely Willard had and wasted no time in cornering her one evening outside in the shadows as she was leaving.

He was no fool and knew she had a plan for a bigger score. He, apparently, had plans of his own that weren't working as well as her own. "There is plenty to go around. I can help you," he said that night. So she arranged to meet him next day for coffee at a small café a good ways out of town.

She was fashionably late just to make him a bit anxious and worrisome. When she first sat down, he tried to make light conversation by asking questions about the last 25-30 years, but she avoided his probes and got to the chase. Then he wanted to know what her plan was to part Phyllis from her money, but again she was not forthcoming. Finally, he leaned forward and inclined his head toward hers conspiratorially, and said, "Okay, you'll agree we both have the same goal and that is to part Phyllis from her money. You won't tell me how you plan to do that, but my guess is that it won't be easy and it isn't foolproof. Am I right?"

She continued to stare at him over her raised coffee cup. His closeness made her skin crawl; the years had not changed that condition. She spoke low, "I do not need my crystal ball to conclude that your personal plan is not working for you. So you thought to tag along on my coattails? Am *I* right?"

"Madam! I'm a schemer and I'm not coming to the table empty-handed. I have a plan that is *really sweet*. But it means we work together and we split 50/50. I assume you can do a séance."

"It's my specialty. Stop the cat and mouse and get to the point." She put her cup down and narrowed her eyes.

For the next hour and a half he laid out his plan meticulously, they discussed it vigorously, fine-tuned every point and emerged with a confident, enthusiastic grin. The table was littered with many coffee cups, the remnants of lunch, dozens of balled up lined paper and a pad full of notes and outline for their final plan. Their mood was a mixture of giddiness, relief and pride much like first time parents at the birth of a son.

Reluctant to even touch Willard, Angelica condescended to shake his hand to solidify the partnership. Each agreed to total secrecy and total anonymity. The plan was in motion.

During the months following, Phyllis became much closer to Madam Angelica, and more dependant. Francine saw her come and go nearly every day as the relationship escalated, but seeing her mother in such good spirits she dismissed her innate feelings of distrust and caution. She honestly believed there was no harm in it and only good things for her mother would come of it.

Priscilla was the only family member or close friend (with the exception of Dr. and Mrs. Hart) that took issue with the relationship between Phyllis and Madam Angelica and was very vocal about it. Francine pleaded with her to hold her tongue, explaining how upsetting it was for Phyllis. She would control herself for a day or two, but her jealousy would not be contained. Francine had to give up for she did not understand the true motive.

When the time was ripe, Madam Angelica proposed the possibility of contacting Frank through a séance, Phyllis couldn't stop talking about it for three days. Francine was now concerned. Until now, the interaction between the seer and her mother seemed harmless enough to Francine; even stimulating for her mother's state of mind. But in a séance, Angelica would have to *deliver!* Francine was certain this business was a bunch of malarkey but her mother didn't and would fully expect the spirit of her father to present himself *physically* in front of her. How could Angelica pull off this fantastic stunt? And if she could, to what purpose? And if she couldn't be convincing, what harm would it do her poor susceptible mother?

There was only one person she could pour her heart and soul out to and who would console her and give her excellent advice . . . Lance. In fact, he had been *advising* her for months and she didn't care about consequences.

CHAPTER XXIII—THE GUESTS

After nearly thirty minutes of constant chatter from the guests that wanted to meet her, Madam Angelica took a polite break to return to the bar to refill her sherry glass. Joe saw her coming and had her drink waiting for her and said, "Your sherry, Angel."

"Excuse me? What did you call me?" Angelica said warily.

"I called you 'Angel' . . . um, you know, Angelica, séance, talking to the spirits or angels," answered Joe.

"Who are you? I've been here often but never have noticed you," queried Angelica.

"Conrad hired me for this gig. I needed a job."

"Then, of course, you wouldn't know not to take familiarities with me. I don't talk to the help, so I would appreciate your not addressing any more comments to me in the future, Mr . . . ." Angelica said curtly.

"Joe. Joe Phoenix," he said as his stare bore into her eyes.

She snatched her sherry and turned away quickly. Hugo noticed but stayed in the shadows and watched her return to the small group surrounding Phyllis.

Phyllis was happy to see her return for her confidence had waned without her by her side. Carl came forward dragging his women. "Nice to see you again, Angelica. My ladies here are a bit nervous about this séance tonight. I told them it is just smoke and mirrors, right?" he said with his usual swagger.

"Carl! Don't you dare poke fun because I will indeed take it personally," pouted Phyllis. "Please, you *must* get in the right frame of mind because you are sitting at the séance table."

"She is absolutely correct," added Angelica. "A positive concentration is vital for successful channeling. The vibes must be there or the attempt to cross over will fail. And *I* will know who is breaking the chain. It will be *your* fault if Phyllis is disappointed." People are so predictable, she thought. They always give me an "out". She could see the fear and distrust in the ladies' eyes and smiled inside as she imagined what they were soon to experience.

For every guest that approached for a word or two, Phyllis would beam with pride and excitement. She had anticipated this event like no other event of her life and had dreamed every night about what she would say to Frank when he appeared.

Arthur Hart had been watching her closely for some time and saw her excitement increase along with her breathing the more agitated she became as the time for the séance came closer. He was becoming alarmed. He made a stop at the bar for a glass of water and headed for Phyllis. She was so happy to see him until he silently handed her two pills with the glass of water.

"Oh, Arthur," she whined, "Is this necessary? I'm really fine. Maybe I've had one too many glasses of champagne, but I'm so excited now that Madam Angelica is here and I'm looking forward to the séance."

"All true words, my darling Phyllis, but take the medication if only to humor a worried old man." Arthur took her hand and kissed it gallantly. Just then Prudence and Prentice stepped into the group so Arthur took the opportunity to pull Madam aside for a brief word.

"Madam Angelica, may I have a quick word," Arthur said to her nearly in a whisper. "You are aware, I believe, that Phyllis has a weak heart." He paused for confirmation and was rewarded with a nod. "You have also observed, I am sure, the level of excitement she has reached since your arrival and the séance has not yet begun." Another nod. "What exactly is going to happen in your séance? You must have the entire scene planned. I just want to know if Phyllis can handle what's going to happen." He was out of breath so Madam Angelica assumed he had said his peace and expected a reply.

"You presume, doctor, that because I am a seer I have absolute knowledge of the future. That is not exactly how the *gift* works. If you have never experience a séance, sir, let me explain briefly. Those that wish to lend their energy to the calling of the spirit will sit around the table set up there," she said as she gestured at the table set up in the open space in front of the patio doors. "We all join hands so the current of life force can complete the circle. The crystal ball allows me to focus and transcend between planes and if all goes well without incident, Frank's spirit will channel through me and appear before us. That is the plan, Dr. Hart, and that is what I expect will happen . . . unless the spirit, Frank, senses some anomaly that would frighten him off. Is that all you wish to know?"

"I sure would like to know just how you plan to accomplish that."

"I told you," she said with her head held high as if affronted, but she dealt with this kind of skepticism all the time. Just stick with the illusion wholeheartedly and innocently. It messes with their minds. "I will do my job, doctor. I suggest you simply do yours." That said she simply dismissed him and any further conversation by turning her attention back to Phyllis and her sisters.

Arthur felt he had just been trampled by a stampeding herd of cattle and headed for the bar to wash the sand and grit from his mouth. He still had no idea what was likely to happen . . . and how.

CHAPTER XXIV—THE SÉANCE

While Phyllis was discussing some issue with her sisters, Angelica nonchalantly scanned the room once more, making mental notes of all the guests she had spoken with, which included nearly everyone, with the exception of Lily and Cassandra Brenner, who had approached her with Carl but had uttered nary a word or sound. She was certain they had held their breath the whole time. As her eyes circled the room, they found Joe's staring fixedly at her alone. Her eyes were captured briefly; she frowned quizzically, and tore her eyes away to return to her surveillance. Ultimately, her eyes were drawn back to Joe who was now at her side with a fresh sherry, which she accepted reluctantly, with an air of haughtiness. Joe turned without a word and disappeared back behind the bar, hidden from view by a group of thirsty guests.

It was time. She glanced toward Hugo in the shadows and nodded imperceptibly and he acknowledged the signal.

Angelica reached over and touched Phyllis' arm lightly. Phyllis reacted as if she had been zapped with a charge of electricity by ending her conversation in mid word and turned immediately to face Angelica.

"I believe the Spirits are receptive now," Angelica said with a low clear voice. "We should begin. Come take your seat at the table and the others will follow." As she moved to guide Phyllis to her seat at one side of the round table, the buzz of conversations quickly tapered off until the room was quiet. After Phyllis was settled, Angelica walked to the opposite side of the table and stood at her seat.

"Ladies and Gentlemen," she announced, "I believe I have everyone's attention. I sense the closeness of the Spirit World. We are ready to begin the Séance."

While Angelica was mentally sorting out the guests, she also made sure the crystal ball, which Hugo had already set up in the middle of the table, was positioned correctly and the chairs were properly placed. She found Hugo had done a thorough job as always.

"Francine," she called out and motioned with her hand as she said, "Would you be so kind as to take the seat at the left of your mother."

"And Ruben . . . please take the seat there by your sister." Ruben frowned but did as she requested.

"Dominique . . . would you be so kind as to sit here by me and next to Ruben. Ralph may sit behind you. Dominique looked at Ralph for assurance and he whispered, "I'm right behind you, sweetheart," and took the seat behind her.

"Priscilla . . . if you would take the seat next to Phyllis . . ."

"Oh no you don't. I am taking the seat next to you so I can keep an eye on you, missy. No arguments either. I will have my way in this," boomed a very suspicious Priscilla.

"I would be honored, Priscilla," cooed Angelica as she continued her seat assignments. "Perhaps Willard would then take the seat next to Phyllis."

"You're not leaving me out of this ring. This last seat is mine. I certainly need to keep my eye on these two anyway. I feel like a rose between two thorns!" Carl quipped.

"The rest may sit in any chairs set up around the outer ring of the table."

Quietly, but quickly, the rest chose their seats. Calvin and Bonnie sat just behind Carl and Willard; Cassandra and Lily sat behind Carl and Priscilla. Prentice and Prudence chose to sit behind Lily and Calvin while Paul sat behind his mother. Ralph sat, as promised, behind Dominique and Helene sat behind Ruben and Arthur and Amanda sat behind Francine to be close to Phyllis if she needed them. Florence took a seat behind the Harts; Christian had wanted to be closer to Francine but settled with the chair behind Amanda and Helene. Sven and Charity took the seats behind Helene and Ralph. Holly and Lance sat behind Phyllis, next to Arthur and in front of the bar where Joe and Conrad stood a bit behind them to the right at the corner of the bar. There were other employees, neighbors and friends who took chairs or stood behind Prudence on one side and Christian on the other. There were no seats directly behind Angelica . . . only the patio doors.

"Will those sitting at the table please join hands," Angelica commanded as she reached out to either side of her and grasped Priscilla's large sweaty hand on one side and Dominique's small trembling one on the other. Fortunately, she thought, the ring that controlled the sphere was on her right hand which held Dominique's small hand and not on her left which was now swallowed up by Priscilla's beefy one.

Per Angelica's request, Conrad had turned the main lights down or off completely so that there was barely enough light to see one's neighbor. That was soon rectified.

"I must ask for complete silence, please," Angelica sternly commanded, "and that means turning off all cell phones. The Spirits are easily deterred."

Angelica closed her eyes and raised her face to the ceiling, but not before a quick glance had revealed Ruben had broken the circle of hands in order to reach in his inside coat pocket, retrieve a flask and down a large swig. "I sense the circle is not complete," she said irritably, with her eyes still closed. "All hands *must* be joined . . . Ruben!"

Ruben was startled, "Um, I'm so sorry. Needed my handkerchief." Ruben smiled confidently at his quick cover.

"Next time you need a handkerchief, I suggest you look in another pocket instead of the one with the flask in it," Angelica said without moving her position. With her head facing the ceiling, and with lashes long and full, it was quite easy for her to part her eyes just a bit to take in the slightly awed expressions on most of the faces. Inwardly, she was smiling to herself. It was so predictable that at least one always broke the circle for some reason which gave her the opportunity to stun. This behavior was so oddly consistent with all her séances, it was a bit eerie even to her. The reaction, too, was almost always the same—even the disbelievers sat up straighter and became more attentive. Yes, this was going to be a piece of cake, she thought.

For several moments Angelica sat erect with her lidded eyes staring blindly at the ceiling. Occasionally, she would let out a soft moan and move her upturned head from side to side.

"I can sense them. There are spirits getting closer. It is time for all around the table to place your clasped hands upon the table top." As she said this, and all responded as directed, Angelica moved her thumb ever so slightly so as not to be detected, and the crystal orb in the center of the table began to glow and continued to increase intensity. Another twitch from her thumb and the globe filled with swirling smoke. A soft breeze emanated from the pulsating orb carrying a fragrance of wet earth and rotting leaves. Faint colors rode on the swirls of smoke. Finally, a low, vibrating hummm filled the room.

"Spirits, come closer," Angelica invited. "There are those here tonight who wish to speak to one of you. I beseech you to make your presence known."

Angelica began to writhe slightly as she repeated her plea. When she felt the moment was right, she activated another button and a low, hollow voice spoke as if from deep inside a well, "Whoooo . . . dooo . . . you . . . seek . . . among . . . us?" Asked the voice. There was a murmur throughout the room and several muffled shrieks. Carl, and a few others, looked everywhere to try to discern the trick but were frustrated when no clue was evident.

Phyllis could no longer control herself, "**Frank! Frank!** Is that you? Please. I want to speak to my husband, Frank!"

"Phyllis, be silent," Angelica said softly, "You will have your chance to speak. Be patient."

"I . . . I . . . yes, of course. I'm so sorry."

Minutes passed and again Angelica began writhing in earnest and spoke to the spirit, "We wish to make contact with Frank N. Stein who has been among you this past year to the day. It is urgent that his beloved wife speak with him and discuss resolutions for her future." She paused briefly to prolong the suspense which was totally unnecessary for some in attendance. Finally, she added, "Please, we beg you . . . we implore you . . . tell us if Frank is there with you."

"He . . . is . . . with . . . us . . ." the hollow voice answered.

Phyllis yelped and drew in her breath, nearly forgetting to keep her hands tightly clasped with her neighbors'. Francine held on tight and reminded her to keep the chain intact. She did not wish for Angelica to scold them again.

"Wait! We must speak with Frank!" Angelica implored anxiously.

"He . . . is . . . coming . . ." said the spirit as the voice trailed off.

No one had noticed the patio doors open; nor could anyone have guessed when it happened. Suddenly, a fine mist crept in from the open doors and coiled around the guests as if to caress each one. A low light followed the mist into the room. All eyes bore into the increasingly heavy mist. There in the mist, backlit by the light, was a shadow coming closer. As the shadow came closer, it took the shape of a robed and hooded figure diffused by the mist. The figure ceased its approach several feet from the entrance and spoke in a low reverberating voice, unemotional and in a monotone.

"I am Frank N. Stein . . . who calls me?"

Madam Angelica, the only person in the assemblage who could not see the vision, opened her eyes and rested her gaze on Phyllis, who was frozen in a wide eyed and opened mouthed posture, as was most of the guests. "Your wife, Phyllis, calls you," she said.

"Phyllis . . . my dear beloved Phyllis . . . is that you?"

Hearing the spirit calling her by name, jolted Phyllis out of her shocked trance and she found her voice. "Frank! Oh, my dear Frank . . . is that really you? I knew you would come to me. I needed you to come."

"I have come . . . what is it you wish of me?"

Phyllis continued rapidly, "Oh, Frank! I've missed you so very much. I'm lost without you. I don't know what to do. What shall I do? I need you to tell me what to do."

"Phyllis, my love . . . soon we shall be together . . . for eternity."

Phyllis gasped. Still, all eyes, except Angelica's, were glued to the apparition in the doorway.

"But first, my dear . . . I have a request of you . . ."

"Anything, Frank. You know I would do anything you say."

"Before I departed the world of the flesh . . . my dear friend, Willard, and I were on the verge of a great discovery."

"Willard! What's this nonsense?" piped in Carl.

"Silence!" whispered Angelica.

"A discovery of monumental importance to humanity. It was my intent to invest my entire personal fortune into the development of this miracle . . . a miracle that could save millions of lives and curtail human suffering. But, alas, I left the mortal world too soon."

"What is it you wish me to do," whispered Phyllis, totally rapt.

"You . . . Phyllis . . . must fulfill my promise to mankind. What are worldly riches compared to eternal paradise?"

"Yes, Frank. But how can I help? What would you have me do?" said Phyllis in earnest.

"You ask me to tell you what you are to do? I say this . . . Leave your fortunes to my dear, trusted friend, Willard Hemlock"

"What! This is a crock," Carl again.

"So that he may continue our work to ease the suffering of humanity."

"Of course, Frank . . . anything you say, Frank. Lance is here . . . I'll change my Will immediately . . . tonight! Is that all right? Is that what you want?" Phyllis said frantically.

"At last . . . I will rest in peace. Come to me soon, Phyllis . . . I am waiting for you . . . ."

The mist became thicker as the figure grew smaller as the light dimmed and lost its shape before it disappeared.

"Wait . . . Frank . . . I love you . . . Frank . . . Frank . . . Wait!! Frank . . . don't go . . ." Phyllis blubbered through sobs and tears.

"Goodbye, my love . . . goodbye . . . g o o d b y e . . . ."

Then, everything happened at once.

CHAPTER XXV—THE MURDER

Suddenly, all the lights went out, including the Crystal Ball, plunging the entire room in complete darkness.

There was a shuffle of feet; chairs moving; a gunshot; a scream; a clank; a thud; and everyone seemed to find their voice at once.

Just as suddenly, all the lights came on displaying a room in chaos. Many of the guests had gotten to their feet. Lily Brenner was lying on her side on the floor. Carl discovered he was bleeding from his forehead. Madam Angelica was not in her seat but the mist was dissipating rapidly and she could be seen kneeling over a prone figure outside on the patio.

A second scream filled the room followed by frantic sobs and cries of "Mother! Mother! Oh, God! Help her, help her . . . someone." Francine was bending over Phyllis whose beautiful dark blue dress was rapidly turning crimson from a fatal stab to the chest from an ice pick.

Arthur and Florence were initially caught up in the confusion but quickly sorted out priorities and responsibilities. Florence headed immediately to Lily only to discover she had merely fainted. Carl's wound was superficial but would need stitches. Being a head wound, it bled shockingly, but a compress would stop the flow in short order. Then she headed out to the patio, which had cleared of the mist but was still shrouded in darkness. She saw a figure in white robes lying on the patio. What appeared to be blood covered a shoulder. Kneeling beside the figure, Angelica had wrapped her arms around the motionless body and was sobbing uncharacteristically. When she saw Florence approaching, she pleaded, "Help him, please help my son."

Arthur had immediately turned his attention to Phyllis but quickly determined his skills could not reverse the reality of death.

As everyone stared at each other in shocked suspension, there came a low moan rapidly getting louder until it reached a high pitched mournful wail. All eyes turned toward the sound coming from a kneeling figure on the floor in front of the bar. Back arched, head raised to the ceiling, folded arms boxed his head and ears, Joe Phoenix continued the horrible wailing, as a wolf would to the moon, and soon folded up double in uncontrollable sobs. "What have I done?" he wailed. "This is all my fault. I am totally to blame. How can I ever live after this?"

Conrad appeared from nowhere and gently consoled Joe and eased him to his feet, supporting his nearly limp frame.

Everyone would have been talking at once if they had known what to say and to whom to say it. Instead they just looked from one to the other and back again, trying to make some sense of the whole scene. The only thing they all found apparent was that Phyllis was *DEAD . . . MURDERED!*

CHAPTER XXVI—THE INTERROGATION

When Police Inspector Cloque Jouseau arrived, Conrad admitted him and immediately escorted him to the lounge where he announced him to the room of guests. The room appeared to the Inspector like a scene from a war movie. He stood in the doorway and took in every detail while Conrad did his best to point out all the attendees and give a brief account of the evening's events from his point of view. The Inspector's stance and demeanor was very much reminiscent of Madam Angelica earlier in the evening.

The guests had broken up into smaller groups; some sitting; some standing. Arthur and Florence had been busy tending to those in need of their services. Carl's nasty gash had been stitched and dressed. Lily, along with several other guests, had been given medication for anxiety. The figure on the patio had been brought inside and his injuries assessed as a gunshot wound to the shoulder, which would need surgery to remove the bullet. He had been identified as Hugo, Angelica's son. He was placed on a settee and a compress applied to the wound. His breathing had steadied but he was still unconscious.

After one last visual circle of the room, the Inspector walked toward the séance table while removing a small notebook and pen from his raincoat pocket, and said, "My condolences to the family. I am Police Inspector Jouseau responding to the call made by Mr. Diddit here, reporting a homicide. May I examine the victim?"

The small group in front of him parted to reveal Phyllis's body still sitting in her chair at the table. The Inspector was assured that nothing had been touched or in any way tampered with except what was needed to ascertain the condition of the body. "That's excellent," he congratulated, "But, of course, all of you have moved from your original spots. Correct?"

"Naturally, Inspector, some of us had to seek medical attention," interjected Carl, who fell into the *take charge* position with ease. "I, myself, sustained a wound to the head which needed stitches. I could have been killed. Poor fella there," Carl continued, motioning to Hugo's form stretched out on the settee, "got the bullet. I must have gotten in the way. Fortunately, he was only injured. Seems quite logical that someone would want to kill that fella as anyone can now see what a fake this séance is."

"Yes, I knew it!" piped in Priscilla. I . . . er . . . think it is in a way fortunate my sister never found out." She raised her already soaked hanky to her eyes and turned away.

After making a few notes, the Inspector tucked the pad and pen in his pocket and withdrew a tape measure and a camera from another. He took careful measurements and several pictures of Phyllis's body from every angle, as well as photographs of the séance table and other parts of the room. He then requested volunteers to remove the body to a sofa in the back part of the salon so as not to be a distraction to his investigation. In the commotion to remove the body, someone kicked an object that went sliding across the floor and came to rest at the Inspectors feet. A gun.

"I would like to recreate the scene as it was before the demise of Mrs. Stein. Therefore, would all of you please take the positions you were occupying at that moment," the Inspector commanded as he bent down to retrieve the gun and examine it. Everyone complied except Joe who was still rocking and moaning in a corner of the room. Just as the Inspector noticed Joe, Conrad whispered into his ear. The inspector nodded and turned his attention to the rest of the group now assembled in their positions.

"So, what happened here tonight?" the Inspector queried.

Several voices spoke at once. The Inspector quickly raised both hands, "Okay, okay, quiet! In most of my cases the witnesses are reluctant to speak. I am happy to know that will not be the case here. Perhaps Dr. Hart would be kind enough to begin and also give us an update on the injuries as well."

"Of course, Inspector," said Arthur, as he rose from his seat. "My name is Arthur Hart and I have been the family physician and close friend to the Stein family since Frank and Phyllis married. My wife and I are Godparents to Ruben and Francine. To begin, I must go back a year. I am sure you are aware of the fire at the Stein-Brenner Plant last year and the tragic death of Frank Stein." The Inspector nodded. "Phyllis took the news of Frank's death extremely hard and I have been treating her for anxiety and depression for the past year. Shortly after the fire, Madam Angelica made her acquaintance with Phyllis and I believe their relationship helped Phyllis get through each day, although I did have concerns as to what motivated Madam Angelica's attentions and just how this would affect Phyllis. When the suggestion of a Séance surfaced recently, I noticed Phyllis' excitability level increase substantially and her blood pressure followed suit. Frankly, I am not a fan of the occult but as long as Madam Angelica's ministrations were innocent enough and her relationship had a positive effect on Phyllis, I was in favor of it. But a Séance, I thought, might be stretching this to the limit. I feared how this all would ultimately affect Phyllis. I certainly wasn't prepared for an ice pick to her heart!"

Arthur choked up and had to turn away, retrieving his still damp handkerchief from his back pocket.

"So, let me get this straight," the Inspector said, taking advantage of the pause, "Mr. Stein died in a fire last year and Mrs. Stein has been seeing a mystic, Madam Angelica, in essence, to help her make sense of his death. And the family accepted this because the relationship helped her depression. But I take it having a séance was a cause for concern. Is that correct?"

Several affirmations could be heard.

Amanda stood up and continued for her husband, "I know Phyllis was very concerned herself about the evening. She was very excited about the possibility of seeing Frank again but also worried that he would not appear. She really was a lost soul this past year. Not at all in her regular routine. We used to attend several luncheons a week and supported many charities. But she rarely went out of the house this past year. To plan this séance was an extreme event for her. Arthur had insisted on having nurse Florence with her these many months in case her nerves got the better of her. And her sister, Priscilla, has been invaluable this past year taking over the daily tasks. I noticed this evening that Phyllis was holding up very well with all the guests and was delighted to see her younger sister and her new husband. When Madam Angelica arrived, her excitement level became frantically elated. And during the Séance, she was totally rapt."

"What happened at the Séance?" ask the Inspector, his eyes resting on Francine.

95

"Well, Madam Angelica called us all to the table and said the spirits are willing, or something like that. She told the ones at the table where to sit . . . well, except Aunt Priscilla insisted on sitting next to Madam Angelica and Carl insisted on taking the last seat . . . there." Francine gestured toward Carl. "The others sat in the rest of the chairs as you see, with some standing. The lights dimmed and the crystal ball lit up and we all joined hands. Or we joined hands first and then the ball lit up, I can't recall. I do remember Madam Angelica chastised my brother for breaking the circle of hands to take a drink"

"Damn, Francine, did you have to mention *that!*" Ruben said angrily.

"I'm trying to remember everything, Ruben. I don't know if it means anything to the Inspector," Francine explained.

"Please go on miss, you are doing fine," the Inspector assured her.

"Well, Madam Angelica called the spirits and got an answer. Then she called specifically for my father . . . for Frank N. Stein. Somehow the patio doors opened . . . personally, I didn't see them open. And mist started to fill the room, and there was a light shining in. Suddenly a figure could be seen in front of the light walking through the mist. It was dressed in a white hooded robe . . . well, we now know it was Hugo there on the settee. He spoke and said he was Frank N. Stein and told my mother she would be joining him soon. Mother asked him to tell her what she should do with her life and the figure told her to leave all her money to Willard who was working on one of my father's formulas that would save the world . . . or something like that. Mother said she would do that . . . she said she would do anything . . . she would change the Will tonight. Then the figure was leaving and was nearly out of sight when all the lights went out and it was pitch black. I heard a gun shot, a scream, a thud, and a clank . . . and some scuffing noises. Just as suddenly, the lights all came back on and Lily had fainted, Carl was bleeding from the forehead and Madam Angelica was crouched over the robed figure which turned out to be her son, Hugo . . . he had been shot. Then I turned and looked . . . looked . . . down . . . mother . . ." Francine crumbled in her seat shaking with sobs.

"Thank you, miss, that was excellent. And you are Mrs. Stein's daughter, Francine, I believe?" asked the Inspector.

"Yes sir," said a very sober Ruben. Francine couldn't talk for crying. "I am her son, Ruben, and this is her daughter, Dominique." Ruben gestured toward Dominique. "My wife, Helene, is here behind me and Dominique's husband, Ralph, sits behind her. You know Mr. and Mrs. Hart already. Behind them is my mother's nurse, Florence Curtain. Beside her is my cousin . . . well, not really my cousin . . . Carl's son, Christian. And then there is Christian's sister, Charity and her husband Sven Svenson. Behind my mother's chair is our lawyer, Lance Knight and his wife, Holly. Sitting next to my mother is Willard Hemlock, who used to work for the company. Beside him is Carlton Brenner, my dad's partner. Then there is my Aunt Priscilla next to Madam Angelica. Calvin and Bonnie Booker, the bookkeeper for the plant, are there and my Aunt Prudence and her husband Prentice Pireet sit behind them. Carl's wife, Lily, and daughter, Cassandra, are behind him and my cousin, Paul, is at the end of the back row there." This is by far the longest speech Ruben had ever made and he relaxed in his chair surprised and exhausted.

"Thank you, Ruben. I have made notes that are sure to come in handy," thanked the Inspector. "Tell me, what happened before Madam Angelica and Mr. Handy arrived. Anything unusual come to mind?"

"Well," said a recovering Francine, "my brother came in loaded to the gills and fell at my mother's feet. But I wouldn't say that was unusual, although my mother was furious."

"How dare you criticize Ruben. So what if he's not his mother's favorite as you are, Francine. He is handling his demons the best he can. Your father is the cause of those demons so naturally he would not be too anxious to come face to face with his father's spirit tonight," said Helene, defensively. Ruben hung his head even lower and blubbered uncontrollably. A groan came from Joe slumped in the corner.

Prudence was next to speak, mostly to redirect the attention from Ruben, "I suppose you could say our arrival was unusual as we were not expected until next week. But it was a happy reunion and not of any great importance where the séance is concerned, except, of course, that the occult is something both my husband and I totally disagree with."

"I see you are sitting at a distance from the Séance table. Is that because of your objections to the séance?" the Inspector reproached.

"Well, yes, I suppose. But had Madam Angelica asked me to sit at the table, I would have done whatever made my sister happy, regardless of my feelings" said Prudence.

Then Arthur said, "There was the Will, of course. Lance had updated Phyllis' Will and we . . . er . . . Amanda and myself . . . were asked to be witnesses. Just routine business and took only a few minutes."

"A Will you say?" repeated the Inspector. "Do you have a copy of this Will, Lance?"

"Why, yes, of course," said Lance, retrieving the Will from his inside suit pocket. "As Arthur said, it was just routine. I finally convinced Phyllis to update the Will she had made when Frank was still alive. It wasn't absolutely necessary but I thought it might help bring some form of closure for Phyllis concerning Frank's death. I also have a copy of Frank's Will and Phyllis's old Will if you wish to see them." Lance handed all copies to the Inspector.

The Inspector read through the Wills quickly and said, "I see by Frank's Will, Mr. Diddit, you have inherited quite a sum and yet you are still in the employ of the household."

"Yes, sir," said Conrad. "It was the condition of the Will that I remain in the service of Phyllis Stein and I was only too glad to do so. Actually, I have touched none of the money so far, except to invest it."

"And you, Francine," said the Inspector, quickly changing directions, "you were given control of the business interests at a yearly salary of $250,000. Is that correct?"

"It was only a formality," added Francine. "The company documents also have such a provision. I have been in training with the help of Lance for most of this year and believe I have the necessary knowledge to protect my family's interests."

"I also see here that a large sum, a million dollars to be exact, was bequeathed to Frank's son, Frank Jr. I take it, Frank was married before." pointed out the Inspector.

Carl offered input this time, "Yes, Inspector, Frank and I both married after graduating from college but his only lasted a couple years, I believe. Wife took off with the kid and he never found them."

The Inspector went on to read further and then commented, "Phyllis old Will as well as the new one leaves Conrad additional property . . . beach-front, no less. You must have been very valuable to the family, Conrad, to deserve to be so singled out so handsomely."

"The feeling was mutual, Inspector," answered Conrad.

"Yes, of course. And I see that the old Will would have left all three children, Dominique, Ruben and Francine, equal shares in the estate. However, in the new Will this is not the case. The Will states:

'I give, devise and bequeath to my daughter, Dominique Baldwin, the token sum of one dollar, as her fortune from her father is more than sufficient to support her in style. In addition, I belatedly give her all my love which I failed so miserably to bestow on her over the years. For this oversight, I am deeply ashamed and honestly regret the years of love we have lost forever. I beg you to forgive me.'

'I give, devise and bequeath to my son, Ruben Stein, the token sum of one dollar, in the fervent hope that having nothing will instill in him the necessary desire to make a success of himself as his father did before him. In addition, I have set up a College Trust Fund of $100,000 (to be used solely on education) in the hope he will return to school. Consider this, your parents will make no further demands on you so you are now free to be the person you chose to be. That is my legacy to you, my dear, sweet son.'

'I give, devise and bequeath to my thoughtful sister, Priscilla Penniless, who I am deeply indebted to for her sacrifices and care she has bestowed upon me when my need was great, the sum of $500,000, absolutely and forever.'

'All the rest, residue and remainder of my property, real personal and mixed of whatever nature and wheresoever situate, I give, devise and bequeath to my beloved daughter, Francine Stein, who has stood by me with understanding and love in my time of deepest turmoil. This bequest is absolute and irrevocable and a sign of my complete faith in her abilities to carry on the Family Empire begun by my dear departed husband, Frank.'

"This is most interesting." The Inspector paused to let that information sink in and then addressed Ruben, "Mr. Stein . . . Ruben, if I may . . . were you aware of the contents of these Wills?"

"No sir. I never gave it much thought. I wasn't much use to my parents. I could never live up to their expectations. But now that you mention it, I believe mother and father did have Wills drawn up years ago, and, of course, father's was read last year. If you mean specifically if I knew I would be, in essence, disinherited? Not exactly, but I knew I had disappointed both my parents; I just wasn't my father and he never understood that." Ruben turned away for a few seconds to quell the emotion welling up inside. When he was in control again, he continued, "If it hadn't been for Uncle Carl offering to take me under his wing and give me a job, I don't think I would be sitting here tonight."

"Well I think it is reprehensible!" piped up Helene. "Ruben has made every effort to achieve the status expected of him. It was Frank and Phyllis' mistake in setting the standard too high. Carl has been more of a father to him than Frank ever was or could be. But to cut him out of the Will is lower than low even for Phyllis."

There was another groan from the corner.

"Dominique! Any comments from you?" the Inspector asked, quickly changing direction.

"I . . . I . . . I loved my mother more than life itself. I would never question anything she did," said Dominique, between sniffles. "It is true. I don't need her money. You see, my father was Arnold Dumbelli. He died in a boating accident when I was an infant. I inherited a good deal of his fortune. And Ralph . . . Ralph will always take care of me." She turned to look at Ralph who wiped a tear from her cheek and held her hand tight.

"Inspector, sir," interjected Ralph, "Dominique has a considerable trust fund, it is true; but I have a business which is doing quite well. Financially, we are very comfortable, even well off, and care nothing for the Stein family fortunes. Just wanted to make that clear to everyone. Thank you."

"Thank you, Mr. Baldwin," said the Inspector turning his attentions to Carl who was smirking a bit over his dead partner's family rivalries.

"Francine, you are very close to your mother. Were you aware of the contents of the new Will?" the Inspector asked.

"It may be hard to believe, Inspector, although I knew Lance was preparing a new Will to update the old one," Francine admitted, "But I did not know the exact contents. Lance had meant to discussed it with me, since I am the head of the household now, but we never got around to it. I think he wanted my agreement so it wouldn't be just my mother's doing. She didn't always have the best judgment as we all saw tonight. But I was aware mother wanted me to take care of everything because Dominique had her own fortune and a husband to take care of her. She didn't believe my brother could take care of anything, and for whatever reason, she didn't want Helene to get her hands on the family fortune. But, I ask you, who deserves to share in our family fortune more? Honestly, Helene has been the most loyal and devoted member of our family and our brother's savior. My brother is not a bad person. He just lacks self confidence."

"And you, Ms. Penniless," continued the Inspector, "It seems that you have just come into a rather large amount of money as well. Perhaps this is no shock to you."

"On the contrary, Inspector," Priscilla said, indignantly, "I had no idea my sister intended to bequeath me anything. Nor did I expect to be hearing her Will quite so soon. I came here last year to take care of my sister . . . not do her in. And I believe I have done the job I came here to do, no matter what anyone else may think. I do know that my sister appreciated my being here."

"Yes, indeed, and I would say this Will verifies that," added the Inspector. "Perhaps your son, Paul, is more interested in the money?"

"Don't you mess with my son. I take good care of him. He can tell you. I see that he gets whatever he wants." Priscilla said, defensively.

"That certainly is correct, Inspector. But I have my own income from working at the plant. Honestly, I had no idea there was a new Will or even that I would have any chance to benefit from it," explained Paul.

"Thank you, all, for clarifying that. So, Mr. Brenner, you and Mr. Stein had known each other for a long time, throughout your school years, I believe?" Carl nodded and was about to speak when the Inspector continued, "And then you started your chemical business as equal partners . . . but with the financial backing of Phyllis? I ask this because newspapers and magazines are not always so accurate as we would wish."

"Yes, you are correct. We are like one big family. I was devastated when Frank died in that fire last year, and Phyllis' death tonight is equally as disturbing. I would like to take this opportunity to extend my condolences to the family and hope they will continue to consider me their special uncle who will always be there for them." Carl finished his speech like a gentleman but with no real sincerity showing in his face, eyes or demeanor. Just a bit of smugness at having been the first to grandstand before the others.

The groan from the corner became a faint laugh.

"Yes, the fire. I read quite a bit about that tragedy last year. I understand you have rebuilt the damaged wing. Have you found someone to replace Frank as research and development scientist? I imagine developing new products is paramount to the continuing success of your business," said the Inspector.

"I am astonished at your knowledge of my business, Inspector," Carl returned. "You must also realize the value to the company of Frank's considerable contributions. His shoes will be hard to fill."

"So, you have not filled the position," retorted the Inspector. "I am amazed you have been able to increase profits this past year with no new products entering the market. Quite a feat especially after your Marketing Manager leaving the company about the same time."

"I should point out, Inspector, that Francine came on board soon after Frank's death. She has been working tirelessly with Lance to get up to speed on the workings of the entire company," Carl countered, defensively. "She and Lance have put in endless hours late into the night to fill the gap caused by the tragedy last year. And I may point out that Ruben has blossomed extremely well to become a huge asset to the company. I am sincerely grateful for all their efforts."

"Yes, to be sure. A busy year, too, I suppose for you, Mr. Booker." The Inspector's quick change caught Calvin by surprise and he bolted upright in his chair as if hit by lightning.

"What? Uh . . . busy . . . busy . . . busy," Calvin stammered wide eyed.

"How do you explain such nice profits under the circumstances?" added the Inspector.

"Well, I . . . I . . . only handle the money, Inspector. I don't have anything to do with the development or marketing of the products we sell. Perhaps it has just been a good year for everyone." Calvin finished with a hiccup, as his whole body rattled as if sliding over a washboard. He quickly crossed his legs and hugged his body to try to keep the shaking to a minimum and hope it wasn't too obvious.

"I think business is just really good," spoke up, Bonnie, as if she knew something the others did not. "There is always loads of people shopping every day, I can tell you that! It is so hard to get waited on, it's so busy." She sat up straight, smiling broadly as if she just solved the greatest mystery in the world.

"Ah, most enlightening," acknowledged the Inspector, "I will have to . . . ah . . . research that."

Carl was amused. Bonnie was always good for a laugh. "If we want to know about the economy, just ask a woman."

"Madam Angelica!" the Inspector switched directions again. "It appears you, madam, are the only one here whose guilt has crashed down upon them so far. I think it is time you tell us your story."

"Sir," she began, "are you accusing me of a crime? It is my business to create an illusion that my client wishes to see. And to see to it that each client comes away from each session with more confidence and a better sense of self than they had previously. I am a professional and therefore have seamless expertise in my field. I would not call this a crime."

"You could argue that point but I would venture to say some may label you a fraud." The Inspector slowly circled the table as he talked until he came to where Angelica was seated. "But let me ask you this, Madam, have you ever had an itch that just couldn't be ignored? I have one now and in my business that tells me there is more here than a busted séance."

"I don't know what you mean, Inspector. Why are you pointing fingers at me when my son lies there unconscious. I would think you would be more concerned with who tried to kill *him*!" screamed Angelica hysterically.

"You are quite right, Madam, we will sort that out in due course."

"If you ask me," piped in Priscilla, "I think Willard was in on this whole séance business from the start. He's been after my sister almost from the day after the fire. I think you should check that out, Inspector."

"Thank you, madam," said the Inspector.

The Inspector continued around the table and stopped in front of Willard. "Mr. Hemlock! I suspect you are in this pretty deep. Conrad has already filled me in on the séance, especially the discourse between our *ghost* here," pointing to Hugo, "and Phyllis. We know now that this séance was contrived, so what I need to know is how *your* name got into the act. Why would Madam Angelica want *you* to get Phyllis' money, unless . . ."

"Okay, okay. You have no idea what it is like to always be at the bottom of the heap, never quite making it to the top. The best I could ever do is hang on the coattails of Carl and Frank. Frank tolerated me okay but Carl here never appreciated nor trusted me. But Frank was the real deal . . . you know . . . honest and legit . . . unlike the rest of us. Yes, you are right to question the business." Carl grabbed his arm and Willard pulled away sharply. "Take your hands off me. Don't you see . . . you're *busted!* You see, Inspector, Carl doesn't really need to fill Frank's place. The plant is just a front for processing and moving drugs . . . illegal drugs!"

Willard hung his head to gather himself for the full confession. "The night of the fire, I was in my office and saw the smoke and flames coming out of the research building. I thought this would be my chance to leave the company. All I had to do was get to Frank's files and steal his newest, most promising formula. I just got out in time before the explosions and before the flames consumed everything. I found out days later that Frank had been in that building. Even if I had known at the time, I couldn't have gotten to him, the flames were so daunting. But, you see, Frank's death opened a new opportunity. If I could get Phyllis to marry me, then I could be top dog at the plant equal to Carl. I could be somebody. However, I hadn't counted on Phyllis being unreceptive. My great plan wasn't going anywhere."

There were angry words exchanged all around the table in response to Willard's revelations. The Inspector was rapidly taking notes.

"I knew Phyllis was seeing a psychic. She would always dismiss me hours before her appointment or simply tell me not to come visit on the day she was to see The Madam. This went on for a month and I was getting angry and frustrated, so I waited outside one day in the hope of having words with this person who was cutting into my game. All of a sudden, there she was, and I stopped her. When she saw me there was shock and fear in her eyes. So, I looked closer at her and saw some familiar features which tickled my memory of long ago college days. It was then I realized I had her." Willard paused for breath and looked over at Angelica whose eyes were spitting fire but her face showed defeat.

"All right, all right!" Madam Angelica shouted desperately. "It is my story so I shall tell it."

"By all means, Angel. I've been waiting a lifetime to hear this." Joe had quietly vacated his corner in response to Hugo's stirring and had been kneeling beside him reveling in the beauty of the young man. But upon hearing Angelica's words, stood for this ultimate confrontation.

"What? Who are you to call me out? You are nobody, barman. Go back to your corner," Angelica said angrily at being interrupted and thrown off her mark.

"Perhaps I'll have a drink to warm up. There certainly is a chill in the air," teased Joe as he walked behind the bar. "Please continue the story everyone is on the edge of their seats waiting for."

"Mr . . . . er . . . Phoenix is it?" questioned the Inspector. "I will allow this interruption, but would appreciate your silence now. You can fully expect to have your turn on the soap box immediately following the Madam." He then turned his attention back to Madam Angelica and bade her continue.

The murmurs died down and all eyes were on Angelica.

CHAPTER XXVII—ANGEL'S STORY

Angelica cleared her throat and with clear resolve began, "For the past twenty five plus years, I have perfected my craft as a mystic by reading tarot cards, rune stones, lifelines and such, barely making a living for my son and myself. Some years ago, I was fortunate to cross paths with a young electronics technician who helped me develop this unique, remote controlled crystal ball, which turned out to be a boon for my business. Séances were the thing! Rich widows especially enjoyed them. We were the best in the business. I saw your faces during the *show*. I had you all . . . even the non-believers. Admit it! I would not be spilling my guts now if Phyllis . . . and my son . . ." She turned aside to regain control.

"The trick was finding a score," she continued. "Where do I find them, you might ask? Why in the society obituaries. I couldn't believe my eyes last year when I came across the name Frank N. Stein . . . a name I knew well. As is my routine, I contacted the widow, Phyllis, and the fish was on the hook."

"How dare you speak so disrespectful of my mother!" Francine cut in. The anger and revulsion in her face was missed by no one. "You horrid creature praying on a most beautiful soul. You are a disgrace to humanity and I charge you with the responsibility of my mother's death. Inspector do you duty and take this *slug* away from my sight." Her hatred vented, she collapsed in tears into her seat as Amanda and Arthur comforted her.

Dominique could only sit there in a shocked daze, staring at nothing in particular, but with tears streaming down her cheeks and holding Ralph's hand. Ruben just sat with his head in his hands. Carl, on the other hand, had his hands full trying to keep Priscilla from launching herself out of her chair after Angelica. Prentice had moved his chair closer to Prudence in order to comfort and subdue her. Lily and Cassandra were practically sitting in the same chair with their arms wrapped around each other, wide eyed and shivering. Calvin was shaking all over and didn't know what to do with his hands while Bonnie, perhaps for the first time in her adult life, sat demurely silent, trying desperately to blend into the woodwork. Conrad had slipped behind the bar to share a stiff drink with Joe who was smiling and shaking his head. Christian and Paul were the only ones, with exception of Joe, sitting comfortably cross-armed in their chairs enjoying the show.

Just then, Hugo stirred and began to regain consciousness. Arthur, Florence, Joe and Angelica ran to his side. All other activity ceased until Arthur announced that Hugo's wound had stopped bleeding. Although he had lost a lot of blood, the bullet was lodged in soft tissue and could easily be removed. Curiously, the one most concerned and relieved was Joe.

Arthur returned to his seat next to Amanda and left Florence with Hugo to administer some pain medication. Joe pulled up a chair and sat at the foot of the settee. Hugo seemed bewildered and cautious with Joe's familiarity.

The Inspector inquired, "Mr. Handy! I trust you are feeling much better. Your . . . er . . . mother has been enlightening us on her trade secrets. Perhaps later you might feel well enough to make some comments of your own."

Hugo looked around, still trying to bring the room in focus and make sense of where he was and what had happened to him.

Angelica returned to her seat and reluctantly continued her story. "So, Inspector and guests, I contacted Phyllis and offered my services. I must say she was a delightful lady but earnestly willing to believe anything I said. She was a most enjoyable and satisfying client. Then I ran into Willard, the snake!"

All eyes turned to Willard as if in agreement with her assessment. Willard first tried to shrink from the stares but then pulled himself together and sat high in his chair ready to take whatever came right on the chin.

"You see, Willard knew me in another life. How he recognized me, I can't imagine because I went to great lengths over the years to change my appearance. I dyed my red hair black; had my nose fixed; straightened some rather crooked teeth and got brown contact lenses to cover my green eyes. I was certain those years were dead and buried. But Willard stood between me and the life I thought I had outrun."

Willard was suddenly filled with a conscience and strangely had the urge to speak. "For what it's worth, Angel, I wouldn't have blown your cover."

"No? You were ready, willing and about to do so minutes ago," she said.

"Well," Willard stammered, "You must concede you are busted anyway and I'm going down with you. Nothing personal. It's just a risk of the trade."

"It is true. I can't put the blame on you for this evening's failure. I was planning something of the sort anyway. You see, Inspector, it was Willard's idea for the ghost to implore Phyllis to change her Will in favor of Willard. It was a long shot but I suppose it was a better scenario than what I was originally planning. So that is how Willard's name got into the Séance. Who would suspect Willard of being an accomplice. No one would ever guess we had once known each other so very long ago. It is so ironic . . ."

Angelica took a long breath and finally made the revelation she dreaded to make. "My real name is Angina . . . Angel for short . . . and I was once known as **Mrs. Frank N. Stein.**"

CHAPTER XXVIII—THE REAL GHOST

Inspector Jouseau moved closer to Angelica. "The question now, madam, is are you *still* Mrs. Frank N. Stein?

"As I recall," Angel said thoughtfully, "We definitely divorced, and I cleaned him out then, what little there was, as I had planned to clean out his fortune now. I figure it should have been mine . . . right?"

"Lance," the Inspector said, "Wasn't there a *Frank N. Stein, Jr.* as a beneficiary in Phyllis' Will?"

Lance was clearly caught off guard and it took him a long minute to respond. "Well, yes . . . ah . . . no . . . actually there is a *Frank N. Stein, Jr.* in Frank's Will. I wondered about that. Frank had never told me personally he had been married before let alone had a child. I just assumed by the Will . . . If I remember correctly, young Frank, or should I say, Hugo, has inherited $1,000,000."

"No, I'm afraid he hasn't inherited . . . yet!" Joe had stood to make this short speech and then proceeded to the bar to mix another drink. "You see, Frank Senior is not deceased . . . not yet, anyway."

All eyes followed his route. The Inspector said, "Joe . . . are you saying *YOU* are Frank N. Stein come back from the dead?" There was a simultaneous intake of breathe from the guests.

Francine was the first to jump out of her chair, "Daddy? How is this possible?"

Ruben sputtered something unintelligible and sat up straight scrutinizing the man behind the bar for the first time that evening. Yes, he could see some resemblance. But how could this be? Everyone at the time was certain he had perished in that horrible fire. He started to stand but was overcome by so many conflicting emotions he collapsed back into his chair visibly shaken.

"If you're still alive, maybe mother is . . ." exclaimed Dominique hopefully but Ralph grabbed her arm to keep her from running to her mother's body.

"No, my love," Ralph spoke softly, "Arthur is certain. You must accept it. But it appears that your stepfather is alive and that is cause for rejoicing."

The shock of Joe's . . . or rather, Frank's . . . revelation washed over Carl and finally he found his voice. "You can't be Frank! The fire . . . the fire totally destroyed everything. Frank was in there . . ."

"Yes, you would know wouldn't you Carl . . . my dearest *friend!* You left me unconscious on the floor and then lit the fire. You saw the room burst into flames so why would you believe I could ever survive such an inferno." Frank stood at the corner of the bar and stared threateningly at Carl. For the first time in their relationship, Frank actually saw fear in Carl's eyes.

"Just how did you manage to escape such certain death, Mr. Stein? And, just as importantly, where have you been for the past year?" Inspector Jouseau stood between Frank and Carl and poised his pen over a fresh page of his half filled notebook.

"Fair questions, Inspector," Frank conceded. "The story is long but I will try to give you the condensed version. I came to with flames licking my feet and legs. I got to my feet and ripped off the bottom of my burning pants legs. The way to the door was impassable but a path to a window was negotiable. When I reached the window, I heard the first explosion, which propelled me through the window, along with half the office. If I had not been in front of the window, I expect I would have been crushed against a wall or other solid structure. As it was, I was badly burned and suspected I had a broken arm and leg. I must have laid there unconscious in the rubble for only a short while as another explosion roused me. I remember feeling the need to seek shelter . . . to hide from some unremembered threat. There was a delivery truck nearby. Somehow I managed to crawl to it and found the back unlocked. I pulled myself in and wrapped myself in old insulation quilts left on the truck floor."

Frank paused and looked around at the intent faces trying to process all the information that they had heard so far. All faces except Carl who could no longer look Frank in the eye. Frank continued, "I don't know how long I lay there unconscious or asleep but when I opened my eyes I couldn't remember anything about the fire or what I was doing in that truck. I tried to move but quickly discovered the injuries I couldn't account for. As my mind began processing all this new information, the truck swerved and I realized I was moving from a place I couldn't remember to a place I couldn't guess. Confused and in a state of panic, I must have passed out once again and didn't wake again until my body registered a lack of movement . . . the truck had stopped. Soon after, the driver opened the rear doors and discovered a stowaway. Somehow I ended up in a hospital somewhere in the mid-west. I had no identification and couldn't remember who I was, so was sent to the indigent ward and my injuries treated. I was very fortunate that a local church charity took up my case and provided the funds needed for the plastic surgery necessary to repair the damage from the burns. The doctors did a magnificent job, don't you think? Hardly any scars show. But with no photograph to use as a guide, they did the best they could; however, I ended up looking quite different from my original self. The bones healed quickly but the burns took considerably longer. But as the days passed, my memory did not recover."

"Then one evening I woke up coughing only to discover my room was on fire, which turned out to have been caused by faulty wiring. The fire was discovered almost immediately and quickly dealt with. The seed of shock from seeing the flames began eroding the wall of self imposed amnesia. In short . . . I started to remember and soon remembered everything. I remembered discovering Carl's little side business in illegal drugs. I was furious he was using our business to process the raw material into illegal marketable substances like cocaine. I demanded to see him. He came to the lab late that evening and I accused him of trafficking. We got into a heated verbal fight. I went to the phone to call the police and that's when Carl picked up something heavy and beamed me with it. I was barely conscious but I remember Carl smashing all the jars of chemicals. When he lit and tossed the match, I remember being so astonished at his unabashed act of cold blooded murder of not just anyone, but a lifetime best friend. He walked out without even looking back."

"With my body healed and my memory restored, I knew my insane hatred for the man who had caused me . . . and no doubt my family . . . such pain demanded revenge. It was then I started to plan my resurrection and retaliation. I spent hours in the library researching what news I could find about my family and the business since the fire. When I read about the impending séance, I had my opening. And when my plan was complete, I contacted Conrad for I needed his help, although I did not fully disclose the true purpose of my awakening. Just weeks before the planned Séance, Conrad and I spent every free minute he had holed up in the gardener's shed in the south meadow refining my plan to surreptitiously re-enter my life. One small snag turned out to be Angel's crystal ball. Conrad went to great lengths to discover the technician who helped develop the sphere and we were able to make a device which would counter all signals and render the ball dark."

At this point Frank ran his hands through his dyed brown hair and started pacing back and forth. "Even the best laid plans can go awry and this one sure did. At the right moment, Conrad pulled the circuit breaker as I deactivated the crystal ball. I quickly stepped around the corner of the bar with the exact target in mind through the darkness. But as I pulled the trigger, I bumped into something and the shot went astray." At this point, Frank looked over at the young man lying on the settee and their eyes locked. The tortured pain on Frank's face transferred all the love and emotion stored up in a hidden place in his heart to his son and his son acknowledged his full comprehension and forgiveness to the man he never knew, until this night, as father. Frank said, in a whisper, to his son, "My God! I could have killed you . . . just because of my foolish hatred and crazy need for revenge. What kind of person am I? I'm no better than Carl . . . or for that matter, any of you on the wrong side of the law. No better than the murderer who killed my dear Phyllis tonight."

Francine stood, rushed to her father and hugged him.

The Inspector raised his pen and turned the page in his notebook. He had one page left. That's all he needed.

CHAPTER XXIX—ANATOMY OF THE MURDER

After Frank's revealing story, everyone sat rather subdued and in deep thought. Much had been revealed tonight—many crimes—but not all had direct influence on discovering the murderer of Phyllis Stein. During this ebb, Inspector Jouseau took the opportunity to review his notes with the practiced eye experienced in putting together the puzzle pieces of a homicide. He was ready to begin.

"In order to commit a murder, a murderer needs three things:

OPPORTUNITY
ACCESS TO A WEAPON
MOTIVE

"When the room was thrown into darkness, this condition gave the killer the *opportunity* to commit the crime cloaked in anonymity. You could say that everyone here was enveloped in darkness, so everyone had *opportunity*. So we must further narrow the field of *opportunity*. Let's consider timing. Conrad tells me the lights were only out for mere seconds which would not be enough time, based on your position relative to the victim, for the majority of you to have committed the crime.

"Let us move on to who had *access to the murder weapon,* which, in this case, was an ice pick, typically kept on or near the bar. Can you verify this Frank?"

Frank turned to examine the top of the bar, "There was an ice pick right there," pointing to the end of the bar. "I used it several times tonight. As a matter of fact, Willard used it to clean his fingernails."

"Is it a crime to be fastidious in one's appearance?" Willard added, defensively.

"The import issue is: Did Willard return the item to the bar after concluding this activity?" the Inspector asked Frank.

"Ah . . . yes, yes. Yes, I am certain I used it after his hygiene respite. The last I remember it was on the bar," concluded Frank.

"Can you give me a time, relative to the beginning of the Séance, the ice pick was last seen on the bar?" added the Inspector.

"Well, let's see," Frank said, thoughtfully, "I would say maybe two minutes before Angel signaled little Frank . . . ah, I mean, Hugo . . . to start the preparations. Conrad was to dim the lights for the Séance too. In fact, I had just made Angel a drink and she was standing at Phyllis' side and almost immediately signaled for the séance. Yes, I think two minutes is fairly accurate, give or take a minute."

"So, we can conclude that the window of opportunity to get the ice pick before the seance was only several minutes. Still a possibility. To get the ice pick after the seance began, would mean taking advantage of the shorter time the lights were out. Equally challenging. But why take the weapon before the seance unless you know the lights are going out, giving opportunity. Only Frank and Conrad knew the lights were going to be off and both of them were busy doing other things."

"I think we can assume the weapon was not taken until the lights went out, giving the murderer the opportunity. So, the murder was not premeditated, but rather spontaneous," the Inspector emphasized. "Therefore, we can presume something happened during the seance that prompted the murderer to murder . . . specifically . . . to murder Phyllis."

"That brings us to *MOTIVE*. Motive is a reason powerful enough to cause an ordinarily reasonable person to ignore all reason and thought of consequences to be compelled to take another person's life. It crosses all class distinctions, selects no gender, favors no race or nationality, sanctions no religious belief, and seeks no level of intelligence. Without motive, there is no incentive and everyone is susceptible to the clutches of the strongest motive."

"Remember, I said *all three—opportunity, access to a weapon, and motive*—MUST be present. You could have the opportunity and motive but not a weapon, unless you're strong enough to use your bare hands, in which case you DO have a weapon, you cannot commit the crime. You might have a weapon and motive but if an opportunity does not exist, you cannot commit the crime. You might have opportunity and a weapon but without a motive to compel you, you would not even consider the crime. So, who among you has all three? Who would want Phyllis dead. Who would want to kill a kind, although weak willed, lady of impeccable reputation and one so highly respected in the community. Who would want to kill a rich . . ." Inspector Jouseau stopped his pacing and looked around the room to see if his words caused a stir. He noticed no change in demeanor.

He again began his pacing and continued his analysis. "As I understand it correctly, the purpose of this Séance was to have Phyllis change her Will in favor of Willard who was prepared to share the windfall with Angelica. But in order to get the money, Phyllis would have to die *after* first changing her Will. Money is always a strong motive for murder. Willard is certainly seated within range of the ice pick and he's sitting close to Phyllis. However, what's the point in killing Phyllis *before* she has had a chance to change her Will in his favor. Opportunity and weapon but no motive."

"Florence, Amanda and Arthur are seated close to Phyllis and not too far away to acquire the ice pick, but they are friends and healers who cared very much for Phyllis and had nothing to gain from her death. We can eliminate them as suspects."

"It would be a real stretch for Ruben to reach the ice pick, but more than that, his motive is very weak. By his own admission, he was not interested in Phyllis' Will nor did he expect any return from it. Likewise, Dominique and Ralph are both too far away to acquire the weapon as well as to use it, it is highly unlikely either are dependant on any inheritance from Phyllis."

"We know that Priscilla would inherit a great deal of money at Phyllis' death, and, indirectly, her son Paul would have access to that money through his mother. But the distance either would have to travel to achieve Phyllis' demise makes the task impossible."

"As unscrupulous as Carl has been revealed to be, the fact that he received an injury roughly at the time of the murder, clearly gives him an alibi, and, likewise, eliminates Hugo who actually received the bullet, and Frank, who was actively firing the shot at that time. Conrad Diddit couldn't have done it as he was occupied at the electric panel."

"A new Will was signed tonight and the major recipient of the inheritance we all now know to be Francine. Although she claims not to know the exact contents of the Will, she does admit to knowing her mother's general intention. It is not easy for a child as loving and caring as Francine is to kill a parent, especially a mother. By her own admittance, she was the head of the house and a huge influence in Phyllis' life as well as having her own interest in the company."

"No! You can't be accusing ME! For no amount of stupid money could I ever be enticed to kill my MOTHER! You call yourself a police detective . . . " ranted Francine, but was cut short by Inspector Jouseau.

"No, Francine. I was not accusing you at all. In fact, I was about to say that, although you are situated next to your mother, it would be nearly impossible for you to negotiate a path to the bar to get the weapon and return to commit the murder in the short time allowed."

"Holly," the Inspector said, sympathetically, "We have not talked with you this evening, but although you are close to both the weapon and the victim, I can see absolutely no reason you would want to ensure Francine would get her inheritance even if you knew anything at all about the new Will, which I doubt you did. But, Lance, you do have every reason to want Phyllis dead."

"Frank said his shot missed its mark because he *bumped into something*. It was you groping for the ice pick and got in his way. And you are the only one here tonight who had absolute knowledge of the contents of Phyllis' Will before the Séance. You alone knew Francine was the major beneficiary and you couldn't risk her losing it. You and Francine have admittedly spent much time together. You want Francine *and* the money. Love and money—a double-barreled motive."

"You, Lance, had the *opportunity, access to the murder weapon, and motive*. I, Inspector Cloque Jouseau, arrest you, Lance Knight, for the murder of Phyllis Stein."

ADDENDUM

"In addition, there will be enough room in the Paddy Wagon for the following people, who need to answer some serious questions at the police station. All of you are advise to keep silent until you can contact your attorney (I suggest someone other than Lance Knight). If you do not have an attorney, one will be appointed for you. And where is this Carolee Russell? I definitely need to have a little talk with her too."

FRANCINE STEIN – ADULTERY

RUBEN STEIN – POSSESSION & SALE OF ILLEGAL DRUGS

PAUL PENNILESS – POSSESSION OF ILLEGAL DRUGS

CARLTON BRENNER – ARSON
                              INSURANCE FRAUD
                              ATTEMPTED MURDER
                              SPOUSAL ABUSE
                              CHILD ABUSE
                              TRAFFICKING IN ILLEGAL DRUGS
                              RACKETEERING

CALVIN BOOKER – EMBEZZLEMENT
                              MONEY LAUNDERING

WILLARD HEMLOCK – THEFT
                              ATTEMPTED EXTORTION
                              DRUG TRAFFICKING

MADAM ANGELICA – EXTORTION & FRAUD

HUGO HANDY – EXTORTION & FRAUD

CONRAD DIDDIT – ACCOMPLICE TO ATTEMPTED MURDER

JOE PHOENIX/FRANK N. STEIN – ATTEMPTED MURDER
CARRYING A CONCEALED WEAPON

The End

PART TWO

THE PLAY

SO . . . YOU WANT TO HAVE A MURDER MYSTERY PARTY!

You have read the story and should have an understanding of the plot, the characters, character relationships and general timetable of events. So now you would like to have a party with your friends acting out the roles of the characters in a play format with a "pretend" murder to solve in the end. How do you begin?

Murder in the Haunted House is not only a story of a murder but it also has all the necessary instructions, materials, plans and guidelines to hold a murder mystery *party play* designed for a casual party atmosphere.

Part One—The Story is merely a framework to help you understand the characters, their relationships to one another and how each personality adds to the drama preceding the murder. You need to grasp the lattice work of individuals in order to find logic in all the intrigues and thus follow that logic to sort out the puzzle in the end.

There is no script per se, nor specific dialogue to speak of (no pun intended) . . . just bits of character information to use as guidelines and certain specific instructions designed for each participant. It is each person's opportunity and responsibility to "become" the character described in their individual personality work-up and ad lib the play within the confines of the specific information and instructions given prior to the event.

By not having a fixed scrip to memorize, which is difficult in itself, each individual may tap their own creativity in providing their own remarks and choosing their own pace. With this method, it is expected that each person will have more freedom to invent and enjoy not only their character but challenge the responses of other characters. It is not so much ACTING but REACTING that is important and enjoyable in this format.

Consequently, the play is unique every time it is performed. The murder story will remain the same but the way it is performed will never be the same twice.

The evening will be filled with spontaneous incidents that will test everyone's abilities to adapt and stay in character, but that is the challenge and enjoyment of putting aside one's self and transforming into another personality. Shyness seems to melt away to be replaced by a shining star. That is truly the most fun and a phenomenon for which I was totally unprepared.

The host and/or hostess should take character parts too in order to be on hand ready to "steer" the evening, especially during the interrogations after the murder, which needs delicate management. During the interrogations, all evidence should be discussed up to a point before the murderer is exposed, if you want to give the guests a chance to guess the murderer. Bear in mind that three conditions must be satisfied in solving any murder case; i.e. OPPORTUNITY—ACCESS TO THE MURDER WEAPON—MOTIVE.

So, take a break in the party after the interrogations for all participants to come to their own conclusions and vote individually who they think the murderer is. Perhaps a small gift might be offered to all with the correct conclusions. Might I suggest a bottle of red wine for each winner? Or simply a certificate (see *Chart 1 in the CHARTS* section) to hand out to those amateur sleuths sharp enough to honor. *Chart 1* is just a suggestion . . . you might have a better idea.

So, shall we start planning the murder mystery party . . .

INSTRUCTIONS FOR THE HOST/HOSTESS

FIRST: REVIEW THE STORY

To make certain this particular murder mystery can be adequately staged and performed in your particular setting, review the story in your mind trying to picture the party taking place. Is there adequate space and configuration of the room, as relationships in staging are critical for this murder mystery. If in your mind you can see it happening, then the answer is "yes" the play will work and you can go on to the next step.

SECOND: PICK A DATE TO HAVE THE PARTY

You know the story and the characters, you must first pick a date for the party. You will want the party date to be far enough ahead to send out invitations, get replies, pair up characters with invitees, send out individual character instructions and still give the characters enough time to get familiar with their character, as well as the other characters, plan what to wear, procure any props needed and perhaps have a general meeting (if convenient) to discuss questions and go over logistics. Some characters will definitely need some kind of rehearsal if only to understand the set up. And you will need the time to study your strategy and design the proper murder scene setting. I suggest at least two to three weeks minimum although more time may be required if you are mailing out invitations and character assignments.

THIRD: SEND OUT INVITATIONS

Your attention is directed to the INVITATION marked as *Chart 2*, along with the news clipping and history byte marked similarly as *Chart 3* located in the *CHARTS* section. Make copies of the invitation and then print the news clipping on the back of the invitation. You are hereby given permission to reproduce those pages for the explicit personal use in the performance of this play in party format. All other copyright laws apply.

Make a list of guests you wish to invite to participate in the play. Although there is a short explanation on the Invitation as to the type of party this is and what will be expected of invitees, you may have more personal convincing to do with some guests. Keep this Invitation Guest List handy for recording responses and other information and notes you will need later when assigning characters.

Mail out or hand carry to each invitee on your guest list a copy of the invitation and the news clipping page as early as possible (you might want to stress early reply). This should allow enough time to get responses so you can make character assignments and send out individual character descriptions and instructions to the guests, giving them ample time to study their character, discuss with you any questions and concerns, and plan their costume.

FOURTH: GUEST LIST

Once you've gotten responses and have followed up on those who did not respond so you have a clear picture of all the guests definitely attending your party, divide the guests into ACTIVE and PASSIVE roles as indicated by their responses. Now, with that divided guest list in hand, find the LIST OF ACTIVE CHARACTERS, the LIST OF PASSIVE CHARACTERS and the LIST OF AUXILIARY CHARACTERS which are marked *Chart 4 and Chart 5* respectively and can be found in the *CHARTS* section. Now you are ready to assign specific characters to specific guests.

FIFTH: ASSIGNING ROLES

First, consider the roles for host and hostess. Typically, the host assumes the role of the butler during the play and then changes character and costume to play the police inspector. In these roles, he has the most control of the play. The hostess would be ideal as Camille Leon in either the maid persona or as reporter/ photographer making a home movie at the same time.

There are quite a number of characters in the story but not all of the characters are necessary for the execution of the plot. Twenty one of those characters are considered by this author to be necessary for the best contribution to the murder plot so are called ACTIVE characters. Additionally, fifteen of the ACTIVE characters are considered KEY characters and represent the minimum characters required for proper implementation of the story. There are six secondary KEY characters that enhance the story even more. The rest are PASSIVE characters. Although they have no necessarily direct influence in the murder story, they add much to the overall entertainment. Nevertheless, they are dispensable if there are not enough guests to play those parts. On the other hand, if you have more guests than written characters, I have provided an auxiliary list of friends of the family, neighbors, and employees of the Stein Brenner Company. If you need even more, simply use the same description as a neighbor but make up a new name. Although these characters have no specific instructions pertinent to the murder play, other than not to do or say anything that would over-ride the other characters and falsely influence the outcome of the intended plot, it is believed to be important for each guest to feel he/she is part of the story and can readily join in the fun as a separate fictional character to trade places with, if only for an evening.

Knowing your guests well will definitely facilitate character selection. It is recommended that you first set the ground-work by making sure each invited guest is comfortable with the type party, will definitely attend, and have given their preference as to ACTIVE or PASSIVE character. Because of the importance of the key characters, it would be wise to stress the need of a commitment and promptness. Illness is something you cannot control, so have a contingency plan to fill a key character(s) if such should be the case at the zero hour.

Obviously it is important that the core characters are on time and in attendance. As a matter of fact, it is just as critical that every guest be on time and stay throughout the murder scene. You would not appreciate your *murder in progress* being interrupted by a late comer. I have had this happen on one occasion and I can tell you that it is a host's nightmare. But the host/hostess should be prepared for such possible catastrophes and have an escape plan. But, first explaining the importance of promptness and commitment could go a long way to avoid those awkward moments.

Begin by making a list of the guests that have agreed to participate in ACTIVE roles. Using the LIST OF ACTIVE CHARACTERS mentioned earlier, compare what you know about the personality, persona and other qualities of each guest with the character descriptions from that list. Try to picture each guest with a character you think is a good match or which guest might have fun playing a particular role. There is no hard fast rule that requires couples to play couples but it is usually helpful and more convenient to assign couples together.

When you have all the ACTIVE characters assigned, begin adding PASSIVE characters using the LIST OF PASSIVE CHARACTERS and matching them to the rest of your guests. As mentioned above, if you should have more guests than characters, use the LIST OF AUXILIARY CHARACTERS to the degree needed.

When you are satisfied with all the assignments, proceed to the next step.

SIXTH: DISTRIBUTING THE INDIVIDUAL CHARACTER INFORMATION TO EACH GUEST

In the *CHARACTERS* section, you will find pages for a booklet of a list of all the characters with a descriptive comment next to each. Each guest should receive a copy of this booklet of *Cast of Characters* along with their individual information packet. If you do not want to take the extra time and effort to precisely print the booklet form, I have provided the list in letter form format. It is easier to reproduce and collate but not as efficient to carry around during the evening as a reference (which is its purpose). You are hereby given permission to reproduce those pages of the booklet *Cast of Characters* for the explicit personal use in the performance of this play in party format. All other copyright laws apply.

The *CHARACTERS* section also contains each individual character's *Personal Instructions*. Each person should receive in a sealed envelope a copy of his/her own personal description and instructions. This information could be very revealing if shared with anyone other than the eyes intended. In order to keep up the spontaneity of the evening and enhance the element of surprise, it is thus very important to stress the confidentiality of those personal documents. Naturally, guests who play husbands and wives, should compare information so there are no conflicting statements offered during the evening. You are hereby given permission to reproduce those pages of *Personal Instructions* for the explicit personal use in the performance of this play in party format. All other copyright laws apply.

Also, there are *General Instructions* in the *CHARACTERS* section that should be included in everyone's package and are designed to give general instructions for each guest to help them in how to perform the role they have been assigned. You are hereby given permission to reproduce those pages of *General Instructions* for the explicit personal use in the performance of this play in party format. All other copyright laws apply.

Lastly, the set-up and seating/standing arrangements for the Séance itself is most critical to the plot and solving of the murder. Included as *Chart 7* in the *CHARTS* section is a *SEATING ARRANGEMENT FOR THE SÉANCE TABLE* and surrounding area. Each person should get a copy of this seat assignment so they are familiar with where they are to be, even though Madam Angelica will direct each of them around the séance table to a specific seat (as shown on the Chart). Those guests not at the séance table will need to know where they are to sit/stand as well. You are hereby given permission to reproduce those pages of the *Seating Arrangement* for the explicit personal use in the performance of this play in party format. All other copyright laws apply.

IN SUMMATION: After assigning character roles, each person should be given a packet including the following:

> *CAST OF CHARACTERS Booklet or List*
> *PERSONALIZED INSTRUCTIONS*
> *GENERAL INSTRUCTIONS*
> *SEATING ARRANGEMENT*
> *Any props specific to a character . . . like Wills for the Lawyer*

SEVENTH: CHARACTER SUPPORT

You have read the story and should understand the whole picture, especially the character interactions and what is required to happen during the evening leading up to the séance, the séance itself, the interrogations of the witnesses and suspects and, lastly, anatomy of the murder or solving of the crime. The individual characters only know a piece of the puzzle—their piece, and possibly their partner's. It is suggested that you follow up on your *CORE* players to make sure each understands their part or has any questions regarding the *STAGING*. It may be necessary to have at least one meeting with the *CRITICAL* characters so they are familiar with the set-up of the area in which the play will be held.

The *CORE CHARACTERS* are as follows, with the *CRITICAL CHARACTERS* identified with an asterisk:

* Phyllis Stein	Paul Penniless	* Dr. Arthur Hart
* Dominique Baldwin	* Carl Brenner	Amanda Hart
Ralph Baldwin	Lily Brenner	* Willard Hemlock
* Ruben Stein	Calvin Booker	* Madam Angelica
* Helene Stein	Bonnie Booker	* Hugo Handy
* Francine Stein	* Lance Knight	* Conrad Diddit
* Priscilla Penniless	Holly Knight	* Joe Phoenix

The character *Inspector Cloque Jouseau* should be played by someone who knows the entire storyline, although his/her part in the *INTERROGATIONS* as well as the *ANATOMY OF THE MURDER* is written out thoroughly. Usually this character is played by the host or hostess because this one part has complete control of the solving of the crime which is the final goal of the party. But if there is another person you trust with this huge responsibility, it is your choice to make.

EIGHTH: STAGING

In this story, STAGING is extremely important. You will need to set up the room with a séance table (round if possible) large enough to seat at least eight people (it is acceptable if the seating is tight). The table should be situated in such a way so that a doorway (either to the outside or to another room or hall) is behind one seat, and a bar (or something equivalent, for serving the drinks) is set up directly opposite. Please refer to the *Seating Arrangement* Chart 7 in the *CHARTS* section.

You will need to find a globe to use as a crystal ball. If you don't have use of a globe lamp, you might use a low light bulb (blue provides a ghostly hue) under a glass globe lamp shade from an overhead fixture. Crunch up some different colored tissue paper for effect if you like but make sure the bulb does not get hot or the tissue could catch fire.

You will also need to run an extension cord to the lamp, making it as inconspicuous as possible. It should be plugged into an outlet that can be controlled by a central or easily accessible source like a switch or circuit breaker, out of sight of the guests.

Most important, and this may take some creative thinking, at a critical point, all the lights must be turned off together (including the globe). At that point, the room should be in **complete darkness**. Check this out ahead of time because many times there is a light source outside the house that may illuminate the room just enough for people to see what is going on. Check the calendar too, as even a full moon produces more light than you can imagine. You may have to close drapes or even put black paper up on the windows to block out street lights etc.

I would suggest that the séance table and chairs be roped off somehow during the time before the séance so that guests don't sit there and disturb the arrangement. Other chairs should be arranged in rows on both sides without the bar and door, but that can be done by Conrad immediately before the séance. Again, refer to Chart 7 (as suggested above) for seat assignments and general layout of the murder scene.

I cannot stress strongly enough the importance of staging to this particular play. Placement of the bar and doors in conjunction with the séance table is critical, as is also the seating. It is especially necessary for the room to become totally dark. As you have read the story first, you should understand the significance of the staging.

As an added thrilling special effect, I suggest using a smoke machine (or dry ice machine) to create a smoky mist through which the ghost can appear. And a pale back light adds a great effect as well. If you don't have these things, or can't borrow or buy them, you might try using dry ice in a bucket placed just outside the doorway where the ghost will appear. This effect will steal the show.

You can be even more creative by adding eerie music during the séance but the volume should be low so as not to drown out the dialogue.

Even though you have a "live" ghost playing the part, there is much the ghost will need to say. You might experiment with taping the voice and dialogue leaving spaces for answers where expected. For this, you will need a taping device and set up a way to play it during the Séance. Trying out different voices should be fun, too, as the recorded voice often sounds stranger than the original spoken voice.

NINTH: PROPS

TABLE (round) AND CHAIRS—As stated earlier, you will need a table (round if possible) and eight chairs for the séance table. Additional chairs for the rest of the guests on either side of the table. Some guests could be standing. Again, see Chart 7. Don't forget a table clothe or covering.

BAR—You will need to set up a BAR for serving drinks on one side of the séance table directly opposite a doorway to either the outside, another room or a hall (whichever is the designated entrance for the ghost.

CRYSTAL BALL—Beg, borrow or buy a globe table lamp or build one from a globe from an overhead light fixture and a low watt cool bulb (try blue).

COLORED TISSUE PAPER—Crumple up some different colored tissue paper inside the globe "crystal ball" for a nice effect.

EXTENSION CORD—You probably will need an extension cord for the crystal ball light. Remember, it should be connected to a source that can be turned off in unison with all other lights. Rehearsal is required.

MURDER WEAPON—You will need two ice picks. One ice pick will be situated on the bar and used during the evening in preparation of drinks for guests. It should remain in open view on the bar until the lights go out; at that time, Conrad will be assigned to take the ice pick and hide it out of view. The other will be used to create a prop that looks like it is embedded in the chest of the victim. To do this, saw off the pick to about two inches from the handle. Cut some red material in roughly a round circle with fluted edges approximately 8-10 inches wide. Find a cork or use one from a wine bottle. Push the cut-off end of the pick through the middle of the material and into the cork at least an inch, leaving about an inch of the pick exposed. The victim will have this hidden in her purse. When the lights go out, she will retrieve the prop and hold the cork end over her heart with one hand under the material. She should smooth out the material over the chest area which is intended to mimic blood.

CAP GUN—Beg, borrow or buy a child's cap gun which will be hidden in the bar for the bartender to shoot during the lights out scene. Be sure to practice with it to make certain it is in working order and will indeed shoot on cue. Yelling "Bang" (as I have been forced to do on one occasion) just doesn't cut it.

SMALL ZIPLOCK BAG FILLED WITH FLOUR—Fill a couple very small ziplock bags with flour to represent cocaine (or have the characters, Paul, Ruben, and Willard, provide their own.

TAPE RECORDER OR CD PLAYER—You will need a recording device if you decide to record the ghost's speech instead of having him memorize the words. You will also need to plan how to conceal it and control its play. I suggest the ghost have control of this device.

CANNED MUSIC SOURCE—If you choose to have mystical music playing during the séance, you will need a source for this music and someone to operate it. The butler character is ideal to handle this.

BRIEFCASE—Actually, this is optional, and could be the responsibility of the Lance Knight character to provide.

WILL—Make two copies of Phyllis' new Will as it appears in *Chart 6*, as well as one copy each of Phyllis and Frank's old Wills, and then include them in the Personal Package for the Lance Knight character. NOTE: You will have to add signatures to Phyllis' OLD Will and Frank's Will as those Wills should have already been signed. Phyllis' NEW Will still needs to be signed and that will happen during the play. You are hereby given permission to reproduce those pages for the explicit personal use in the performance of this play in party format. All other copyright laws apply.

PAD AND PEN—Inspector Cloque Jouseau needs a pad and pen/pencil for his interrogations. Since this character is typically played by the host, it will be your job to supply this prop.

CHARACTER PROPS—Some of the characters may have need of props and special costume items. Make it known that you are available to assist in searching for and procuring these items.

TENTH: A RECORD FOR POSTERITY

If your party set-up can accommodate a person to video record the event, all the more fun to share. Camille Leon is the character available for the role of TV reporter whose job it would be to try to go around the room during the evening interviewing each character briefly while recording their responses. Sometimes both a reporter *and* cameraman would be necessary or more useful. If you have the resources for the reporter to have a microphone, this would be an additional nice touch as all the rest of the characters could hear the actual interviews and possibly gather more information.

ELEVENTH: REFRESHMENTS

Now that all the murder mystery details are in motion, it is time to discuss what refreshments you wish to serve. Probably, you have not scheduled the party during the dinner hour, so no need to provide a dinner menu by any means, unless it is your choice. So, what is appropriate for a Séance?

First consider the size of the room or area available. Much space will be taken up by the séance setting. Physical bodies could be as few as fourteen or as many as forty or more. Typically, chips and dips and such could be put around on smaller side tables. Depending on the size of the bar set-up, hors d'oeuvres could be place on one end of the bar. The butler could be utilized to walk around with a tray of hors d'oeuvres. Perhaps Camille could be a maid and do the same . . . perfect role for the hostess.

Another suggestion would be to serve chips and dips and the like during the murder mystery part; and then after the murderer is revealed, serve dessert and coffee. Perfect time to discuss the play and decide just how many types of crimes had been committed by the various characters besides murder. First on the list might be the writing of this play . . . just joking, I hope.

THE CHARACTERS

GENERAL INSTRUCTIONS
FOR THE PLAYERS

Welcome to the murder mystery party play *Murder in the Haunted House.*

Each invitee, like yourself, is assigned the role of one of the characters in this murder mystery play. There is no script . . . no dialogue to learn. Everyone is given a character study of their character and data about their life. Also, depending on the role played, instructions will be given of specific acts, encounters, or conversations that need to take place during the evening. Each person has the freedom to develop their character as they see the character based upon the information given. For one evening, leave your inhibitions at home and come transform into a brand new person for an exciting adventure . . . and **Murder!**

As a character, the following information may be helpful in understanding your character, the role you are to play and how you are to interact with the others at the party in order to accomplish your piece of the plot and enjoy the journey.

PLEASE READ ALL THE INFORMATION PACKET . . . Obviously you need to learn about your own character; but you should also familiarize yourself with the background information for all characters, especially the characters your character should know well and will need to interact with. If you are in command of the information, you are more comfortable in your part. And don't forget to study these General Instructions . . . they are important too.

STUDY YOUR PART . . . and the parts of all characters you are to relate to during the evening. Get the feel of your character's personality as well as background. Try to get in your character's head, so to speak . . . and get into your character's skin. Use your guidelines to create a new life so you can be prepared to interact with others.

PLAN THE EXECUTION OF YOUR SPECIAL INSTRUCTIONS . . . If you are given specific things to do or people to interact with, you must plan your evening to get these accomplished by specific times or, in most cases, before the Séance begins. Generally, you are given lots of latitude with how you accomplish your individual instructions; but if your instructions are very specific, please follow closely.

PLAN FOR THE UNEXPECTED . . . The other characters and non-character "guests" (if any) are likely and encouraged to ask questions of you, some of which may be outside the information given you. You are allowed to "wing it" and make up information as long as it is not outside the perimeters of probability for your character or might possibly interfere with or contradict any other part of the play.

ACT AND REACT . . . It is important to get into the mind and personality of your character as well as be familiar with ALL information, so you are prepared to **REACT** to any "surprises" as your character might react, based on the guidelines of your role. You **ACT** when you are completing the assigned instructions and just being your character . . . You **REACT** at all other times to the environment around you. And try to stay "in character" throughout the evening.

SOCIALIZE WITH THE OTHER CHARACTERS AND (if present) NON-CHARACTER GUESTS . . . Before, during and after executing your specific special instructions, initiate conversations with others, always keeping in character, of course. You are encouraged to talk about yourself or the general situation, and especially to ask questions of others . . . put them on the spot if you wish. Get people talking about the Séance or each other. This brings out lots of information that may be needed later. Just make certain you stay within the perimeters of your character based on the information provided.

PLAN A MODE OF DRESS . . . This is "high society" . . . it is suggested that you dress "rich". This can be the fun part of getting in character. In some cases, your role may call for various "props". You are encouraged to be inventive and develop a character you feel matches the description given. If you have any questions, call and discuss them with the host/hostess.

SURPRISE! . . . To keep the mystery of the evening intact and to make it fun and fascinating, hopefully, for all, it is advised that you keep your character's personal instructions (and any "privileged" information) completely private until you MUST share them during the evening. Exceptions will be those incidents where you may wish to rehearse planned interactions with husband/wife relationships. Encountering "surprises" should give each of you a chance to participate in the fun of the mystery . . . whether you are a character or non-character guest.

TO TELL THE TRUTH . . . After the murder, during the interrogations, you are required to answer the questions truthfully to the extent that you have individual knowledge from what you've read, observed and overheard during the evening, continuing to remain "in character". Only exceptions are those characters that are specifically asked to respond a certain way in their Personal Instructions . . . and, of course, the murderer who will naturally deny the crime until found out in the end.

CLUES . . . You may be questioned for any clues you may have observed. But please feel free to offer information on anything you have heard or observed during the evening. Such participation is very helpful to the interrogator.

NON-CHARACTER GUESTS . . . All parties are unique. Some are small enough to only include the "essential" characters to the play. Some are large enough to use all the characters. Some are played for a larger group where there are too many people to all have a written part. These people are "Non-character Guests". These guests should feel they are part of the play, although they have no written part, by inviting them as "friends of the family", "employees", or whatever suits the play. They need not be just observers but should be encouraged by the characters in the play to get involved and participate simply by asking them questions or striking up a conversation. It can be fun catching them by surprise just to see their reaction. All guests, whether a character or non-character, should be given a Guest List booklet or list with brief information about each character in order to familiarize themselves with the characters of the play and the purpose of the evening. Don't ignore the non-characters . . . get them involved and see what happens.

REMEMBER—BE your character. Stay in character throughout the evening (if at all possible), **ACT** and **REACT**, complete all assigned tasks, observe the other characters for clues, socialize and above all, HAVE FUN!

CAST OF CHARACTERS

PHYLLIS STEIN. . . . . Widow of Frank N. Stein
DOMINIQUE DUMBELLI BALDWIN . . . . Phyllis' daughter from her first marriage
RALPH BALDWIN . . . . Dominique's husband
RUBEN STEIN . . . . Phyllis and Frank's son
HELENE STEIN . . . . Ruben's wife
FRANCINE STEIN . . . . Phyllis and Frank's daughter
PRISCILLA PENNILESS . . . . Phyllis' younger sister
PAUL PENNILESS. . . . . Priscilla's only son
PRUDENCE PIREET. . . . . Phyllis & Priscilla's youngest sister
PRENTICE PIREET . . . . Prudence's new husband
CARLTON BRENNER . . . . Frank N. Stein's business partner
LILY BRENNER. . . . . Carlton's second wife
CHRISTIAN BRENNER. . . . . Carlton's son by his first wife
CASSANDRA BRENNER. . . . . Christian's twin sister
CHARITY BRENNER SVENSON . . . . Carlton's youngest daughter by his first wife
PROFESSOR SVEN SVENSON. . . . . Charity's brand new husband
CALVIN BOOKER. . . . . Business Controller
BONNIE BOOKER . . . . Calvin's wife
LANCE KNIGHT. . . . . Business and Personal Lawyer
HOLLY KNIGHT. . . . . Lance's wife
DR. ARTHUR HART . . . . Family Doctor
AMANDA HART . . . . Arthur's wife and Phyllis' dear friend
FLORENCE CURTAIN. . . . . Phyllis's nurse
WILLARD HEMLOCK. . . . . Frank and Carlton's college friend
MADAM ANGELICA . . . . Séance Conductor and Medium
HUGO HANDY . . . . Madam Angelica's Bodyguard and Chauffeur
TILLY TOYLER . . . . Carlton's Secretary
WALLACE WINGATE . . . . Company Purchasing Agent
WINTER WINGATE. . . . . Wallace's Wife
DANNY DINGO . . . . Company Transit Director
DOTTIE DINGO . . . . Danny's Wife
MIKAL MAESTRO . . . . Symphony Conductor
MARTHA MAESTRO . . . . Mikal's Wife
FELIX FARNUM . . . . Neighbor
FANNY FARNUM . . . . Neighbor's Wife
CONRAD DIDDIT. . . . . Stein Family Butler
JOE PHOENIX . . . . Bartender
FRANK'S SPIRIT . . . . Séance Spirit
INSPECTOR CLOQUE JOUSEAU . . . . Police Inspector (Host)
CAMILLE LEON . . . . Network News Reporter or Maid (Hostess)

CAST OF CHARACTERS BOOKLET

The following pages contain short descriptions of each character in the story and a few more if you need them. The pages are arranged so that you can print one page and back it up with the next page, continuing until the end of the booklet. Assemble the pages (making note of the page numbers) and fold the set of pages in half. Tie a ribbon around the center fold to hold the booklet together or use your creativity to achieve that purpose.

Each of your guests should receive one of these booklets with their character package before the party. Additional copies should be on hand at the time of the party for those who forgot theirs or for other non-character guests, if any.

Quick reference of the booklet keeps the characters straight in the guests' minds and there are places for notes that could be a big help as the evening progresses.

Also provided, at the end of the booklet, is the same *Cast of Characters* list but in an 8 ½ x 11 format. This format is easier to print and assemble but it is larger and more bulky to carry around at the party. It is your choice as to which to use.

You are hereby given permission to reproduce those pages of the *Cast of Characters* for the explicit personal use in the performance of this play in party format. All other copyright laws apply.

MURDER
IN THE
HAUNTED HOUSE

A MURDER MYSTERY PARTY PLAY
WRITTEN BY
CAROLEE RUSSELL

A
Russell
'Riginal

NOTES

NOTES

Welcome to

MURDER in the HAUNTED HOUSE

This is a murder mystery "party play."

It is not a scripted play where the characters have to learn "lines" . . . but rather a play where the characters are given a set of "guidelines" and bits of personal information to use in developing their own interpretation of the character they are to play.

They are not given lines but must ad lib, keeping within the guidelines and information given them.

So . . . every time this play is performed in a party atmosphere, it will be unique. This is your chance to step outside yourself and become another person.

It is YOUR play!

Go have fun with it!

LIST OF CRIMES YOU NOTICED
(besides writing this play)

CAST OF CHARACTERS

PHYLLIS STEIN............Widow of Frank N. Stein
DOMINIQUE..BALDWIN....Phyllis' daughter
RALPH BALDWIN............Dominique's husband
RUBEN STEIN.............Phyllis and Frank's son
HELENE STEIN.............Ruben's wife
FRANCINE STEIN............Phyllis & Frank's daughter
PRISCILLA PENNILESS......Phyllis' younger sister
PAUL PENNILESS...........Priscilla's only son
PRUDENCE PIREET..........Phyllis's youngest sister
PRENTICE PIREET...........Prudence husband
CARLTON BRENNER..........Frank's business partner
LILY BRENNER............Carlton's second wife
CHRISTIAN BRENNER........Carlton's son
CASSANDRA BRENNER........Christian's twin sister
CHARITY SVENSON.........Carlton's youngest
PROF. SVEN SVENSON.......Charity's husband
FLORENCE CURTAIN.........Phyllis's nurse
DR. ARTHUR HART..........Family Doctor
AMANDA HART.............Arthur's wife
CALVIN BOOKER...........Business Controller
BONNIE BOOKER..........Calvin's wife
LANCE KNIGHT............Business/Personal Lawyer
HOLLY KNIGHT...........Lance's wife
WILLARD HEMLOCK........Frank & Carlton's college
                       friend
MADAM ANGELICA.........Séance Conductor and
                       Medium
HUGO HANDY.............Madam Angelica's
                       Bodyguard & Chauffeur

TILLY TOYLER.............Carlton's Secretary
WALLACE WINGATE.......Purchasing Agent
WINTER WINGATE...........Wallace's Wife
DANNY DINGO..............Transport Director
DOTTIE DINGO...............Danny's Wife
MIKAL MAESTRO..........Symphony Conductor
MARTHA MAESTRO........Mikal's Wife
FELIX FARNUM..............Neighbor
FANNY FARNUM............Felix's Wife
CONRAD DIDDIT.........Stein Family Butler
JOE PHOENIX...............Bartender
FRANK'S SPIRIT............Séance Spirit
CAMILLE LEON.............Network News Reporter
         or Maid (Hostess)
INSP. CLOQUE JOUSEAU...Police Inspector (Host)

AND POSSIBLY OTHER SOULS

CONRAD DIDDIT is the family Butler and devoted servant for nearly 30 years ad well as close friend and confidante to Frank.

JOE PHOENIX is the bartender and temporary servant hired by the butler solely for this evening's event.

FRANK'S GHOST is expected to make an appearance.

CAMILLE LEON is a Newspaper Reporter and Photographer for the Lightning Gazette who has been following this story since the fire a year ago. She bribed Priscilla to allow her access to this Séance. She hopes this will be the story of a lifetime . . . and not the end of her career. With the occult one never knows what the future holds.

INSPECTOR CLOQUE JOUSEAU is the police homicide detective called to the scene by the butler to solve the murder.

AND POSSIBLY OTHER SOULS

MIKAL MAESTRO is the Conductor of the town Symphony. He and his wife met the Steins because Frank and Phyllis served on the Symphony Board of Directors and they became fast friends even though Mikal's head is completely full of music with room for little else. Mikal took Frank's death very hard and, although his head tells him this Séance stuff is a fake, his heart wants to believe in the possibility.

MARTHA MAESTRO is Mikal's wife and mother of his seven children. It was Phyllis who convinced her to get help with the children so she could get out and get a life. So she joined Phyllis and Amanda in many of their social and charitable endeavors. She is terrified of the occult.

FELIX FARNUM is a long-time neighbor and close friend of the Stein family. Their children grew up with the Stein children. They are here tonight to give Phyllis their full support.

FANNY FARNUM is Felix's wife and one of Phyllis' best friends. She loves to laugh and tell jokes. They've been bridge partners at the Marathon Duplicate Bridge Group for ten years and she's been lost without her this past year. She hopes tonight she can talk Phyllis into coming back to the group.

"ONE YEAR AGO TODAY, CHEMICAL MANUFACTURER FRANK N. STEIN TRAGICALLY PERISHED IN AN EXPLOSION AND INTENSE FIRE WHICH DESTROYED THE RRESEARCH WING OF THE STEIN-BRENNR CHEMICAL PLANT

Such was the headline of the *Lightning Gazette*. Phyllis Stein did not need to be reminded of the gruesome, painful details of her husband's death. A year had not been enough time for her to recover from the horrifying shock and devastating loss of her dear husband. Unable to cope, she sank deeper into depression, alienating herself from family and friends, and becoming emotionally and physically drained to a point of threatening her health. The only people she could turn to for consolation and understanding, it seemed, were her younger daughter, Francine, who was a soothing comfort to her during this tragic time, and Madam Angelica, a mystic of some note, whom Phyllis met shortly after her husband's demise. It was Madam Angelica who had given Phyllis hope . . . hope of making contact with Frank's spirit in the Other World . . . hope of speaking with him and hearing his comforting words . . . hope of sorting out the confusion of her life. HOPE in the form of a SÉANCE!

*

Frank had not been her only husband nor she his only wife. Her first husband was billionaire Arnold Dumbelli of the Madison Avenue Dumbelli's Training Pants fortune, who had died suddenly in a yachting accident less than a year after they were married. Since his body was never recovered, a Memorial Service was held at the spot where Arnold's boat capsized in Long Island Sound. That marriage had made Phyllis a rich widow and had produced a healthy baby girl, Dominique. But because of Phyllis' immaturity and insecurity, neither brought her any joy.

Her second marriage to Bruce Brassiere, heir to the Itty Bitty Titty Brassiere fortune, was equally disconcerting and ended in a "hushed" annulment due to irreconcilable "likenesses" . . both preferred the company of women in the afternoons and men in the evenings. The family managed to keep the scandal from the newspapers and made it monetarily worth her while to cooperate in this. Bruce was too wrapped up in the family business to put up much resistance. It comes as no surprise that there were no children from this marriage.

Then she met Frank! He was tall and handsome and full of enthusiasm about his future plans in the chemical research/manufacturing field. His easy charm and flashing smile just melted her heart. His first marriage to his college sweetheart had ended in a bitter, ugly divorce only a year before he met Phyllis. The legal entanglements had left him penniless, without a job and worse . . without his young son to whom he had been devoted. His ex-wife had disappeared after the divorce taking the boy with her and all efforts to find them had failed. Frank was just getting his life together after the divorce and contemplating starting a chemical company with his college buddy, Carlton Brenner, when he met Phyllis. It was love at first "site" . . since they both were in the Fairwinds Real Estate Office looking over property. They merged. With Phyllis' financial backing, Frank was able to join Carl in building a chemical research/manufacturing empire. Frank and Phyllis' long marriage had seemed all peaks and few valleys and produced a son, Ruben, and a daughter, Francine. It was a blissful union with staggering financial and social success.

And then the fire. . .

TILLY TOYLER is Carlton's Secretary and an extremely efficient one. She is like a no-nonsense machine at work and at home as well. That could account for why she remains unmarried in her mid forties. She is also the office gossip and is never without her steno pad. She brought a steno pad tonight to take copious notes about the Séance . . or anything else that seems interesting;

WALLACE WINGATE is Purchasing Agent for the Stein-Brenner Company. He misses Frank and the friendship he gave everyone at the plant. Work this past year has been a real drudge, but he is in too deep to quit. He's terrified of Carl and Carl's "friends".

WINTER WINGATE is the daughter of a mobster in Chicago. She's "one of them" and Wallace regrets the day he met her but divorce is not an option. Winter loves parties . . any party. She's never heard of a séance and never had her palm read. She's disappointed there will be no dancing tonight.

DANNY DINGO serves as Company Transit Director and is Head of the local Teamsters. He has total charge of everything coming in and out of the plant. He thinks of only two things: work and football. He doesn't know what "social" means but Carl insisted he be at the séance . . just in case . . despite his discomfort.

DOTTIE DINGO is Danny's wife and a "real blond" but with a figure worth showing off . . and she does. She has the license on swinging hips and low cut tops. Bonnie Booker hates her.

MADAM ANGELICA had been attracted by the headline newspaper article a year ago on the Stein-Brenner Plant fire and had contrived a meeting with Phyllis some time after. She has been seeing Phyllis for the better part of a year trying to console her and win her confidence . . . with unbelievable success and rewards. Phyllis completely believes in Madam Angelica and the occult. Madam Angelica suggested a Séance to contact Frank in the hope that his spirit's presence would have a desirable influence on Phyllis. Drumming up business in this social circle wouldn't be bad either.

HUGO HANDY is Madam Angelica's bodyguard and chauffeur. He is a disturbing presence in the shadowy background, poised for possible action from, shall we say, unbelievers.

PHYLLIS STEIN

Phyllis Stein is gathering together her family and dearest friends to share with her what could very well be the most exciting evening of her life.

Because of the overwhelming depression that followed her husband's death last year, Phyllis had been willingly guided toward her salvation by Madam Angelica's counsel and is convinced tonight's Séance will bring Frank's Spirit to her to show her the direction her life should take. Having lost the security of her husband's protection and support, she desperately needs to hear his reassuring words and guidance.

The following are her invited guests (not many of whom share Phyllis' confidence and enthusiasm for this evening's event).

DOMINIQUE DUMBELLI JOHANSON O'REILLY SCHWARTZ GONZALES WELLINGTON SUBARU GUNDERMANN CHANG POLANSKI JONES BALDWIN is Phyllis' daughter by her first husband, Arnold Dumbelli, who died suddenly in a yachting accident when Dominique was less than a month old. Phyllis had been very young, immature and insecure during Dominique's early years and had left her upbringing pretty much to nannies and other servants. Dominique has never recovered from the apparent rejection which has resulted in a love/hate relationship. Her search for the love that was denied her in her youth has led her through many marriages . . . all doomed to failure. Her present union is with Ralph Baldwin who has the gift of controlling Dominique's whining and temper tantrums. Dominique sees this evening as another form of her mother's rejection in favor of her step-father and step-sister, Francine, and she is convinced Madam Angelica is responsible.

RALPH BALDWIN is Dominique's present husband. A simple man with simple tastes, he is drawn to the bird with the broken wing...that is Dominique. He loves her despite her flaws, or perhaps because of them. He understands her and is devoted to easing her pain with soft words or a gentle touch... Few know how highly intelligent and well read he is, or that he has an innate sense of the inner struggles of others. Outwardly, he's unremarkable and seems to disappear in plain sight. People are constantly bumping into him. He might be a "cellophane man" but his eye misses nothing. Despite his limited talents and low-keyed personality, his piano moving business is flourishing...a real accomplishment for him, especially since he can't even carry a tune. He expects this evening to be an amusing distraction and hopes Dominique won't cause too much trouble.

WILLARD HEMLOCK belongs to the family who established Hemlock College, which was the only means he had of acquiring a college degree although not necessarily an academic education. As the last male in the Hemlock line, the family was very tolerant of his meager scholastic abilities, but that's not to say he wasn't smart in other ways ...smart like a fox. His "creative ideas" are not always of a legitimate nature and over the years he has become a successful con-man and manipulator. To most people, he is an obnoxious, creepy weasel; but fearing his tactics, most men tolerated him, take care not to rile him or simply leave him alone. Willard had the acuity to perceive great potential in associating himself with and insinuating himself onto his college buddies, Frank and Carl. So, when he heard that Frank and Carl were forming their own business, he wheedled himself onto the payroll as a marketing rep. The association had not panned out quite the way he had hoped, so after the fire he left the company to woo Phyllis for her obvious attributes . . . money! Her obsession with Frank, however, is a larger obstacle than he anticipated. Think of Uriah Heap and you have Willard.

LANCE KNIGHT is a young, Wall-Street type lawyer. He has been with the Stein-Brenner Company for nearly ten years as well as being the Stein's personal lawyer and family friend. He has done well in those years owing, in no small part, to his wit, charm and good looks as well as his education and talent. He should thank his wife for his education, but he feels he has paid the price. They married very young, sooner than he had planned, and the years and his success have caused him to drift from the person he once was in High School, much like a caterpillar becoming a butterfly; whereas his wife is still the person she was when she fell in love with Lance. Her clinging is getting on his nerves. His life so far has been governed by fateful consequences causing him to make the wrong decisions for the right reasons. He would now rather make the right decisions for the wrong reasons. His head is into getting ahead so his social skills have suffered, although the right woman could change that. His attendance tonight is business as well as social.

HOLLY KNIGHT had married Lance, her high school sweetheart, immediately after graduation, as most of her friends were doing, but in her case it was more urgent and necessary. Shortly after their wedding, she had a miscarriage and the ensuing complications rendered her sterile. To hold onto Lance, the love of her life, she agreed to work in order to put him through college and law school. It was a tremendous sacrifice but she was certain it would be worth it. What she hadn't anticipated was the metamorphosis resulting from an education. It hurt to admit, but she no longer fitted into Lance's life. She is trying to reinvent herself to try to rekindle the romance of long ago. She feels she is in need of spiritual guidance ... perhaps tonight's the Knight ... er ... night!

RUBEN STEIN is the first child of Phyllis and Frank and the obvious choice to take over the business from his father. As a child, Ruben quickly realized he lacked the talent his father had for business. He is only of average intelligence, with an inferiority complex topping out at zero, and is easily dominated and manipulated. He believes he is a disappointment to his family. To cover his inadequacies, he drinks . . . a lot! His overwhelming jealousy of Francine threatens to consume him. His ambitious wife constantly pushes and nags him to excel so he can take over the business, but it only contributes to his smothering pressures. His mother, not understanding his deep identity problems, has no patience with his behavior, especially since his father's death. "Uncle" Carl is the only one that has given him a chance. He thinks this Séance business is stupid . . . but can't quite understand why he fears it.

HELENE STEIN is from the wrong side of the tracks and ambitious. In High School, Helene was a force to be reckoned with...strong and confident. All the girls idolized her and followed wherever she led them. Smiling does not come naturally to her. She usually got what she wanted, and she wanted Ruben for the potential he represented. She misjudged Ruben's dynamics, so if her hunger for money and status is to be sated, she has to be the power behind the throne. Over the years this has been an enormous challenge but her efforts continue. She will not admit having made a mistake, so she is still trying to reinvent Ruben. Frank had recognized her selfish ambitions and his disdain had been an obstacle for her. With him gone, her attentions have focused on Phyllis who has not been too receptive in her right state of mind. Tonight's Séance may put Phyllis in the right mood and present any number of favorable possibilities.

FRANCINE STEIN is Phyllis and Frank's youngest child. She has looks, charm, wit, brains and fortitude . . . just like her father. Women envy her and men are mesmerized by her. The darling! Self-assured and very together for her young age, she has devoted her life to the family and the family business. She has the talent Ruben lacks and feels a bit embarrassed about that, causing her to be sympathetic towards him which seems to anger him more. Her father's death forced her into the business sooner than expected, but, with Lance Knight's help, she has excelled at the challenge. She loves her mother and treats her with understanding and sincerity and her pampering has earned her much favor. She seems so perfect and well adjusted. Despite her obvious perfections, she is still exciting and non-intimidating to men and could have her pick. She's very good at dodging them too. She does not believe in the occult, but is afraid of what the outcome of this séance will do to her mother. Never one to succumb to gloom and doom, she indulges her mother by her presence at this Séance, but is determined to party and have fun.

Page 9

CALVIN BOOKER is a paranoid Don Knotts of the accounting world. He started with the company early on and is now it's Controller. As a young accountant, this nervous, shy man had been captivated by an exotic dancer during a bachelor party for a friend. He madly pursued her promising he was her ticket into the polite society, she married him. The years following had been, for Calvin, a desperate struggle to make good on his promise. His life has not taken all the turns and directions he had hoped. He is a nervous, worried, frightened man who doesn't want to believe in the spirit world but is awfully afraid that it exists.

BONNIE BOOKER, a former stripper, had expected big things from Calvin, hoping to climb the social ladder to respectability . . . at least high enough to outdistance her nefarious beginnings. Far from being a "My Fair Lady", she nevertheless considers herself a success (not realizing one can't make a silk purse out of a sow's ear) and cares nothing about how Calvin manages financially. After all, she can't count up to three with mittens on. She loves being the social butterfly, hobnobbing with the rich and sometimes famous, oblivious to the frowns and sharp remarks. It is obvious she did *not* have Professor Higgins as a teacher as she still dresses garishly and is loud and crass. Tonight's Séance should be a "real hoot!"

Page 16

ARTHUR HART has been the friend and family doctor of both the Stein and Brenner families since Frank and Phyllis needed a blood test in order to marry. He not only delivered both Ruben and Francine but he and his wife, Amanda, stood as Godparents for both children. He took Frank's death especially hard, mostly because of the nature of the incident. Because the Plant was full of highly flammable chemicals, the fire was so intense that everything was reduced to ashes. Not even a bone fragment could be recovered for burial. This was so devastating to Phyllis that Arthur is seriously concerned about her health . . . mental as well as physical. A year had done nothing to relieve her depression. Her obsession with this Madam Angelica person worries him. He does not believe in spirits (unless they are the "liquid" kind) and fears what failure of this evening might do to Phyllis.

AMANDA HART is the devoted and patient wife of a busy doctor as well as Phyllis' closest friend and confidant . . until Madam Angelica showed up. She is extremely active . in community affairs and local charity functions as was Phyllis before Frank's death. She is very jealous of the attention this Madam is getting and wants to get Phyllis out of her depression and back into their old routines. She secretly hopes this fake Séance falls flat, for she doesn't believe in this business for a minute.

PRISCILLA PENNILESS, Phyllis' younger sister, is all the things Phyllis is not . . . strong-willed, domineering, organized, quick-minded, stern and POOR. Though not as fortunate in her life as Phyllis, she loves her sister but is often frustrated and annoyed with her behavior. She wasted no time moving herself and her son, Paul, into the mansion with Phyllis after the fire and completely took over the running of the household, bossing the servants and the children. Paul, however, is the apple of her eye . . he can do no wrong . . . her life is devoted to him, and her personality completely changes to doting mother when he's with her. Otherwise, to others, it's her way or the highway. Her biggest concern is Phyllis' fanatical preoccupation with this Madam Angelica person and she's not too pleased with the attention that creep, Willard Hemlock, is giving her sister. She plans to keep a close eye on the proceedings tonight

PAUL PENNILESS is Priscilla's only child . . . her pride and joy. Paul is useless. One might go so far as to say he is a bum, a freeloader and an opportunist for all occasions. He inherited these genes from his shiftless father who abandoned the family when Paul was still in diapers. Paul is wholly arrogant from being spoiled and enjoys using people, especially his mother, who pets him and gives him everything she can . . and then some. He believes he should not have to spend much effort to make a buck but a con game is more his style. He is having a high time living off his Aunt Phyllis and isn't beyond considering a little incest with his cousin, Francine . . after all, the royals did it. And tonight he feels royal

PRUDENCE PIREET is the youngest sister of Phyllis and Priscilla. Shy little Prudence has been a prim and proper history teacher...well..forever. Always with her nose in a book she had little time or desire for personal relationships. Harassed by her colleagues to "get a life", she finally agreed to a vacation cruise ... a choice that would dramatically change her life. There she met Prentice. She has only been married a few days and is bursting with pride over her splendid good fortune. She has always felt rather distant to her rich relative, Phyllis, but under present circumstances, she is anxious to become reacquainted with her older sister. In short, Prudence has finally blossomed.

PRENTICE PIREET met Prudence on a cruise to the Bahamas and was captivated by her femininity and knowledge of world events. Within days they were married by the Ship's Captain and spent the remaining time on the cruise honeymooning. Although his family has "old" money, he has become a success on his own merits as a businessman and politician. In fact, he has just been approached to run for the Senate which is only one step closer to his goal..President! Prentice is considered the "catch of the season" in the media, but he considers himself the lucky one to find a partner so interesting and well read as to be the perfect marriage partner for his political aspirations. He's not handsome so much as distinguished, refined and well educated. His comportment is commanding; he knows how to "work a room." Still, he is out of his element at this séance and worries what the association with these gypsies might do to his future plans. Those Democrats can dig up anything.

CHARITY BRENNER SVENSON is Carl's daughter by his first wife. She is a typical "Valley Girl". While living with her maternal grandparents in California, she attended an exclusive finishing school and private college. While in college she met and married her theology Professor, Sven Svenson. Currently, they are returning from their honeymoon in Sweden where she met his family, and plan to spend some time with Carl and Lily before returning to California. She is proud as punch over her "catch" and tonight she gets to show him off.

PROFESSOR SVEN SVENSON is the son of one of Sweden's richest merchants. Not having to worry about earning money, he decided he would concentrate on gaining power...power molding inquisitive minds. So he became a college professor in the field he thought wielded the most influence...religion. His only weakness is Charity. He is "totally smitten." He loves Charity but he's not sure he can endure this Séance which is contrary to all he believes.

FLORENCE CURTAIN is Phyllis' personal live-in nurse. Because of Phyllis' declining health, Nurse Curtain has been retained for the past six months at Dr. Hart's insistence. She tries to do her job but Priscilla is constantly intervening. She's not used to this treatment and hopes the little men in White Coats will come soon and take Phyllis to where she belongs so she, Florence, can go on to a more rewarding position. This Séance might just turn out to be a moving experience.

CHRISTIAN BRENNER is Carl's first child and heir ...not necessarily apparent. Christian, typical of the second generation rich, does not share his father's interest in business but prefers to spend his time and his father's money on the race car circuit. Surprisingly, he is good at it, which is the only reason Carl continues to support him. He has his "groupies" on the circuit so his ego is well stoked. He relishes the adoration which has made him audacious. His life is one big party. He likes "Auntie" Phyllis and family, especially Francine. This Séance business is a new one on him, but what the hell...he's a good sport.

CASSANDRA BRENNER is Christian's twin sister and thus feels an unusual kinship with him. But even with this special bond, she has not shared all her secrets with him. Secrets that have shaken her sanity. If only she had been allowed to go with her younger sister, Charity, to be raised by her maternal grandparents after her mother died. She is completely antisocial and afraid of her own shadow. Her life has improved since Lily married her father. She now has someone to cling to and share her burdens with. She's especially interested in this Séance. She could very well be Madam Angelica's next client. M o t h e r ....!

CARLTON BRENNER grew up with Frank and both chose Hemlock College for it's chemistry program. Being the youngest of seven brothers, Carl saw no future in entering the family's highly successful perfume manufacturing business. His aim was for a quick trip to the top of the heap. Obsessed with money and power, Carl would do most anything to get more of both...and has. During a chance reunion with Frank shortly after Frank's divorce, it occurred to him that Frank's excellent scholastic record could be the catalyst he needed to achieve his dreams, so he suggested a partnership. Frank jumped at the chance to work with his best buddy. With no financial support from Carl's family, having been disinherited for his rebellion from the family, and Frank's divorce cleaning his pockets, Phyllis had been the answer to their prayers. Their business prospered and they both became billionaires. That was enough for Frank but Carl compulsively hungers for more. His friends at *Lobo's* have been very helpful. He acts the suave gentleman with flair and flash but beneath this surface he is tough, cold and cruel, akin to Dorian Gray. His first wife could probably tell you the extent of that ... if she were still alive. Always suspicious, he is uneasy about this Séance.

LILY BRENNER had been Carl's secretary some years ago and married Carl shortly after his wife died...hmmm. A timid, feminine woman, she was instinctively drawn to the dominating power Carl exuded. Now she is afraid of it and of him. No, not just afraid...terrified. She found that Cassandra was likewise traumatized, so they naturally cling to each other out of desperation and the hope that it might double their strength or at least provide comfort. Social functions make her nervous and uncomfortable. She believes in ghosts!

CHARACTER
LIST

MURDER IN THE HAUNTED HOUSE

CHARACTER LIST

PHYLLIS STEIN is gathering together her family and dearest friends to share with her what could very well be the most exciting evening of her life. Because of the overwhelming depression that followed her husband's death last year, Phyllis had willingly been guided toward her salvation by Madam Angelica, a local sere and fortune teller. For these many months, she has sought Madam Angelica's counsel and is convinced tonight's Séance will bring Frank's Spirit to her to show her the direction her life should take. Having lost the security of her husband's protection and support, she desperately needs to hear his reassuring words and guidance.

The following are her invited guests (not many of whom share Phyllis' confidence and enthusiasm for this evening's event):

DOMINIQUE DUMBELLI JOHANSON O'REILLY SCHWARTZ GONZALES WELLINGTON SUBARU GUNDERMANN CHANG POLANSKI JONES BALDWIN is Phyllis' daughter by her first husband, Arnold Dumbelli, who died suddenly in a yachting accident when Dominique was less than a month old. Phyllis had been very young, immature and insecure during Dominique's early years and had left her upbringing pretty much to nannies and other servants. Dominique has never recovered from the apparent rejection which has resulted in a love/hate relationship. Her search for the love that was denied her in her youth has led her through many marriages . . . all doomed to failure. Her present union is with Ralph Baldwin who has the gift of controlling Dominique's whining and temper tantrums. Dominique sees this evening as another form of her mother's rejection in favor of her step-father and step-sister, Francine, and she is convinced Madam Angelica is responsible.

RALPH BALDWIN is Dominique's present husband. A simple man with simple tastes, he is drawn to the bird with the broken wing . . . that is Dominique. He loves her despite her flaws or perhaps because of them. He understands her and is devoted to easing her pain with soft words or a gentle touch. Few know how highly intelligent and well read he is, or that he has an innate sense of the inner struggles of others. Outwardly, he's unremarkable and seems to disappear in plain sight. People are constantly bumping into him. He might be a "cellophane man" but his eye misses nothing. Despite his limited talents and low-keyed personality, his piano moving business is flourishing . . . a real accomplishment for him, especially since he can't even carry a tune. He expects this evening to be an amusing distraction and hopes Dominique won't cause too much trouble.

RUBEN STEIN is the first child of Phyllis and Frank and the obvious choice to take over the business from his father. As a child, Ruben quickly realized he lacked the talent his father had for business. He is only of average intelligence, with an inferiority complex topping out at zero, and is easily dominated and manipulated. He believes he is a disappointment to his family. To cover his inadequacies, he drinks . . . a lot! His overwhelming jealousy of Francine threatens to consume him. His ambitious wife constantly pushes and nags him to excel so he can take over the business, but it only contributes to his smothering pressures. His mother, not understanding his deep identity problems, has no patience with his behavior, especially since his father's death. "Uncle" Carl is the only one that has given him a chance. He thinks this Séance business is stupid . . . but can't quite understand why he fears it.

HELENE STEIN is from the wrong side of the tracks and ambitious. In High School, Helene was a force to be reckoned with . . . strong and confident. All the girls idolized her and followed wherever she led them. Smiling does not come naturally to her. She usually got what she wanted, and she wanted Ruben for the potential he represented. She misjudged Ruben's dynamics, so if her hunger for money and status is to be sated, she has to be the power behind the throne. Over the years this has been an enormous challenge but her efforts continue. She will not admit having made a mistake, so she is still trying to reinvent Ruben. Frank had recognized her selfish ambitions and his disdain had been an obstacle for her. With him gone, her attentions have focused on Phyllis who has not been too receptive in her state of mind. Tonight's Séance may present possibilities.

FRANCINE STEIN is Phyllis and Frank's youngest child. She has looks, charm, wit, brains and fortitude . . . just like her father. Women envy her and men are mesmerized by her. The darling! Self-assured and very together for her young age, she has devoted her life to the family and the family business. She has the talent Ruben lacks and feels a bit embarrassed about that, causing her to be sympathetic towards him which seems to anger him more. Her father's death forced her into the business sooner than expected, but with Lance Knight's help, she has excelled at the challenge. She loves her mother and treats her with understanding and sincerity and her pampering has earned her much favor. She seems so perfect and well adjusted. Despite her obvious perfections, she is still exciting and non-intimidating to men and could have her pick. She's very good at dodging them too. She does not believe in the occult, but is afraid of what the outcome of this séance will do to her mother. Never one to succumb to gloom and doom, she indulges her mother by her presence at this Séance, but is determined to party and have fun.

PRISCILLA PENNILESS, Phyllis' younger sister, is all the things Phyllis is not . . . strong-willed, domineering, organized, quick-minded, stern and POOR. Though not as fortunate in her life as Phyllis, she loves her sister but is often frustrated and annoyed with her behavior. She wasted no time moving herself and her son, Paul, into the mansion with Phyllis after the fire and completely took over the running of the household, bossing the servants and the children. Paul, however, is the apple of her eye . . . he can do no wrong . . . her life is devoted to him, and her personality completely changes to doting mother when he's with her. Otherwise, to others, it's her way or the highway. Her biggest concern is Phyllis' fanatical preoccupation with this Madam Angelica person and she's not too pleased with the attention that creep, Willard Hemlock, is giving her sister. She plans to keep a close eye on the proceedings tonight.

PAUL PENNILESS is Priscilla's only child . . . her pride and joy. Paul is useless. One might go so far as to say he is a bum, a freeloader and an opportunist for all occasions. He inherited these genes from his shiftless father who abandoned the family when Paul was still in diapers. Paul is wholly arrogant from being spoiled and enjoys using people, especially his mother, who pets him and gives him everything she can . . . and then some. He believes he should not have to spend much effort to make a buck but a con game is more his style. He is having a high time living off his Aunt Phyllis and isn't beyond considering a little incest with his cousin, Francine . . . after all, the royals did it. And tonight he feels royal.

PRUDENCE PIREET is the youngest sister of Phyllis and Priscilla. Shy little Prudence has been a prim and proper history teacher . . . well . . . forever. Always with her nose in a book she had little time or desire for personal relationships. Harassed by her colleagues to "get a life," she finally agreed to a vacation cruise . . . choice that would dramatically change her life. There she met Prentice. She has only been married a few days and is bursting with pride over her splendid good fortune. She has always felt rather distant to her rich relative, Phyllis, but under present circumstances, she is anxious to become reacquainted with her older sister. In short, Prudence has finally blossomed.

PRENTICE PIREET met Prudence on a cruise to the Bahamas and was captivated by her femininity and knowledge of world events. Within days they were married by the Ship's Captain and spent the remaining time on the cruise honeymooning. Although his family has "old" money, he has become a success on his own merits as a businessman and politician. In fact, he has just been approached to run for the Senate which is only one step closer to his goal . . . President! Prentice is considered the "catch of the season" in the media but he considers himself the lucky one to find a partner so interesting and well read as to be the perfect marriage partner for his political aspirations. He's not handsome so much as distinguished, refined and well educated. His comportment is commanding; he knows how to "work a room." Still, he is out of his element at this séance and worries what the association with these gypsies might do to his future plans. Those Democrats can dig up anything.

CARLTON BRENNER grew up with Frank and both chose Hemlock College for it's chemistry program. Being the youngest of seven brothers, Carl saw no future in entering the family's highly successful perfume manufacturing business. His aim was for a quick trip to the top of the heap. Obsessed with money and power, Carl would do most anything to get more of both . . . and has. During a chance reunion with Frank shortly after Frank's divorce, it occurred to him that Frank's excellent scholastic record could be the catalyst he needed to achieve his dreams, so he suggested a partnership. Frank jumped at the chance to work with his best buddy. With no financial support from Carl's family, having been disinherited for his rebellion from the family, and Frank's divorce cleaning his pockets, Phyllis had been the answer to their prayers. Their business prospered and they both became billionaires. That was enough for Frank but Carl compulsively hungers for more. His friends at *Lobo's* have been very helpful. He acts the suave gentleman with flash and flair but beneath this surface he is tough, cold and cruel, akin to Dorian Grey. His first wife could probably tell you the extent of that . . . if she were still alive. Always suspicious, he is uneasy about this Séance.

LILY BRENNER had been Carl's secretary some years ago and married Carl shortly after his wife died . . . hmmm. A timid, feminine woman, she was instinctively drawn to the dominating power Carl exuded. Now she is afraid of it and of him. No, not just afraid . . . terrified. She found that Cassandra was likewise traumatized, so they naturally clung to each other out of desperation and the hope that it might double their strength or at least provide comfort. Social functions make her nervous and uncomfortable. She believes in ghosts!

CHRISTIAN BRENNER is Carl's first child and heir . . . not necessarily apparent. Christian, typical of the second generation rich, does not share his father's interest in business but prefers to spend his time and his father's money on the race car circuit. Surprisingly, he is good at it, which is the only reason Carl continues to support him. He has his "groupies" on the circuit so his ego is well stoked. He relishes the adoration which has made him audacious. His life is one big party. He likes "Auntie" Phyllis and family, especially Francine. This Séance business is a new one on him, but what the hell . . . he's a good sport.

CASSANDRA BRENNER is Christian's twin sister and thus feels an unusual kinship with him. But even with this special bond, she has not shared all her secrets with him. Secrets that have shaken her sanity. If only she had been allowed to go with her younger sister, Charity, to be raised by her maternal grandparents after her mother died. She is completely antisocial and afraid of her own shadow. Her life has improved since Lily married her father. She now has someone to cling to and share her burdens with. She's especially interested in this Séance. She could very well be Madam Angelica's next client. M o t h e r . . . . !

CHARITY BRENNER SVENSON is Carl's youngest daughter by his first wife. She is a typical "Valley Girl". While living with her maternal grandparents in

California, she attended an exclusive finishing school and private college. While in college she met and married her theology Professor, Sven Svenson. Currently, they are returning from their honeymoon in Sweden where she met his family, and plan to spend some time with Carl and Lily before returning to California. She is proud as punch over her "catch" and tonight she gets to totally show him off.

PROFESSOR SVEN SVENSON is the son of one of Sweden's richest merchants. Not having to worry about earning money, he decided he would concentrate on gaining power . . . power molding inquisitive minds. So he became a college professor in the field he thought wielded the most influence . . . religion. However, he thinks he has more "power" than he actually has. He has far too much pride and more than an equal amount of prejudice. His weakness is Charity. He is totally smitten. He loves Charity but he's not sure he can endure this Séance which is contrary to all he believes . . . or thinks he believes.

LANCE KNIGHT is a young, Wall-Street type lawyer. He has been with the Stein-Brenner Company for nearly ten years as well as being the Stein's personal lawyer and family friend. He has done well in those years owing, in no small part, to his wit, charm and good looks as well as his education and talent. He should thank his wife for his education, but he feels he has paid the price. They married very young, sooner than he had planned, and the years and his success have caused him to drift from the person he once was in High School, much like a caterpillar becoming a butterfly; whereas his wife is still the person she was when she fell in love with Lance. Her clinging is getting on his nerves. His life so far has been governed by fateful consequences causing him to make the wrong decisions for the right reasons. He would now rather make the right decisions for the wrong reasons. His head is into getting ahead so his social skills have suffered, although the right woman could change that. His attendance tonight is business as well as social.

HOLLY KNIGHT had married Lance, her high school sweetheart, immediately after graduation, as most of her friends were doing, but in her case it was more urgent and necessary. Shortly after their wedding, she had a miscarriage and the ensuing complications rendered her sterile. To hold onto Lance, the love of her life, she agreed to work in order to put him through college and law school. It was a tremendous sacrifice but she was certain it would be worth it. What she hadn't anticipated was the metamorphosis resulting from an education. It hurt to admit, but she no longer fitted into Lance's life. She is trying to reinvent herself to try to rekindle the romance of long ago. She feels she is in need of spiritual guidance . . . perhaps tonight's the Knight . . er . . . night!

ARTHUR HART has been the friend and family doctor of both the Stein and Brenner families since Frank and Phyllis needed a blood test in order to marry. He not only delivered both Ruben and Francine but he and his wife, Amanda, stood as Godparents for both children. He took Frank's death especially hard, mostly because of the nature of the incident. Because the Plant was full of highly flammable chemicals, the fire was so intense that everything was reduced to ashes. Not even a bone fragment could be recovered for burial. This was so devastating to Phyllis that Arthur is seriously concerned about her health . . . mental as well as physical. A year had done nothing to relieve her depression. Her obsession with this Madam Angelica person worries him. He does not believe in spirits (unless they are the "liquid" kind) and fears what failure of this evening might do to her.

AMANDA HART is the devoted and patient wife of a busy doctor as well as Phyllis' closest friend and confidant . . . until Madam Angelica showed up. She is extremely active in community affairs and local charity functions as was Phyllis before Frank's death. She is very jealous of the attention this Madam is getting and wants to get Phyllis out of her depression and back into their old routines. She secretly hopes this fake Séance falls flat, for she doesn't believe in this business for a minute.

FLORENCE CURTAIN is Phyllis' personal live-in nurse. Because of Phyllis' declining health, Nurse Curtain has been retained for the past six months at Dr. Hart's insistence. She tries to do her job but Priscilla is constantly intervening. She's not used to this treatment and hopes the little men in White Coats will come soon and take Phyllis to where she belongs so she, Florence, can go on to a more rewarding position. All things considered, she would even rather be in Brooklyn . . . in the winter! This Séance might just turn out to be a moving experience.

CALVIN BOOKER is a paranoid Don Knotts of the accounting world. He started with the company early on and is now it's Controller. As a young accountant, this nervous, shy man had been captivated by an exotic dancer during a bachelor party for a friend. He madly pursued her promising her the moon. Believing he was her ticket into polite society, she married him. The years following had been, for Calvin, a desperate struggle to make good on his promise. His life has not taken all the turns and directions he had hoped. He is a nervous, worried, frightened man who doesn't want to believe in the spirit world but is awfully afraid that it exists.

BONNIE BOOKER, a former stripper, had expected big things from Calvin, hoping to climb the social ladder to respectability . . . at least high enough to outdistance her nefarious beginnings. Far from being a "My Fair Lady", she nevertheless considers herself a success and cares nothing about how Calvin manages financially. After all, she can't count up to three with mittens on. She loves being the social butterfly, hobnobbing with the rich and sometimes famous, oblivious to the frowns and sharp remarks. It is obvious she did *not* have Professor Higgins as a teacher as she still dresses garishly and is loud and crass. Tonight's Séance should be a "real hoot!"

WILLARD HEMLOCK belongs to the family who established Hemlock College, which was the only means he had of acquiring a college degree although not necessarily an academic education. As the last male in the Hemlock line, the family was very tolerant of his meager scholastic abilities, but that's not to say he wasn't smart in other ways . . . smart like a fox. His "creative ideas" are not always of a legitimate nature and over the years he has become a successful con-man and manipulator. To most people, he is an obnoxious, creepy weasel; but fearing his tactics, most men tolerated him, take care not to rile him or simply leave him alone. Willard had the acuity to perceive great potential in associating himself with and insinuating himself onto his college buddies, Frank and Carl. So, when he heard that Frank and Carl were forming their own business, he wheedled himself onto the payroll as a marketing rep. The association had not panned out quite the way he had hoped, so after the fire he left the company to woo Phyllis for her obvious attributes . . . money! Her obsession with Frank, however, is a larger obstacle than he anticipated. Think of Uriah Heep and you have Willard.

MADAM ANGELICA had been attracted by the headline newspaper article a year ago on the Stein-Brenner Plant fire and had contrived a meeting with Phyllis some time after. She has been seeing Phyllis for the better part of a year trying to console her and win her confidence . . . with unbelievable success and rewards. Phyllis completely believes in Madam Angelica and the occult. Madam Angelica suggested a Séance to contact Frank in the hope that his spirit's presence would have a desirable influence on Phyllis. Drumming up business in this social circle wouldn't be bad either.

HUGO HANDY is Madam Angelica's bodyguard and chauffeur. He is a disturbing presence in the shadowy background, poised for possible action from, shall we say, unbelievers.

TILLY TOYLER is Carlton's Secretary and an extremely efficient one. She is like a no-nonsense machine at work and at home as well. That could account for why she remains unmarried in her mid forties. She is also the office gossip and is never without her steno pad. She brought a steno pad tonight to take copious notes about the séance . . . or anything else that seems interesting.

WALLACE WINGATE is Purchasing Agent for the Stein-Brenner Company. He misses Frank and the friendship he gave everyone at the plant. Work this past year has been a real drudge, but he is in too deep to quit. He's terrified of Carl and Carl's "friends."

WINTER WINGATE is the daughter of a mobster in Chicago. She's "one of them" and Wallace regrets the day he met her but divorce is not an option. Winter loves parties . . . any party. She's never heard of a séance and never had her palm read. She's disappointed there will be no dancing tonight.

DANNY DINGO serves as Company Transit Director and is Head of the local Teamsters. He has total charge of everything coming in and going out of the plant. He thinks of only two things: work and football. He doesn't know what "social" means but Carl insisted he be at the séance . . . just in case . . . despite his discomfort.

DOTTIE DINGO is Danny's wife and a "real blond" but with a figure worth showing off . . . and she does. She has the license on swinging hips and low cut tops. Bonnie Booker hates her.

MIKAL MAESTRO is the Conductor of the town Symphony. He and his wife met the Steins because Frank and Phyllis served on the Symphony Board of Directors and they became fast friends even though Mikal's head is completely full of music with room for little else. Mikal took Frank's death very hard and, although his head tells him this Séance stuff is a fake, his heart wants to believe in the possibility.

MARTHA MAESTRO is Mikal's wife and mother of his seven children. It was Phyllis who convinced her to get help with the children so she could get out and get a life. So she joined Phyllis and Amanda in many of their social and charitable endeavors. She is terrified of the occult.

FELIX FARNUM is a long-time neighbor and close friend of he Stein family. Their children grew up with the Stein children. They are here tonight to give Phyllis their full support.

FANNY FARNUM is Felix's wife and one of Phyllis' best friends. She loves to laugh and tell jokes. They've been bridge partners at the Marathon Duplicate Bridge Group for ten years and she's been lost without her this past year. She hopes tonight she can talk Phyllis into coming back to the group.

CONRAD DIDDIT is the Stein family butler and devoted servant for nearly 30 years as well as close friend and confidante to Frank.

JOE PHOENIX is the bartender and temporary servant hired by the butler solely for this evening's event.

FRANK'S GHOST is expected to make an appearance.

CAMILLE LEON is a Newspaper Reporter and Photographer for the Lightning Gazette who has been following this story since the fire a year ago. She bribed Priscilla to allow her access to this Séance. She hopes this will be the story of a lifetime . . . and not the end of her career. With the occult one never knows what the future holds.

INSPECTOR CLOQUE JOUSEAU is the Police Homicide Detective called to the scene by the butler to solve the murder.

AND PERHAPS OTHER SOULS . . .

PERSONAL
INSTRUCTIONS

Personal Instructions are for your eyes only except where you might want to review relationships with your spouse or someone else you must specifically relate to. If you have certain instructed tasks to perform within a time frame, please see that they are accomplished . . . usually before the Séance.
Enjoy having fun with your character and the rest of the Cast.

PHYLLIS STEIN—PERSONAL INSTRUCTIONS

> **PHYLLIS STEIN** is gathering together her family and dearest friends to share with her what could very well be the most exciting evening of her life. Because of the overwhelming depression that followed her husband's death last year, Phyllis had willingly been guided toward her salvation by Madam Angelica, a local sere and fortune teller. For these many months, she has sought Madam Angelica's counsel and is convinced tonight's Séance will bring Frank's Spirit to her to show her the direction her life should take. Having lost the security of her husband's protection and support, she desperately needs to hear his reassuring words and guidance.

You come from a low middle class family whose uneducated and unskilled parents both worked hard at any thankless job they were luck enough to get—sometimes two—just to make ends meet. The best the family lived was when both your parents worked at the local factory that made spare parts for mannequins until the factory went out of business. Having three daughters was a financial burden but they were good parents and did the best they could to provide for most of your needs. But the one thing you needed most of all was their attention. You, being the oldest, had the responsibility of caring for your two younger sisters, which gave you little time for a social life. Your school mates thought you were a bit shy but actually you didn't talk much because you didn't have anything you thought was worth saying. Despite your quietness, your classmates liked you because you were comfortable to be around and because you were gorgeous and attracted the boys. You were never more than a C student which gave you a complex. You were born under the sign of Libra which meant you can never seem to make a decision, which explains a lot over a lifetime.

Like your girlfriends, you yearned for a "Prince" to sweep you off your feet and take you away from all this and treat you like a Princess. Don't know about the Prince part (until Frank) but you did manage to get the CASH to live like a Princess.

You can make up names and family experiences, any details about your life if it is reasonably within the guidelines set forth here. Be sure you cross-check any information that would be a shared experience, so there isn't any conflicts of information. If for some reason there is a conflict, just claim you didn't remember it that way, after all, your sisters are younger and raised under a different set of circumstances as well as being different in personalities.

You married Arnold Dumbelli when you were 17 . . . and a little pregnant. Soon after Dominique was born, Arnold died in a boating accident. His death left you and Dominique quite rich, as his family were the Madison Avenue Dumbelli's who made a fortune in Training Pants, among other endeavors, but you were too weak emotionally and immature to know how to deal with wealth, widowhood and motherhood. You left the running of your life and the upbringing of your child to others.

You married again at 20 to Bruce Brassiere . . . another fortune. He turned out to be gay. Of course, the family knew it and that's why they manipulated innocent you to marry Bruce hoping to add respectability to the situation. They didn't count on you needing a real man in your life, so when they sensed a rebellion from you, the family paid you handsomely to keep silent, and the marriage was quietly annulled.

At 22 you met Frank at the Fairwinds Real Estate Office and fell instantly in love. After a very short interval, you married him and assisted him financially to start his business with Carl. He completely dominated your life and you loved it. He took care of you like a Prince should care for his Princess. Ruben was born a year later and he turned out to be a disappointment as both you and Frank tried to push him beyond his limits. He could not cope with the stress and became a problem child. You never understood that you and especially Frank were the cause of Ruben's behavior. Seven years later, Francine was born and has been the sunshine in your life ever since. You were married roughly 28 years before the fire happened.

The fire last year, which took your husband's life, has destroyed your near perfect world . . . and the stress is destroying your health. You lean almost totally on Francine for comfort and understanding. Dr. Hart has been treating you and will be on hand tonight (possibly along with Nurse Curtain) with medication from time to time (candy). When offered the "pills", take them obediently.

After the fire, you allowed your younger sister, Priscilla, and her son, Paul, to move in with you and run the household since you could not. You resent her interference, but you feel you have no choice . . . being nearly totally helpless and in a constant state of nervous exhaustion. You pay her handsomely for her services. It is almost impossible for you to make a decision . . . any decision. You have trouble deciding which side of the bread you should butter. Frank always took care of everything.

Willard Hemlock has been trying desperately to court you for the better part of a year but you are too obsessed with Frank to feel for anyone else . . . but nothing will deter him. He has become nearly a fixture around the mansion. Nevertheless, you depend on him a great deal and are very thankful for his presence. Make a point of having him sit to your right at the Séance for support.

Shortly after the fire, you received a call from Madam Angelica who offered to counsel you regarding the Spirit World which started a long alliance resulting ultimately in this Séance. She has helped bring some comfort and hope back into your life. You are so excited about this Séance and the possibility of speaking to Frank's spirit that you can hardly concentrate on anything else. People have, and possibly will again, warn you of the futility of this Madam and her Séance, but you are completely in the clutches of Madam Angelica and are determined not to listen to anyone. Defend Madam Angelica vigorously.

You will begin the evening in a place of prominence to receive your guests. You greet people and talk with them but most of your conversation is about Frank and Madam Angelica's attempt tonight to reach his spirit. Act excited, nervous, confused, flighty and sometimes teary but remember to be the gracious socialite which you have become. Others will try to discuss other matters but somehow you always seem to get it back to Frank and the Séance.

Expect to induce the following additional interactions:

Dominique: Act irritated and uninterested in whatever she has to say and make excuses to be elsewhere giving her the brush-off. (You never really got close to Dominique for some reason only an analyst could know, despite her efforts to win your love and approval.)

Ruben: He is a disappointment to you and you cannot understand nor tolerate his behavior. He should be loud and abusive to you and you argue and find fault at every confrontation as one would with a rebellious teenager although he is nearly thirty. Show your embarrassment of his behavior, make excuses and apologize to other people.

Francine: She is you pet and obvious favorite. Show her love and a lot of attention and devotion. She is your support . . . you lean on her. Show your dependency on her by asking her to come do things for you . . . get drinks, handkerchiefs, etc.

Priscilla: You are putty in her hands, only occasionally putting up a fuss. She will try to run the whole evening . . . act only a little irritated and put up only minimal resistance but always defend Madam Angelica.

Carlton (you call him Junior): You consider him the closest of friends besides being partners in business . . . like family. But you've always distrusted him for some reason you can't put your finger on. You relate well with him, probably because you and Frank have shared so much with him over the years.

Lance: Lance is a bright young fellow and you like him a lot . . . you wish Ruben could be more like him and frequently say so. He has been like another son since he started with the company nearly ten years ago. Tonight, he will corner you at some point to have you sign your new Will. Choose 2-4 people . . . the Harts . . . Nurse Curtain . . . and Holly Knight, perhaps . . . to be your witnesses. Take them to a private corner for a quick review of the Will and the signing. (Tell no one of the contents of the Will . . . telling the witnesses only that it is a routine update of your Will after Frank's death, at the advice of your lawyer).

Amanda: She is your closest friend and up until the fire you had been quite active with her in various charities. She will try to get you reinvolved tonight so you may have to invent charities to discuss. Tell her you just are not ready but depending on what Frank says tonight in the Séance, you may feel differently tomorrow.

Madam Angelica: Get excited when she arrives and rush to greet her. Fawn over her and introduce her around admiringly with idolatry in your eyes.

Joe the Bartender: Joe will serve you a drink during the evening when there are people near you. Look at him familiarly and ask, "Do I know you . . . have you served me before? Your eyes look so familiar." He says he has served you before and you say you hope he will be available to serve you again.

SEANCE: Madam Angelica and/or Conrad will indicate it is time and call all characters to their seats . . . see attached *Seating Arrangement* for your assigned seat. During the Séance, Frank's ghost will appear. Memorize the attached short dialogue or have a cheat-sheet handy.

The lights (all of them I hope) will go out and everything will be black. A gun will go off. A woman (not you) will scream. You will be stabbed! Not REALLY, but to make it look like it, you will conceal in your purse (which you will have on your lap) an ice pick attached to red material (the Host will provide you with this prop, which is an ice pick with all but two inches of the pick cut off and punched through a 6" x 8" fluted edged red material—to look like blood—into a wine bottle cork). You will spread the material over your chest and hold it there with your hand under the material holding the cork (rehearse this). You are dead! . . . so make yourself as comfortable in the chair as you can, head down or back, and wait out the rest of the proceedings. Try not to laugh. If you would prefer not to sit in the chair playing dead until the crime is solved, talk with the hostess ahead of time and perhaps several of the men can carry you to a sofa or couch so you can be comfortable but still hear what is going on.

During the evening, don't forget to **ACT and REACT**!

DOMINIQUE DUMBELLI JOHANSON O'REILLY SCHWARTZ GONZALES WELLINGTON SUBARU GUNDERMANN CHANG POLANSKI JONES BALDWIN—PERSONAL INSTRUCTIONS

> **DOMINIQUE...BALDWIN** is Phyllis' daughter by her first husband, Arnold Dumbelli, who died suddenly in a yachting accident when Dominique was less than a month old. Phyllis had been very young, immature and insecure during Dominique's early years and had left her upbringing pretty much to nannies and other servants. Dominique has never recovered from the apparent rejection which has resulted in a love/hate relationship. Her search for the love that was denied her in her youth has led her through many marriages... all doomed to failure. Her present union is with Ralph Baldwin who has the gift of controlling Dominique's whining and temper tantrums. Dominique sees this evening as another form of her mother's rejection in favor of her step-father and step-sister, Francine, and she is convinced Madam Angelica is responsible.

Your dead father, Arnold Dumbelli (who died in a boating accident shortly after you were born), provided very well for you in his Will and you are a rich woman in your own right, so you really have no interest in your mother's money or your step-father's money. You have been married many times, searching for the love that your mother seems to deny you and only your mother can give you... so each marriage has failed (you can make up interesting stories about your past husbands, if you are asked). Ralph is the best one of the lot and most tolerant and understanding of your situation. He is also rather dull... and unruffled by your tantrums of frustration. You are a whiner and complainer but Ralph knows just the words or touch to settle you down.

You have grown up with a love-hate relationship with your mother for as a child you were practically raised by nannies and servants. You are constantly trying to get your mother's attention and approval but your efforts always turn into arguments, criticisms and confrontations, which leave you stomping off angrily. To cover your true insecurities, you appear argumentative... with nearly everyone... especially your mother. You are jealous of Francine and have compassion for Ruben who you can identify with. You take out your frustrations on Ralph and also make your complaints known to any guest who will listen. You think you love your mother, but, in fact, you are obsessed with seeking love and approval from your mother.

The tragedy in the relationship between you and your mother is that you believe that your mother is perfect, totally flawless and faultless. So it has to be your fault, you must not be good enough, so your life has been a constant battle to find the one thing that will make your mother accept and love you. But the quest has resulted in failure after failure.

All your life you have never truly experienced *love*, therefore, you have never learned to recognize love in any form. Even the love for your mother is not love at all, but a mixture of jealousy, obsession and irrational focus to share in normal relationships. Even your marriages were acts of desperation to love and be loved. Men obviously are attracted to your physical beauty but also to a hint of schoolgirl's innocence mixed with curiosity. However, usually after just a few short months of marriage, the ugliness within erodes the relationship. Since you do not really understand love, a broken relationship does not affect your heart . . . but it does affect your head. It means another failure . . . another rejection. Ralph, however, seems to understand the root of your problems and is compelled to act as your protector and consoler. You aren't really aware of it, but for the first time in your life, you have found love and are, in fact, *in* love.

Complain to anyone who'll listen that your mother won't pay attention to you . . . that you know what's best for her but she won't listen. Tell everyone how dumb this Séance is and that it will only make matters worse. Be hateful and argumentative with almost everyone . . . except Ruben who you try to get to agree with you . . . and, of course, Ralph, although you do sometimes tend to try to boss him around.

When the Séance is announced, proceed to the Séance table and sit in the seat assigned to you as per the attached *Seating Arrangement*. React as your character would to the Séance. <u>REMAIN SEATED</u> throughout the Séance but by all means REACT . . . screaming is good . . . moaning too.

During interrogations, you must tell the truth. Answer all questions honestly as you feel your character would based on the information given and that which you may have observed during the evening . . . all in character, of course. Feel free to volunteer anything you saw or heard during the evening that you think may be important in solving the crime.

ACT and REACT

RALPH BALDWIN—PERSONAL INSTRUCTIONS

> **RALPH BALDWIN** is Dominique's present husband. A simple man with simple tastes, he is drawn to the bird with the broken wing . . . that is Dominique. He loves her despite her flaws or perhaps because of them. He understands her and is devoted to easing her pain with soft words or a gentle touch. Few know how highly intelligent and well read he is, or that he has an innate sense of the inner struggles of others. Outwardly, he's unremarkable and seems to disappear in plain sight. People are constantly bumping into him. He might be a "cellophane man" but his eye misses nothing. Despite his limited talents and low-keyed personality, his piano moving business is flourishing . . . a real accomplishment for him, especially since he can't even carry a tune. He expects this evening to be an amusing distraction and hopes Dominique won't cause too much trouble.

You are basically easy going and undemonstrative . . . not much ruffles you. You met Dominique and immediately understood her problems with her mother and was attracted to her vulnerability, which makes you very patient and understanding (you try to comfort her using soft words and a gentle touch). You knew she was well off financially when you married her but money isn't really important to you beyond having a roof over your head, food to eat and clothes on your back. Your own piano moving business takes care of that pretty well.

Dominique will argue with you and try to pick fights but you don't rise to the bait (you know it is just frustration talking). You allow her to henpeck you and find it amusing. You pay your respects to your mother-in-law but basically you can mill around amongst the guests and discuss topics you think your character might discuss . . . you are very well read so should not have a problem with a choice of topics . . . the Séance could be an apt topic or your piano moving business. Make light of "society" and too much money. You don't believe in ghosts or mystics and séances. You are here tonight determined to protect Dominique from further hurt . . . and also to enjoy the "show".

When the Séance is announced, sit in the seat assigned as per the attached *Seating Arrangement*. React as your character would during the Séance. <u>REMAIN SEATED</u> throughout the Séance but react as you think your character would. Remember, your first thought is to protect Dominique.

During interrogations, you must tell the truth. Answer all questions honestly as you feel your character would based on the information given and that which you may have observed during the evening . . . all in character, of course. Feel free to volunteer anything you saw or heard during the evening that you think may be important in solving the crime.

ACT and REACT

RUBEN STEIN—PERSONAL INSTRUCTIONS

> **RUBEN STEIN** is the first child of Phyllis and Frank and the obvious choice to take over the business from his father. As a child, Ruben quickly realized he lacked the talent his father had for business. He is only of average intelligence, with an inferiority complex topping out at zero, and is easily dominated and manipulated. He believes he is a disappointment to his family. To cover his inadequacies, he drinks . . . a lot! His overwhelming jealousy of Francine threatens to consume him. His ambitious wife constantly pushes and nags him to excel so he can take over the business, but it only contributes to his smothering pressures. His mother, not understanding his deep identity problems, has no patience with his behavior, especially since his father's death. "Uncle" Carl is the only one that has given him a chance. He thinks this Séance business is stupid . . . but can't quite understand why he fears it.

Inwardly, you have a weak nature, average to low IQ, low self-esteem, feel sorry for yourself, and are a manic-depressive. Outwardly, you are loud, boorish, argumentative, impatient and an alcoholic. You have limited talents in the business world. Your father pushed you into the business, but fear of failure kept you from working hard at it. Your wife is also pushing you which adds to your stress. All this stress through the years has warped your social personality. To compensate for your insecurities, you are loud and boastful and brush off criticism (which you think everyone is giving you) much as a cow brushes away annoying flies . . . but inwardly you crumble. You were coerst into marrying Helene but envy her strength and drive which also adds to your identity problems. (Talk over, with your wife, and make up how you met and discuss how you should relate to one another.)

Since you couldn't cut the mustard under your father's tutelage, Uncle Carl took you under his wing . . . and you sold your soul to him. He gave you something you could do . . . push drugs . . . illegal drugs that he is secretly processing at the plant. Carry a couple of small plastic bags of flour and try to sell this "coke" to some of the "likely" guests. Paul is one of your biggest customers, as he is a secondary pusher . . . make a hit on him tonight so that one or two people see (don't be TOO obvious). You are beginning to get careless (especially when you are drinking) and this troubles Carl . . . deeply. He will chastise you. Act angry and act rebuffed.

When you enter this evening, seek out your mother and try to give her a hug, but you have started the party early and are well on your way to being intoxicated, so you stumble and nearly fall at her feet . . . or actually fall if you like, and need assistance getting up, laughing all the time. Your condition turns her off and you get hurt and angry. Sulk off complaining loudly that nobody cares . . . that calls for a drink (I caution you not to over-do it for REAL, however).

Go through the evening in a high (but surly and angry) manner around the guests (acting intoxicated) but when you are not talking to anyone be very quiet and solemn. Sometimes your anger gets peaked and you explode in a loud temper outburst. The only one that seems sympathetic is your half-sister, Dominique. You know she has her own rejection and identity problems. Commiserate with her. Do a "mother likes you best" routine on Francine. Avoid her and talk to others about "your sis, goody two shoes," or something similar. Make light of the Séance as all a big joke.

Complete all of the above before Séance time, which should make for a very good time. When the Séance is announced, sit in the seat assigned you per the attached *Seating Arrangement*. Your reaction during the Séance is to cry softly like a baby saying quietly "I'm sorry, Daddy," over and over. <u>REMAIN SEATED</u> throughout Séance.

During interrogations, you must tell the truth. Answer all questions honestly as you feel your character would based on the information given and that which you may have observed during the evening . . . all in character, of course. Feel free to volunteer anything you saw or heard during the evening that you think may be important in solving the crime.

ACT and REACT

HELENE STEIN—PERSONAL INSTRUCTIONS

> **HELENE STEIN** is from the wrong side of the tracks and ambitious. In High School, Helene was a force to be reckoned with . . . strong and confident. All the girls idolized her and followed wherever she led them. Smiling does not come naturally to her. She usually got what she wanted, and she wanted Ruben for the potential he represented. She misjudged Ruben's dynamics, so if her hunger for money and status is to be sated, she has to be the power behind the throne. Over the years this has been an enormous challenge but her efforts continue. She will not admit having made a mistake, so she is still trying to reinvent Ruben. Frank had recognized her selfish ambitions and his disdain had been an obstacle for her. With him gone, her attentions have focused on Phyllis who has not been too receptive in her state of mind. Tonight's Séance may present possibilities.

You came from a lower class background and hated it. You vowed to improve your social and financial situation so right out of High School you coerced Ruben to agree to marry you after graduation and convinced his parents that if they allowed you both to marry now, you would see to it that Ruben excelled at college. The task turned out to be unattainable and your ego took a bruising. You fully expected to remake Ruben into the son his father wanted and live happily ever rich after. It hasn't been as easy as you had hoped because Frank saw you for what you are. You refuse to give up, you have merely redirected your efforts toward other family members (Phyllis and Francine) and business interests (Carl). Use tonight to campaign for Ruben with these people.

You are strong-willed, cunning, domineering, and very pushy trying to maintain your husband's place in the family, in business and in society. You apologize and make vague excuses for your husband's behavior trying to pacify the impact on society. You manipulate your husband, although he ignores your efforts in public. You are money hungry and very waspish. You have no sense of humor but are ingratiating when necessary.

Generally, use the evening to promote Ruben; but when he does something that embarrasses you, quietly, with anger and a frown, condemn him under your breath with ice in your words. At other times, try to make points with other family members and Carl Brenner . . . but most especially, Phyllis. Make wild promises that Ruben can improve and perform . . . you will see to it.

When the Séance is announced, sit in the seat assigned to you as per the attached *Seating Arrangement.* Carry a small purse and place it on your lap during the Séance. React as your character might to the Séance. <u>REMAIN SEATED</u> throughout the Séance. Stand when you hear a scream.

During interrogations, you must tell the truth. Answer all questions honestly as you feel your character would based on the information given and that which you may have observed during the evening . . . all in character, of course. Feel free to volunteer anything you saw or heard during the evening that you think may be important in solving the crime.

ACT and REACT

FRANCINE STEIN—PERSONAL INSTRUCTIONS

FRANCINE STEIN is Phyllis and Frank's youngest child. She has looks, charm, wit, brains and fortitude . . . just like her father. Women envy her and men are mesmerized by her. The darling! Self-assured and very together for her young age, she has devoted her life to the family and the family business. She has the talent Ruben lacks and feels a bit embarrassed about that, causing her to be sympathetic towards him which seems to anger him more. Her father's death forced her into the business sooner than expected, but with Lance Knight's help, she has excelled at the challenge. She loves her mother and treats her with understanding and sincerity and her pampering has earned her much favor. She seems so perfect and well adjusted. Despite her obvious perfections, she is still exciting and non-intimidating to men and could have her pick. She's very good at dodging them too. She does not believe in the occult, but is afraid of what the outcome of this séance will do to her mother. Never one to succumb to gloom and doom, she indulges her mother by her presence at this Séance, but is determined to party and have fun.

You are smart, sassy, witty, attractive, stylish and together. You are young . . . just out of college . . . and have never been married. You are very interested in the family business and want to be a career woman. Since your father's death, you have been running his side of the business and handling all financial matters since your brother, Ruben, is nearly useless in these areas and works mostly at Carl's direction. Lance Knight volunteered to assist you in getting on board with the company functions and finances.

You have fun this evening and flirt lightly with the men. Your cousin, Paul, will make passes at you . . . treat them lightly but not seriously . . . with a smile and a joke. Christian also may make a pass but you only have eyes for one person—Lance Knight.

You have been having an affair with Lance Knight, the family lawyer, for at least six months. He's married, but that doesn't bother you . . . you know the Knights have nothing in common (as you have observed their relationship since Lance first came on board at the company and also became the Stein family lawyer) and it is only a matter of time before the marriage is over, at least, Lance has said as much. You both are discrete; however, this evening, keep your conversation light and innocent . . . but show admiration in your eyes and be coy. Be seen together several times talking . . . find a time to discretely disappear together for a short time. Avoid his wife.

During the evening you fuss over and pamper your mother and act very loving and concerned with her welfare. Common sense tells you this Séance is a joke but your mother won't listen. The doctor will give her medication from time to time . . . question him about it. You know your brother and sister are jealous of you and may attempt to draw you into arguments. You have no patience for that but don't know how to appease them.

Now that you have filled your father's shoes at the plant, you have gotten a closer look at "Uncle" Carl and you feel he has a dark side. You are suspicious and distrustful of his business practices. Your father handled the Research but Carl handled the manufacturing and marketing. You might question him about something suspicious you saw at the plant . . . like odd shipping orders or employees you don't recognize or even accounts that don't jibe). Also, you have noticed some discrepancies in the ledgers and question Calvin about them. Carl should ask you if you know what Frank was working on at the plant before his death. You tell him you have no idea . . . ask what it is all about and why does he want to know.

Holly Knight will ask your advice on how she can get Lance interested in her again . . . that she knows she must be at fault but what can she do to make a better marriage . . . make excuses like you must see to your mother or you must talk to so-and-so. Or, if you like, give advice a go . . . you know it won't matter. Or you can simply admit that, having never been married, you are not the expert to ask . . . and more away.

Complete all of the above before the Séance. When the Séance is announced, please take your seat at the Séance table per the attached *Seating Arrangement*. Carry a small purse and place it on your lap during the Séance. React as your character might to the Séance but <u>REMAIN SEATED</u> during the Séance until something major happens that your character should REACT to.

During interrogations, you must tell the truth. Answer all questions honestly as you feel your character would based on the information given and that which you may have observed during the evening . . . all in character, of course. The exception is that you will not outwardly admit to having an affair with Lance but say "Lance has been a family friend for years and for the past year we have naturally worked closely together on business matters so, of course, we are very close" (or something of that sort). Stutter and act nervous to give suspicion that you are lying. All in character, of course.

ACT and REACT

PRISCILLA PENNILESS—PERSONAL INSTRUCTIONS

PRISCILLA PENNILESS, Phyllis' younger sister, is all the things Phyllis is not . . . strong-willed, domineering, organized, quick-minded, stern and POOR. Though not as fortunate in her life as Phyllis, she loves her sister but is often frustrated and annoyed with her behavior. She wasted no time moving herself and her son, Paul, into the mansion with Phyllis after the fire and completely took over the running of the household, bossing the servants and the children. Paul, however, is the apple of her eye . . . he can do no wrong . . . her life is devoted to him, and her personality completely changes to doting mother when he's with her. Otherwise, to others, it's her way or the highway. Her biggest concern is Phyllis' fanatical preoccupation with this Madam Angelica person and she's not too pleased with the attention that creep, Willard Hemlock, is giving her sister. She plans to keep a close eye on the proceedings tonight.

You come from a low middle class family whose uneducated and unskilled parents both worked hard at any thankless job they were luck enough to get—sometimes two—just to make ends meet. The best the family lived was when both your parents worked at the local factory that made spare parts for mannequins until the factory went out of business. Having three daughters was a financial burden but they were good parents and did the best they could to provide for most of your needs . . . except their time. Phyllis practically raised you and your sister, Prudence. You learned early in life to depend on only one person . . . yourself.

When Phyllis got married and left the household for greener pastures, you fought resentment and felt alone. You and Prudence have nothing in common—she was a book person and you are not. At the first opportunity, age sixteen,—a proposal from a young sailor you hardly knew—you left home too, only to find out you married beneath you. He turned out to be a shiftless, abusive alcoholic. Again the burden of keeping up the household fell on you. It only made you tougher. Then Paul came along and gave you a reason for your life. One night, in a drunken rage, your husband beat you one last time, shouted words only sailors knew, and went after the infant. You became a tiger protecting her cub and lashed back, nearly killing him. That night, he took all the money and anything of any value and left never to come back. You shed no tears. That's when your life began.

You are strong-willed, hard working, cynical, suspicious, hard-headed, bossy and overbearing. You are the opposite side of the coin from your older sister, Phyllis. You love her because she is family, but you can't help envying her good fortune in life . . . financial good fortune as well as emotional good fortune in having so many wonderful years of marriage to Frank. You also have a younger sister (the baby) Prudence, who was an old maid school teacher until recently. You haven't had much contact with her over the years.

Your son, Paul, is just like his father . . . a shiftless bum . . . but you are blind to Paul's faults for he is the light of your life . . . only HE can bring out the soft spot in you. You dote on him and deny him nothing.

When Frank died, you saw a chance to capitalize on the situation and get some financial security for once in your life. You and Paul moved into the mansion and took over running the entire household for your ailing, despondent, widowed sister. You have made yourself indispensable to her. You are certain that deep down inside she appreciates your help for she has agreed to a considerable monthly allowance for your services. To be fair, you expect no handouts . . . you do your very best to earn your keep. That means you are a terror of a taskmaster. You run the servants with an iron fist, ordering them around, finding fault . . . sort of like Leona Helmsley, the Queen of Mean. You criticize the children too and even recommend to Phyllis what she should and shouldn't do. Your nose is in everybody's business whether it concerns you and the family or not . . . you think it is expected of you as part of your "job". You don't smile much . . . unless you are talking to Paul. And he has you completely wrapped around his finger . . . and knows it. Your task tonight is to become just such a character.

You hate Madam Angelica's interference and are suspicious of her methods. You see her as a threat to your position of influence with Phyllis. Confront Madam Angelica, calling her a witch and say she's a fake.

To Paul you are sweet . . . pampering him . . . straighten his clothes or pat down his hair with a loving smile. He will ask you for money, giving you some excuse (any excuse is sufficient for you). Have $200 of play money stuck in your pocket or bra or somewhere ready to give him. Do this where it can be observed. Act the proud mother.

Complete all of the above before the Séance. When the Séance is announced, go to the Séance table area and when Madam Angelica begins telling people where to sit, you pipe in with "You're not telling me where to sit. I'm sitting right here beside you (on her left) so I can keep a sharp eye on you and this hoax." You don't believe in ghosts but you are overwhelmed by what happens . . . leaving you wide eyed with your mouth open, astonished, and breathing in gasps making "oh, oh, oh" noises. <u>REMAIN SEATED</u> throughout the séance.

During interrogations, you must tell the truth, Answer all questions honestly as you feel your character would based on the information given and that which you may have observed during the evening . . . all in character, of course. Feel free to volunteer anything you saw or heard during the evening that you think may be important in solving the crime.

ACT and REACT

PAUL PENNILESS—PERSONAL INSTRUCTIONS

> **PAUL PENNILESS** is Priscilla's only child . . . her pride and joy. Paul is useless. One might go so far as to say he is a bum, a freeloader and an opportunist for all occasions. He inherited these genes from his shiftless father who abandoned the family when Paul was still in diapers. Paul is wholly arrogant from being spoiled and enjoys using people, especially his mother, who pets him and gives him everything she can . . . and then some. He believes he should not have to spend much effort to make a buck but a con game is more his style. He is having a high time living off his Aunt Phyllis and isn't beyond considering a little incest with his cousin, Francine . . . after all, the royals did it. And tonight he feels royal.

You are Priscilla's pampered son and a ne're-do-well. You are the light of your mother's life and you know it. Like your father (who abandoned you when you were a baby), you are shiftless and lazy as well as an opportunist and rebellious delinquent (even though you're in your thirties). You and your mother are poor relations so you have enjoyed living with your rich aunt this past year and love the feel of richness. This life is for you. You are charming and smooth, with a bit of arrogance and audacity. You feel like the singer Tom Jones and expect all the ladies secretly want to toss their panties at you, but you're only interested in Francine's panties. Enjoy the party and go around flattering all the ladies, young and older, but hit on Francine. Go up to your mother when she's talking with some guests and tell her you need some money . . . make up some reason. She's used to this, you do it all the time. Actually, you're hooked on cocaine, as well as pushing it on the streets. Cousin Ruben is your supplier. Try to be secretive tonight, but make sure a couple of people see Ruben sell you the stuff. Accomplish this before the Séance . . . after you get money from mom.

Make jokes about the Séance during the evening.

During the Séance, sit in the seat marked on the attached *Seating Arrangement*. React to the Séance as your character might based on the information given here but <u>REMAIN SEATED</u> throughout the Séance.

During interrogations, you must tell the truth. Answer all questions honestly as you feel your character would based on the information given and that which you may have observed during the evening . . . all in character, of course. Feel free to volunteer anything you saw or heard during the evening that you think may be important in solving the crime.

ACT and REACT

PRUDENCE PIREET—PERSONAL INSTRUCTIONS

> **PRUDENCE PIREET** is the youngest sister of Phyllis and Priscilla. Shy little Prudence has been a prim and proper history teacher…well…forever. Always with her nose in a book she had little time or desire for personal relationships. Harassed by her colleagues to "get a life," she finally agreed to a vacation cruise . . . choice that would dramatically change her life. There she met Prentice. She has only been married a few months and is bursting with pride over her splendid good fortune. She has always felt rather distant to her rich relative, Phyllis, but under present circumstances, she is anxious to become reacquainted with her older sister. In short, Prudence has finally blossomed.

You come from a low middle class family whose uneducated and unskilled parents both worked hard at any thankless job they were luck enough to get—sometimes two—just to make ends meet. The best the family lived was when both your parents worked at the local factory that made spare parts for mannequins until the factory went out of business. Having three daughters was a financial burden but they were good parents and did the best they could to provide for most of your needs. Unfortunately, they weren't around much so Phyllis was burdened with raising you and Priscilla. You thought Phyllis did a good job but she always seemed a bit light-headed to you. Priscilla was the loud one but she spent lots of time with friends instead of at home. You were a book worm and loved school and learning. You always had some school project or assignment you were happily working on. Never gave anyone any trouble.

At seventeen, Phyllis was the first to leave the nest and went on to a better life. Not long after, Priscilla left home too to marry, but not so fortunately. You had no interest in much else except learning and teaching. Dutifully, you took care of your ailing parents until their death and remained in the same house until your colleagues coerced you to take a cruise. There you met Prentice and felt such a comfort being with him that was unlike anything you had felt before. You married on board ship knowing very little about his life except that his interest was in politics. He was certainly worth waiting for and you haven't been happier. Now you feel you have gained an equality with your sister Phyllis and you are anxious to become reacquainted with her and show off Prentice.

Despite your low beginnings, you have always had a graceful comportment and composure and a sweet personality. Perhaps the confidence an education brings forth also is responsible for elegance of stature associated with being a "lady." You dress plain and simple with little make-up or adornments, but your beauty glows, fueled by love.

You almost can't control your excitement at being here tonight and go around introducing Prentice to everyone.

During the Séance, sit in the seat marked on the attached *Seating Arrangement*. React to the Séance as your character might based on the information given here but <u>REMAIN SEATED</u> throughout the Séance.

During interrogations, you must tell the truth. Answer all questions honestly as you feel your character would based on the information given and that which you may have observed during the evening . . . all in character, of course. Feel free to volunteer anything you saw or heard during the evening that you think may be important in solving the crime.

ACT and REACT

PRENTICE PIREET—PERSONAL INSTRUCTIONS

> **PRENTICE PIREET** met Prudence on a cruise to the Bahamas and was captivated by her femininity and knowledge of world events. Within days they were married by the Ship's Captain and spent the remaining time on the cruise honeymooning. Although his family has "old" money, he has become a success on his own merits as a businessman and politician. In fact, he has just been approached to run for the Senate which is only one step closer to his goal…President! Prentice is considered the "catch of the season" in the media but he considers himself the lucky one to find a partner so interesting and well read as to be the perfect marriage partner for his political aspirations. He's not handsome so much as distinguished, refined and well educated. His comportment is commanding; he knows how to "work a room." Still, he is out of his element at this séance and worries what the association with these gypsies might do to his future plans. Those Democrats can dig up anything.

You come from a family of "old" money. Have fun making up stories about them. You are highly educated and an entrepreneur who has made a fortune of your own. Your real interest, as well as your family's, is politics. You are running for Senator (you pick the particulars) and hope to progress some day to a Presidential nomination.

When you met Prudence, you knew almost immediately she was the right woman to be by your side in the political world. Her confident personality, elegant stature, education and intellect overwhelmed you and you knew you wanted her for your wife. She accepted you for the same reasons.

Prudence will want to introduce you around. You are encouraged to work out together your story of how you met and also about your past. When you realize there will be a séance tonight, you are visibly uncomfortable because you are worried how the media will handle your presence here.

During the Séance, sit in the seat marked on the attached *Seating Arrangement*. React to the Séance as your character might based on the information given here but <u>REMAIN SEATED</u> throughout the Séance.

During interrogations, you must tell the truth. Answer all questions honestly as you feel your character would based on the information given and that which you may have observed during the evening . . . all in character, of course. Feel free to volunteer anything you saw or heard during the evening that you think may be important in solving the crime.

ACT and REACT

CARLTON BRENNER, JR.—PERSONAL INSTRUCTIONS

> **CARLTON BRENNER** grew up with Frank and both chose Hemlock College for it's chemistry program. Being the youngest of seven brothers, Carl saw no future in entering the family's highly successful perfume manufacturing business. His aim was for a quick trip to the top of the heap. Obsessed with money and power, Carl would do most anything to get more of both . . . and has. During a chance reunion with Frank shortly after Frank's divorce, it occurred to him that Frank's excellent scholastic record could be the catalyst he needed to achieve his dreams, so he suggested a partnership. Frank jumped at the chance to work with his best buddy. With no financial support from Carl's family, having been disinherited for his rebellion from the family, and Frank's divorce cleaning his pockets, Phyllis had been the answer to their prayers. Their business prospered and they both became billionaires. That was enough for Frank but Carl compulsively hungers for more. His friends at *Lobo's* have been very helpful. He acts the suave gentleman with flash and flair but beneath this surface he is tough, cold and cruel, akin to Dorian Grey. His first wife could probably tell you the extent of that . . . if she were still alive. Always suspicious, he is uneasy about this Séance.

Your family is very prominent in the California social scene but you chose, much to their chagrin, to make it on your own . . . with the help of Frank, and more specifically, Phyllis's money. On the outside, you are the picture of genteel aristocracy and a gentleman of social grace . . . but inwardly, you are hard, cruel, devious, selfish and a wife beater.

Since you can remember, you have been hungry for money and power (not necessarily in that order). It has grown over the years like a malignancy. You have secrets. For years you have had underworld connections through your association with Louis Botalinni, owner of "Lobo's"; and, under cover of the Chemical Company, have been trafficking in illegal drugs for years . . . unbeknownst to Frank. Last year, Frank stumbled upon your secret and the two of you had a brutal confrontation in the Research Lab. You knocked Frank out and, thinking quickly, poured highly flammable chemicals over the entire room and set it ablaze . . . murder and arson being the only plausible solution to protecting your drug empire. the heat was so intense and the explosions so violent, nothing was left of that wing of the plant.

The insurance company's inspectors agreed it was an accident and covered all the damage. You were quickly back in business . . . no one the wiser.

You were surprised but glad that weasel, Willard, quit the Company after the fire. You saw him running from the fire and at first was afraid he had seen or overheard you and Frank . . . but since a year has gone by and no blackmail threats (as that would certainly be his operation), you are fairly certain he didn't have anything on you. You recognize his little game with Phyllis (trying to marry her for her money). Engage in conversation with Willard and ask him how it is going with Phyllis . . . that you know his game and admire his resourcefulness but doubt seriously he will be successful as you know Phyllis well.

Calvin Booker is in to you up to his neck. Back when you were just getting into drugs, you discovered Calvin was embezzling money from the Company. You confronted him and threatened exposure unless he helped you launder the profits from the drug trade for a small cut of the action to boot. He was terrified but had no choice but to agree. Obsessed with fears of detection and prosecution, he's been a pain in the ass, albeit a necessary instrument, since then. He needs constant badgering and harassing . . . you can't stand his whining and need to rebuke him several times this evening, threatening to "fit him with cement galoshes" . . . say this low key but nonetheless audible to a couple people.

Ruben is becoming a problem too. Frank tried to bring Ruben into the business after his graduation from college and was totally frustrated with Ruben's lack of performance. Perceptively, you understood the boy's identity problem and offered to apprentice Ruben somewhere in your half of the Company's responsibility. At that time you were heavy into drug processing and trafficking. Pushing drugs suited Ruben's abilities perfectly, and Ruben jumped at the opportunity. Frank never knew what Ruben was doing, only that he seemed content working with Carl and stayed out of Frank's hair. The problem is Ruben is getting careless . . . selling too openly and too "close to home." Find a time to chastise him roughly and threateningly, being sure some guests overhear.

Francine could be a problem too. She's a sharp cookie and could very easily uncover your "secrets" as her father had. You might discuss business with her, in a prying way. Reflect on the past year that she has taken over Frank's responsibilities. Ask her if she knows what Frank was working on at the time of his death. You are pretty certain he had some very exciting breakthroughs but because the Research Lab and adjacent offices burned, you have no idea what it was. The Company should have the benefit of those discoveries if she has any information in that area. Lance has been with her a great deal of the time helping her assimilate the complexities of the business. Tease her about seeing a lot of Lance, with a wink. Again, let someone hear your conversation.

Years of honing your own claws has made you wise to the ulterior motives of others. You are fairly certain Madam Angelica is not legit. At least something about her is familiar but you just can't put your finger on it. Ask her if you two have ever met. Also, ask her pointed questions about her techniques in this mystic business, giving her a little bit of a hard time . . . amusingly.

As for Lily, you are getting tired of her, as you did your first wife, Elizabeth Victoria Worthington. Sometimes she annoys you (being too weak) and you verbally abuse her (forgetting for an instant where you are, you come close to hitting her . . . as you would at home). It amazes you that she still hangs around, although you notice she is obviously afraid of you, which pleases you. Maybe that's why YOU still keep HER around. Obviously, too, she is afraid of this Séance and you think that's silly . . . but you think everything about Lily is silly. Nevertheless, she is good company for Cassandra, who you have abused all her life, and now everything about her irritates you.

Your first wife, Elizabeth, gave you three children. Shortly after your marriage, she presented you with twins, Christian and Cassandra. You were too busy making your fortune to bother much with them. Christian is a socialite and race car driver (he costs you money) . . . Cassandra is a shy introvert and completely useless to you (she's afraid of you). Some years later, Elizabeth gave you another daughter, Charity . . . a real cutie. Then Elizabeth died and you didn't want to be burdened with the raising the infant. Elizabeth's parents in California gladly offered to raise her.

This is a big part with lots of things to do. Please complete everything before the Séance. Have a good time strutting around acting like the king pin.

When the Séance is announced, you and Lily go to the table and sit in the seats marked in the attached *Seating Arrangement*. Frank's ghost will appear. Act incredulous, saying something like "No! No! It can't be!" Be agitated and just slightly disruptive, but don't leave your seat. When all the lights go black, stand up (**don't move away from your spot**, however) lean on the table and say "Hey, what's happening here? What's going on?" Have a ketchup packet in your pocket, open it and smear some on your forehead.

During interrogations, answer all questions honestly as you feel your character would based on the information given and that which you may have observed during the evening . . . all in character, of course. Feel free to volunteer anything you saw or heard during the evening that you think may be important in solving the crime.

During the interrogations, you must tell the truth. All your past sins MUST come out.

You might be asked if you have filled Frank's position in the company. Tell the Inspector you are waiting for the lab to be finished and up and running. Also, stress that Francine has come on board and that she and Lance have worked long hours getting her up to speed on the workings of the company and she has been invaluable.

You might be asked if you have replaced Willard's position and say that Ruben has taken over many of his duties and is doing a wonderful job.

Later, your drug dealings will be uncovered and your part in the fire. Admit everything.

Reluctantly admit all the information above as your character would. It is important to ACT and REACT as your character might . . . for there are some surprises in store.

ACT and REACT

LILY BRENNER—PERSONAL INSTRUCTIONS

LILY BRENNER had been Carl's secretary some years ago and married Carl shortly after his wife died . . . hmmm. A timid, feminine woman, she was instinctively drawn to the dominating power Carl exuded. Now she is afraid of it and of him. No, not just afraid . . . terrified. She found that Cassandra was likewise traumatized, so they naturally clung to each other out of desperation and the hope that it might double their strength or at least provide comfort. Social functions make her nervous and uncomfortable. She believes in ghosts!

You were originally attracted to Carl because of his strength and power (which you lack) but mostly because he was exciting and wined and dined you, opening worlds you only dreamed about. Marrying him changed a good deal of that . . . for now you are quite acquainted with his dark side. He sometimes abuses you. Although you are afraid of him, you can't imagine a life without him because when he is in a good mood, he's wonderful. Carl has been married before . . . to Elizabeth Victoria Worthington. They had three children . . . twins Christian (a socialite and race car driver) and Cassandra (a shy introvert) . . . and a daughter, Charity. raised by her maternal grandparents and spoiled rotten. Your information is rather sketchy about Elizabeth's death.

You are basically a timid person and soft spoken. You go out of your way to try to please people. Marrying Carl was a big change socially for you and you are still trying to assimilate. You totally identify with weak, shy and abused Cassandra, and you both often cling to each other for comfort and in imagined protection. Try to ingratiate yourself to Phyllis and Amanda Hart (tell her you are interested in some of her charities and offer to get involved).

You act the dutiful but subservient wife when in Carl's presence, trying not to make him angry. You never get too far away from him during the evening . . . although he abuses you, he is your strength.

You are a believer . . . in ghosts that is. And you are terribly anxious about this evening . . . a good conversation topic with the guests.

When the Séance is announced, cower behind Carl as you go to the table. Sit behind Carl next to Cassandra as in the attached *Seating Arrangement*.

During the Séance, show your fear and nervousness with low yelps or gasps (not too loud). Wiggle in your seat cling to Cassandra. Stay in you seat until you hear a gunshot. Scream as loudly as you can and faint to the floor (carefully). Hopefully, someone will come to your rescue and you revive (if no one comes . . . slowly come out of it anyway . . . wouldn't want you to miss anything).

During interrogations, you must tell the truth. Answer all questions honestly as you feel your character would based on the information given and that which you may have observed during the evening . . . all in character, of course. Feel free to volunteer anything you saw or heard during the evening that you think may be important in solving the crime.

ACT and REACT

CHRISTIAN BRENNER—PERSONAL INSTRUCTIONS

> **CHRISTIAN BRENNER** is Carl's first child and heir…not necessarily apparent. Christian, typical of the second generation rich, does not share his father's interest in business but prefers to spend his time and his father's money on the race car circuit. Surprisingly, he is good at it, which is the only reason Carl continues to support him. He has his "groupies" on the circuit so his ego is well stoked. He relishes the adoration which has made him audacious. His life is one big party. He likes "Auntie" Phyllis and family, especially Francine. This Séance business is a new one on him, but what the hell…he's a good sport.

You've grown up with all the money you ever needed and a father that lets you do anything you please. You are arrogant, audacious and self-assured but sociable, interesting and likeable.

You went to college for the social life (barely making C's), but working for a living does not interest you and your father has not demanded it of you . . . he has his own life and doesn't bother much with you except provide for your every need. You suppose he does this because you DO have a talent for racing.

Your passion is car racing . . . and you are good at it. (Make up your own stories about this). Sports is almost the only thing that interests you . . . that and women. You like Dominique and Francine (you might "try a few lines on her" to see if anything develops) and sympathize with Ruben. They are, after all, "family".

You are extremely close with your twin sister, Cassandra, who is very shy and reclusive. You are very protective of her. You are the children of Carl and his first wife, Elizabeth Victoria Worthington. Unlike your sister, Cassandra, you aren't a fan of Lily . . . it isn't that you hate her or anything . . . it's just that she isn't your mother. You like your little sister, Charity, but think she is immature and silly.

Tonight, socialize in character and ask questions about what's going on. Talk racing and sports. Ruben may try to sell you some "coke," but your father has trained you well . . . you just say "NO."

Complete the above before the Séance is announced. When the Séance is announced, sit in the assigned seat as per the attached *Seating Arrangement*. <u>REMAIN SEATED</u> throughout the Séance and react as your character might to what happens.

During interrogations, you must tell the truth. Answer all questions honestly as you feel your character would based on the information given and that which you may have observed during the evening . . . all in character, of course. Feel free to volunteer anything you saw or heard during the evening that you think may be important in solving the crime.

ACT and REACT

CASSANDRA BRENNER—PERSONAL INSTRUCTIONS

> **CASSANDRA BRENNER** is Christian's twin sister and thus feels an unusual kinship with him. But even with this special bond, she has not shared all her secrets with him. Secrets that have shaken her sanity. If only she had been allowed to go with her younger sister, Charity, to be raised by her maternal grandparents after her mother died. She is completely antisocial and afraid of her own shadow. Her life has improved since Lily married her father. She now has someone to cling to and share her burdens with. She's especially interested in this Séance. She could very well be Madam Angelica's next client. M o t h e r . . . . !

You are the twin sister of Christian and the child of Carlton Brenner and his first wife Elizabeth Victoria Worthington of California. You are shy and unsure of yourself and very afraid of your father as he abuses you. When he married Lily, you found out she was as afraid of him as you and a bond grew between you. Often you literally cling to each other for comfort. You trust and share your feelings with Lily and only one other person . . . Christian. You like your little sister, Charity, but have nothing in common with her.

Tonight, you are only attending this Séance because your father demanded it (and you are deathly afraid of your father). You act shy but polite. Stay near Lily like her shadow, often with arms around each other. Go around wide eyed and fearful.

You are very curious about this Séance and get enough nerve to approach Madam Angelica to ask if it is possible to contact your dead mother, Elizabeth. Play this up.

When the Séance is announced, take the seat assigned to you as per the attached *Seating Arrangement*. Show curiosity and wide-eyed anticipation. <u>REMAIN SEATED</u> throughout the Séance and react as you character might to what happens afterward. You can scream if you want.

During interrogations, you must tell the truth. Answer all questions honestly as you feel your character would based on the information given and that which you may have observed during the evening . . . all in character, of course. Feel free to volunteer anything you saw or heard during the evening that you think may be important in solving the crime.

ACT and REACT

CHARITY BRENNER SVENSON—PERSONAL INSTRUCTIONS

> **CHARITY BRENNER SVENSON** is Carl's youngest daughter by his first wife. She is a typical "Valley Girl". While living with her maternal grandparents in California, she attended an exclusive finishing school and private college. While in college she met and married her theology Professor, Sven Svenson. Currently, they are returning from their honeymoon in Sweden where she met his family, and plan to spend some time with Carl and Lily before returning to California. She is proud as punch over her "catch" and tonight she gets to totally show him off.

You are a spoiled, ultra snobby, rich kid . . . a typical "Valley Girl" who grew up believing she was better than anyone else and attended an exclusive California boarding school near your maternal grandparents.

Your mother was Carl's first wife . . . Elizabeth Victoria Worthington, daughter of Walter Oliver Worthington, owner of W.O.W. Import/Export, Ltd. Your mother died when you were an infant and your father allowed your maternal grandparents to raise you. Your grandmother was very attentive to you, taking special care to teach you all the social graces . . . how to be better than anyone else. Despite being raised away from your family, you are the apple of your father's eye, although he has precious little time to give you and has rarely seen you over the years. Even so, you can easily wrap him around your little finger. You think the world completely revolves around you. You have a brother and sister (twins Christian (a socialite and race car driver) and Cassandra (a shy introvert) but they are older and have very little in common with you . . . you almost think of them as not REALLY family. Your father is the only really IMPORTANT person.

That is until you met Sven. He was your Theology Professor at Ambrosia College. From the moment you laid eyes on him, you knew you had met God! You had to have him as yours exclusively and set about weaving your web to entrap him. With your beauty, charm and sex appeal, the task was easy . . . Sven had no chance. You had a huge wedding (took up the entire social page of the local newspaper) and took off for a honeymoon in Sweden to meet Sven's family. (Prepare some stories along these lines to tell people . . . of course, they must jibe with Sven so rehearse ahead of time.)

You are here, tonight, to introduce Sven to your father (who missed the wedding) and show off your "catch" to everyone. Introduce him around to the guests and talk about your school life, California, Sven, the wedding, the honeymoon, and basically YOU. Have fun with this.

When the Séance is announced, you and Sven go to the seats indicated in the attached *Seating Arrangement*. Sven will refuse to sit near the circle of the devil and demands to sit in the back row. <u>REMAIN SEATED</u> throughout the Séance and react as your character might to what happens afterward.

During interrogations, you must tell the truth. Answer all questions honestly as you feel your character would based on the information given and that which you may have observed during the evening . . . all in character, of course. Feel free to volunteer anything you saw or heard during the evening that you think may be important in solving the crime.

ACT and REACT

PROFESSOR SVEN SVENSON—PERSONAL INSTRUCTIONS

> **PROFESSOR SVEN SVENSON** is the son of one of Sweden's richest merchants. Not having to worry about earning money, he decided he would concentrate on gaining power . . . power molding inquisitive minds. So he became a college professor in the field he thought wielded the most influence . . . religion. However, he thinks he has more "power" than he actually has. He has far too much pride and more than an equal amount of prejudice. His weakness is Charity. He is totally smitten. He loves Charity but he's not sure he can endure this Séance which is contrary to all he believes . . . or thinks he believes.

Influenced by wealth, education, and association with religion, you truly believe you are a disciple of God if not God incarnate. You are proud, puritanistic and opinionated. Your only weakness is of the flesh . . . Charity.

Your family are prominent in shipping with headquarters in Stockholm. The family lives on a compound on Lake Limmaren, not far from Norrtalje. Check it out for some background fodder.

You met Charity while teaching Theology at Ambrosia College, an exclusive women's college in California. She was your student and a girl who was used to getting what she wanted . . . she wanted you. You have recently married and spent your honeymoon introducing Charity to your homeland and family in Sweden. You are now here to meet Charity's father and family friends. Charity's mother died many years ago and she has spend most of her life attending schools in California and being raised by her maternal grandparents.

Charity will introduce you around this evening. Be cordial but haughty and proud. You field is religion so are most comfortable talking about that subject (that may take some preparation). You are especially agitated about this evening's event, the Séance . . . you see it as devil worship . . . so voice your displeasure among the guests. It may be a good touch to carry a Bible and weal a large cross . . . hold it up to Madam Angelica like one would to a vampire, if indeed there are vampires . . .

saying something like "Get thee gone, ye witch." How's your Swedish accent? Dress all in black, like a preacher might.

You have an advocate in Dr. Hart regarding religion and this Séance. Have a discussion with him regarding same.

When the Séance is announced, proceed to the area with Charity but refuse to sit near the "circle of the devil." Take the seat indicated in the attached *Seating Arrangement*. <u>REMAIN SEATED</u> throughout the Séance and react as your character might to what happens.

During interrogations, you must tell the truth. Answer all questions honestly as you feel your character would based on the information given and that which you may have observed during the evening . . . all in character, of course. Feel free to volunteer anything you saw or heard during the evening that you think may be important in solving the crime.

ACT and REACT

FLORENCE CURTAIN—PHYLLIS' NURSE

> **FLORENCE CURTAIN** is Phyllis' personal live-in nurse. Because of Phyllis' declining health, Nurse Curtain has been retained for the past six months at Dr. Hart's insistence. She tries to do her job but Priscilla is constantly intervening. She's not used to this treatment and hopes the little men in White Coats will come soon and take Phyllis to where she belongs so she, Florence, can go on to a more rewarding position. All things considered, she would even rather be in Brooklyn . . . in the winter! This Séance might just turn out to be a moving experience.

Six months ago, on the advice of Dr. Hart, you were hired as a private nurse for Phyllis Stein at a handsome salary. If it weren't for the salary, you would be gone!

Your purpose is to monitor Phyllis for her vitals and signs of significantly deep depression. You then report to Dr. Hart any irregularities you think he should be aware of. Phyllis is not happy having you constantly fussing over her and, frankly, you think it unnecessary too.

The problem is Priscilla. She is like a bull dog protecting its master. Time and time again, when you are trying to do your job, Priscilla interferes. You have complained but no one seems to be able to control Priscilla. So you're stuck.

You are actually looking forward to this Séance and think it will be interesting to see how Madam Angelica pulls this off. You think they all should be put in the looney bin . . . except maybe Francine. She seems to have her head on straight . . . but spends far too much time with Lance. She should get out and meet some nice single boys and have some fun.

When the Séance is announced, you go to the seats indicated in the attached *Seating Arrangement.* <u>REMAIN SEATED</u> throughout the Séance and react as your character might to what happens. Your services will be needed after the Séance.

During interrogations, you must tell the truth. Answer all questions honestly as you feel your character would based on the information given and that which you may have observed during the evening . . . all in character, of course. Feel free to volunteer anything you saw or heard during the evening that you think may be important in solving the crime.

ACT and REACT

DR. ARTHUR HART—PERSONAL INSTRUCTIONS

> **ARTHUR HART** has been the friend and family doctor of both the Stein and Brenner families since Frank and Phyllis needed a blood test in order to marry. He not only delivered both Ruben and Francine but he and his wife, Amanda, stood as Godparents for both children. He took Frank's death especially hard, mostly because of the nature of the incident. Because the Plant was full of highly flammable chemicals, the fire was so intense that everything was reduced to ashes. Not even a bone fragment could be recovered for burial. This was so devastating to Phyllis that Arthur is seriously concerned about her health . . . mental as well as physical. A year had done nothing to relieve her depression. Her obsession with this Madam Angelica person worries him. He does not believe in spirits (unless they are the "liquid" kind) and fears what failure of this evening might do to Phyllis.

You are a typical old time, old fashion family doctor. You really care about your patients and still managed to get rich (of course, it didn't hurt being the third generation doctor who's grandfather bought Exxon at $5). You are a "father image" type . . . puffing on a pipe will help the image. Provide something that looks like a doctor's bag and vials to keep your "pills" (candy) in? A stethoscope would be a plus, as well as a blood pressure monitor and anything else you can think of to help play the part of a doctor.

You are deeply concerned about Phyllis's health, having seen it deteriorate over the past year despite your efforts to help. This is the first time since before Frank's death you have see Phyllis even a little excited and enthused about anything. Always the realist, you have no faith or belief in Séances or the occult (being deeply religious) and have tried in vain to convince Phyllis of the folly in this endeavor. Naturally, she ignored you and continues to ignore your advice this evening.

Not deterred, you stay close to her so that you will be on hand should she get a bit over-excited or unusually morose wherein you step forward and administer medication (in the form of tic tac candy or other such pill-looking candy) which you insist she take. Do this several times during the evening.

Talk to people about your fears concerning the trauma you expect the failure of this Séance to have on Phyllis. Enlist the support of Priscilla and Francine. Corner Madam Angelica and tell her how risky her interloping may be. Also, you have an advocate in Professor Svenson regarding religion and this Séance. Have a discussion with him regarding same. All this in front of witnesses, of course, and in character.

Complete all of the above before the Séance. When the Séance is announced, insist Phyllis take one more pill to calm her and then sit with Amanda in the designated seats per the attached *Seating Arrangement*. <u>REMAIN SEATED</u> and agitated throughout the Séance and react as your doctor character would to the events that follow. But, of course, enjoy the "show."

When the time comes, you will be called upon to examine the victim and pronounce death. It is possible there will be other demands for your services. Comply as your character would.

During interrogations, you must tell the truth. Answer all questions honestly as you feel your character would based on the information given and that which you may have observed during the evening . . . all in character, of course. Feel free to volunteer anything you saw or heard during the evening that you think may be important in solving the crime.

ACT and REACT

AMANDA HART—PERSONAL INSTRUCTIONS

> **AMANDA HART** is the devoted and patient wife of a busy doctor as well as Phyllis' closest friend and confidant . . . until Madam Angelica showed up. She is extremely active in community affairs and local charity functions as was Phyllis before Frank's death. She is very jealous of the attention this Madam is getting and wants to get Phyllis out of her depression and back into their old routines. She secretly hopes this fake Séance falls flat, for she doesn't believe in this business for a minute.

You have been Phyllis's best friend ever since she attended her first social tea as Mrs. Frank N. Stein. You both took to each other right away and, through your efforts, Phyllis became involved in all the social activities and functions with you. Your pet projects became her pet projects . . . you pet charities became her pet charities (these you can make up ahead of time or wing it). Since Frank's death, Phyllis has completely dropped out of the social scene and curtailed all of her former activities, including having little contact with you or any of her other friends. This has been unbearable for you.

You see this evening as an opportunity to work on getting Phyllis out of her doldrums and back with the living. Make several attempts to talk her into getting back involved . . . she will give excuses.

You are jealous of the amount of time Phyllis has devoted to this Madam Angelica person, so you immediately dislike and distrust her . . . letting everyone know it. Enlist others' help in trying to get Phyllis to put the past behind her and get on with her life.

Obvious topics of conversations: your charities and activities in the social and country club set . . . Madam Angelica and this "fake" Séance . . . your life as a doctor's wife.

When the Séance is announced, take your assigned seat next to Arthur per the attached *Seating Arrangement*. Carry a small purse and hold it in your lap during the Séance. <u>REMAIN SEATED</u> throughout the Séance and react as your character might to what happens.

During interrogations, you must tell the truth. Answer all questions honestly as you feel your character would based on the information given and that which you may have observed during the evening . . . all in character, of course. Feel free to volunteer anything you saw or heard during the evening that you think may be important in solving the crime.

ACT and REACT

CALVIN BOOKER—PERSONAL INSTRUCTIONS

> **CALVIN BOOKER** is a paranoid Don Knotts of the accounting world. He started with the company early on and is now it's Controller. As a young accountant, this nervous, shy man had been captivated by an exotic dancer during a bachelor party for a friend. He madly pursued her promising her the moon. Believing he was her ticket into polite society, she married him. The years following had been, for Calvin, a desperate struggle to make good on his promise. His life has not taken all the turns and directions he had hoped. He is a nervous, worried, frightened man who doesn't want to believe in the spirit world but is awfully afraid that it exists.

You are a rather timid, bashful, bookish person. In school you were considered a "nerd." You're much like a less confident Don Knotts.

You are caught between a rock and a hard place. Many years ago you were hired as an accountant at the plant in hopes of becoming an important figure in your field. You have done that but certainly not in the manner you had planned or expected. Early in your career you attended a stag party at the Cheek2Cheek Club and became mesmerized by a stripper named Bonnie (her "stage" name was "Belle"). You became obsessed with her. You promised her everything her heart could desire if only she would marry you. She took you at your word. Thereafter, you felt compelled to follow through on your promise because you were afraid she would leave you. Her spending quickly outdistanced your promotions and salary and soon you were desperately in debt. You were forced to start embezzling from the Company.

Unfortunately, it was Carl who found you out and threatened you with prison and social disgrace . . . unless . . . you helped him by laundering the profits from his illegal drug business he was initiating. You were terrified of prison but more terrified of losing Bonnie so there was no choice but to comply. (The 10% cut wasn't bad, however, even if it was dirty money.) The resulting allegiance made a nervous, sniveling, ulcer-ridden piece of jelly out of you. Carry a handkerchief and continually use it to wipe your forehead and neck (sweat!).

With each passing day you are becoming more and more paranoid and unstable under the pressure of Carl's thumb . . . being asked to do more and more nasty things. Whine and complain to Carl you want out . . . plead with him that you can't take anymore . . . but again he threatens you into submission. Make sure there are witnesses to this confrontation.

Francine may question you about a discrepancy she noticed in the ledgers. Act extremely nervous and stutter something like . . . it must be a simple mistake . . . or you're sure she is mistaken . . . or there must be a simple explanation . . . you'll look into it first thing Monday . . . or all of the above.

In conversations with other people, you act nervous and preoccupied. But you dote on your wife when she floats by. Almost anything and everything startles you. You are afraid Madam Angelica is for real and maybe even can read minds . . . yours, maybe. Tentatively question her about her abilities.

Accomplish all of the above before the Séance. When the Séance is called, you and Bonnie take the assigned seats as per the attached *Seating Arrangement*. Continue to act nervous and frightened during the Séance. <u>REMAIN SEATED</u> throughout the Séance and react as your character might to what happens.

During interrogations, you must tell the truth. Your sins MUST be revealed, almost to your relief. Answer questions honestly (even enthusiastically) as your character would based on the information given and that which you may have observed during the evening. Blame your sins on Carl. Cry.

ACT and REACT

BONNIE BOOKER—PERSONAL INSTRUCTIONS

BONNIE BOOKER, a former stripper, had expected big things from Calvin, hoping to climb the social ladder to respectability . . . at least high enough to outdistance her nefarious beginnings. Far from being a "My Fair Lady", she nevertheless considers herself a success and cares nothing about how Calvin manages financially. After all, she can't count up to three with mittens on. She loves being the social butterfly, hobnobbing with the rich and sometimes famous, oblivious to the frowns and sharp remarks. It is obvious she did *not* have Professor Higgins as a teacher as she still dresses garishly and is loud and crass. Tonight's Séance should be a "real hoot!"

You were making your living doing the bump and grind at the Cheek2Cheek Club when a stag party came in . . . not much different than the thousands before . . . except this one had a misplaced, pathetic, little sweet man in it. He was obviously so taken with you that you danced the whole evening just to him. He begged you to go out with him and on a whim you accepted. He treated you so gently, so lavishly, so admiringly, and so lovingly and with class that you realized he could be your ticket out of the "business" so you married him.

Although you are in society now, you can't quite shake the ex-stripper in you. You're proof that one can't make a silk purse out of a sow's ear. Being uneducated, unrefined and a bit of an airhead, even charm school couldn't completely smooth the rough edges . . . your kind of crude oil can never be refined. Even Professor Higgins couldn't make you a "My Fair Lady." But, since you have been to charm school, you now think you have class, so you go around showing off and trying to act the real lady (which emphasizes more that you are not) . . . obviously falling way short of your goal but you're ignorant of your shortcomings and fully believe you are pulling it off, completely unaware of and unaffected by the cringes, smirks and snobby looks. You like to be the center of attention. You never quite got off the stage . . . except on this stage you don't take your clothes off.

You are used to ordering Calvin around . . . and he's used to step-and-fetching whatever you need or want. You don't even know what a Séance is so have fun with that.

If there is a character named "Dottie Dingo" at the party, show obvious hate, jealousy and distaste for her. She has on less clothes than you . . . perhaps.

When the Séance is announced, sit next to Calvin in the assigned seats per the attached *Seating Arrangement*. Sit back and enjoy the show . . . comforting Calvin as needed. <u>REMAIN SEATED</u> throughout the Séance and react as your character might to what happens.

During interrogations, you must tell the truth. Answer all questions honestly as you feel your character would based on the information given and that which you may have observed during the evening . . . all in character, of course. Feel free to volunteer anything you saw or heard during the evening that you think may be important in solving the crime.

ACT and REACT

LANCE KNIGHT—PERSONAL INSTRUCTIONS

> **LANCE KNIGHT** is a young, Wall-Street type lawyer. He has been with the Stein-Brenner Company for nearly ten years as well as being the Stein's personal lawyer and family friend. He has done well in those years owing, in no small part, to his wit, charm and good looks as well as his education and talent. He should thank his wife for his education, but he feels he has paid the price. They married very young, sooner than he had planned, and the years and his success have caused him to drift from the person he once was in High School, much like a caterpillar becoming a butterfly; whereas his wife is still the person she was when she fell in love with Lance. Her clinging is getting on his nerves. His life so far has been governed by fateful consequences causing him to make the wrong decisions for the right reasons. He would now rather make the right decisions for the wrong reasons. His head is into getting ahead so his social skills have suffered, although the right woman could change that. His attendance tonight is business as well as social.

You are dashing, confident, ambitious, self-reliant, aggressive, well educated (thanks to Holly, who worked to put you through school) and a successful corporate lawyer. You have been both a close family friend of the Steins since joining the Company nearly ten years ago.

You watched Francine grow from an early teenager to a beautiful, talented, stimulating young woman who has completely stolen your heart. She is a special "treasure." Your marriage, for you, has been a charade for years. The gap between you and Holly grows ever wider with the passing years. You plan to divorce Holly and marry Francine . . . beautiful, brainy and heir to an empire!. For nearly a year, unbeknownst to Holly . . . or anyone else for that matter . . . you have been having a discreet affair with Francine. You both have agreed to keep your secret until you can divorce Holly, so this evening keep your conversations light and innocent . . . but show admiration in your eyes . . . be coy . . . position yourself fairly near her as often as you can . . . constantly look for her or at her. Be seen together a couple of times talking . . . business, Phyllis' condition, this Séance, family etc. Once during the evening, discreetly leave the room with Francine, returning shortly thereafter . . . making sure at least one person notices.

Mill around this evening talking about law or the Séance etc. Pick out a couple of people and talk about marriage and mention the fact that you and Holly have nothing in common anymore and you are considering calling it quits (you figure this is a good time and place to begin to lay the groundwork). Any conversation with Holly act bored, impatient and uninterested, finding some reason to break off the conversation and move away. Do this a couple of times with witnesses.

Sometime during the evening, go to Phyllis and suggest you two take care of business if she has a minute. Now that Frank is dead, you have prepared a new Will for Phyllis with updates and changes per her wishes. Have her select witnesses (perhaps the Harts, Nurse Curtain, Holly) from the guests and all of you go to a private corner or another room to review the new Will. Mention nothing about the actual contents of the Will . . . only have Phyllis read it over and ask her if it meets with her approval and complies with her wishes. Have her sign and date the Will and the witnesses sign attesting her signature. Fold and put the copies in your pocket and all return to the other guests. (You will be called upon later to produce the old Wills and this new one.)

Complete all of the above before the Séance. When the Séance is announced, you and Holly sit in the assigned seats per the attached *Seating Arrangement* (this is important). Frank's ghost will appear and instruct Phyllis to change her Will and leave everything to Willard Hemlock. You are horrified and panic overtakes you (but you don't show it) . . . you truly love Francine but the thought of losing her inheritance is unthinkable . . . especially to Willard! What's with that, you think.

Fate steps in . . . all the lights will go out (hopefully to pitch black, so be careful) . . . giving you the opportunity you need. YOU ARE TO MURDER PHYLLIS! Since you are close to the bar and to Phyllis, under cover of darkness, you take the ice pick from the bar and stab Phyllis in the chest. Actually, you will only seem to go through the motions for safety reasons . . . Phyllis will already have a prop ice pick in her purse and put it into place herself, while the bartender will hide the one on the bar. You will just stand up, lean over your chair and reach for the pretend ice pick, then lean toward where Phyllis is seated (all this very quickly). Just so you will be prepared and not startled, a cap gun will go off quite near you. Be sure you are in your seat when the lights go on . . . in fact, be comforting your wife asking if she is all right.

During interrogations, act natural and innocent, being eager to assist in any way you can. The bartender will say he tripped on something (you) . . . you say it must have been your chair since you felt it jostled. Do not admit to anything more than a close relationship with Francine . . . after all, you see quite a bit of her being a close family friend as well as working together at the plant.

You will, no doubt, be asked to produce the Wills . . . do so willingly. You will be asked who else knew of the content of the old Wills and who knew of the new Will and its content . . . answer, "To my knowledge, only Phyllis and those witnessing the signing this evening . . . although the witnesses may not actually be aware of the contents unless they had read any part while signing. It is possible, however, Phyllis may have discussed the Will with any number of people prior to or during this evening." You are allowed to give testimony to anything you may have observed during the evening to help throw suspicion somewhere else; for instance, Conrad had much to gain and even Priscilla.

NOTE: Reveal to NO ONE before the conclusion that you are the murderer . . . not even Holly . . . Francine . . . or even Phyllis. And during the interrogations, you are the only one that can lie. Stay low-keyed and willing to help the Inspector. If you perceive suspicion is falling on you, be astonished and reaffirm how much affection you had for Phyllis. Throw blame onto someone else . . . always in character.

Sorry, but you aren't going to get away with murder . . . you will eventually be found out at the conclusion. When the accusing finger points at you, you must breakdown and tell all . . . You're unhappy married life . . . one mistake as a teenager ruined your life . . . love for Francine . . . and the desire for success.

HOLLY KNIGHT—PERSONAL INSTRUCTIONS

HOLLY KNIGHT had married Lance, her high school sweetheart, immediately after graduation, as most of her friends were doing, but in her case it was more urgent and necessary. Shortly after their wedding, she had a miscarriage and the ensuing complications rendered her sterile. To hold onto Lance, the love of her life, she agreed to work in order to put him through college and law school. It was a tremendous sacrifice but she was certain it would be worth it. What she hadn't anticipated was the metamorphosis resulting from an education. It hurt to admit, but she no longer fitted into Lance's life. She is trying to reinvent herself to try to rekindle the romance of long ago. She feels she is in need of spiritual guidance . . . perhaps tonight's the Knight . . . er . . . night!

You and Lance married young because of a surprise pregnancy; but after you lost the baby, you continued working to put Lance through Law School. An education changed him quite dramatically but you remained the hardworking, socially stunted homemaker. Your relationship has deteriorated progressively for the past ten years. You don't fully understand what has gone wrong in the marriage but you believe it must be your fault . . . you must not be a good wife. So you try to please Lance by bringing him food to taste . . . a drink . . . try to make conversation about the Séance or his work. But he will brush you off . . . you look hurt, perhaps with tears in your eyes . . . but you never show anger. You know Lance is having an affair with Francine, because you went looking for him one night and saw them through a window at the plant. But you think it is your fault and, if you change, he will come back to you.

Mention to people that you wished you had gotten an education too so you and Lance would have more in common. But you know you aren't nearly as intelligent as he. Otherwise, mill around making conversation with anyone. Confide in Charity and Prudence (overheard by guests) about your problem with Lance and ask advice. What can you do to get him interested in you again . . . could it be he is just overworked at the plant? Listen attentively. Ask Madam Angelica if she has advice . . . or could she possibly tell you what the future holds for you. Complete all of the above before the Séance.

When the Séance is announced, take your seat beside Lance as per the attached *Seating Arrangement.* Carry a small purse and place it on your lap during the Séance. <u>REMAIN SEATED</u> throughout the Séance and react as your character might to what happens.

During interrogations, you must tell the truth. Answer all questions honestly as you feel your character would based on the information given and that which you may have observed during the evening . . . all in character, of course. Feel free to volunteer anything you saw or heard during the evening that you think may be important in solving the crime.

ACT and REACT

WILLARD HEMLOCK—PERSONAL INSTRUCTIONS

WILLARD HEMLOCK belongs to the family who established Hemlock College, which was the only means he had of acquiring a college degree although not necessarily an academic education. As the last male in the Hemlock line, the family was very tolerant of his meager scholastic abilities, but that's not to say he wasn't smart in other ways . . . smart like a fox. His "creative ideas" are not always of a legitimate nature and over the years he has become a successful con-man and manipulator. To most people, he is an obnoxious, creepy weasel; but fearing his tactics, most men tolerated him, take care not to rile him or simply leave him alone. Willard had the acuity to perceive great potential in associating himself with and insinuating himself onto his college buddies, Frank and Carl. So, when he heard that Frank and Carl were forming their own business, he wheedled himself onto the payroll as a marketing rep. The association had not panned out quite the way he had hoped, so after the fire he left the company to woo Phyllis for her obvious attributes . . . money! Her obsession with Frank, however, is a larger obstacle than he anticipated. Think of Uriah Heep and you have Willard.

You act important like the creepy weasel you are (nothing personal). You know people don't really like you but you delight in making them squirm and act like they like you in public. Not very book smart, you are a natural con man. You think of yourself as a ladies man and are sugary sweet to the ladies (leeringly . . . like a dirty old man). Lick you lips a lot and roll your hands sort of like Uriah Heep in "David Copperfield".

You used Carl and Frank for as much as you could. Carl frightens you because you've seen just how cruel and unabashed he can be. Carl has been processing and dispatching illegal drugs right under Frank's nose for years and you are in on it too. You had been trying to cut your ties with Carl but the right time never presented itself . . . until the fire. You were in the plant last year when the fire started. Instead of going for help, you took the opportunity to make off with several files containing critical formulas. After you heard of Frank's death, you decided to quit the Company and pursue Phyllis for her money in order to set you up in business based on the formulas. Marrying Phyllis was a good idea but she's not interested.

Despite your leaving the plant, Carl still has his hand on you. And the truth of it is, you need the money right now.

One evening while visiting the mansion, you got a glimpse of the Mystic Phyllis was seeing . . . Madam Angelica. You not only recognized her scam but you recognized her (though just barely . . . she had changed so much). She is Frank's first wife, Angina, also known as Angel. You had met Frank and Angel while attending Hemlock College. Privately, you threatened to expose her if she didn't cut you in . . . and you had a plan bigger than hers. Although Phyllis was not receptive to marriage, she was receptive to the dribble Angelica preached and it was even easier to convince her to have a Séance. The plan was to have the ghost of Frank (with the help of Frank's long lost son) to convince gullible Phyllis to change her Will, leaving everything to Willard. She is in poor health anyway, so it shouldn't be difficult to finish her off once the Will is changed.

During the evening, you are very attentive to Phyllis, as usual. Mill around among the guests and act boorish and crude. Avoid Angelica so you don't call attention to your association.

When the Séance is called, you sit in the seat shown in the attached *Seating Arrangement*. REACT as your character would to the Séance. <u>REMAIN SEATED</u> throughout the Séance then fall back off your chair in fright.

During interrogations, you must tell the truth. Answer all questions honestly as you feel your character would based on the information given and that which you may have observed during the evening . . . all in character, of course. Feel free to volunteer anything you saw or heard during the evening that you think may be important in solving the crime.

All your crimes in the above information will need to be revealed. Admit all, like the coward you are. You'll be relieved.

ACT and REACT

MADAM ANGELICA—PERSONAL INSTRUCTIONS

> **MADAM ANGELICA** had been attracted by the headline newspaper article a year ago on the Stein-Brenner Plant fire and had contrived a meeting with Phyllis some time after. She has been seeing Phyllis for the better part of a year trying to console her and win her confidence . . . with unbelievable success and rewards. Phyllis completely believes in Madam Angelica and the occult. Madam Angelica suggested a Séance to contact Frank in the hope that his spirit's presence would have a desirable influence on Phyllis. Drumming up business in this social circle wouldn't be bad either.

You've been a "mystic" for many years and have made a lucrative living from it. Your usual modus operandi is to scan the obituaries selecting the names of the richest and most recent widows . . . then you move in with your sly tongue and fancy ghost show. Each "mark" is usually good for many thousands of dollars . . . often into six figures, when all is counted.

You were only in this town a few weeks when you couldn't believe your eyes . . . there was "Frank N. Stein" in the obits of the local newspaper. Frank was your first husband. You were a freshman at Hemlock college when you met Frank, a senior, and by mid year you were pregnant and planning a wedding. Little Frank. was born that summer and two horrendous years later the union ended in a bitter divorce. You took Little Frank (which is what everyone called him) as far away as possible and never cared if you ever saw or heard of Frank again . . . until you read his obituary. You are astonished at how rich he had become . . . when you were married to him, he had nothing. You felt you really have a right to his money and, from what you could learn of his wife, she would be a real easy hit.

You were right . . . the contact was easy . . . Phyllis was a real dishrag. But the fly in the ointment turned out to be running into Willard Hemlock who recognized you from college, despite the ravages of time, over indulgence and enhancement surgery. Thank goodness Carl had not recognized you. But Willard had an excellent plan . . . one that should net you far more than you could have managed yourself . . . and the irony pleases you immensely.

The "Piece de Resistance", which tickles you the most, is that Frank's son, Frank, Jr., will play the part of Frank's ghost. During the evening, he acts as your chauffeur and bodyguard, Hugo Handy (a stage name), staying mute and formidable. But as the Séance begins, he slips away to play the ghost.

So, for nearly a year, you have been counseling Phyllis and have gained her absolute and complete confidence . . . she is putty in your hands. You are convinced that whatever Frank's spirit says to her she will heed. This is going to be a piece of cake.

You were hard, tough, rough and shrewd as Angel, which is what Frank used to call you . . . and it had amused you to use the professional name Angelica . . . Madam Angelica . . . your real name, Angina Pectoris Stein, had no zing . . . in fact, it sounds like a middle eastern country. As Madam Angelica you act cool, reserved, serene, mysterious and confident. You can make up stories about other séance experiences. You must make people believe you are the next step to God. Dress like an elegant gypsy with black veil/scarf over your head, or a shawl, heavy make-up, and lots of jewelry

You will arrive in a grand manor with Hugo (Frank, Jr.) hovering in the shadows nearby (up until the Séance). Many of the people at this gathering tonight have heard of you but few have met you. Pay particular attention to Phyllis, reassuring her of tonight. Mill around trying to drum up business with the guests. Several of the characters may approach you with questions or condemnations. Handle them with confidence and dignity as you choose but be prepared for ad libs.

Have little to do with Willard as you don't want to draw attention to your complicity. Also avoid Carl as he may recognize you. If you encounter him and he says something, tell him you two have met in another life (which isn't far from the truth).

The bartender, Joe Phoenix, will call you "Angel" . . . act startled and indignant at the familiarity of hired help . . . so admonish him for taking such familiar liberties, telling him you are "Madam Angelica".

At an appropriate time, the butler will approach you and ask if he should prepare for the Séance. Nod, Yes. He will take care of the details and announce that everyone should be seated for the Séance. Nod to Hugo as his sign to do his thing. You proceed to your seat (indicated on the attached *Seating Arrangement*) and remain standing until everyone is seated. Start by telling people where to sit around the table (as per the *Seating Arrangement*) . . . Phyllis first. Priscilla should butt in and demand to sit where she wants . . . next to you. Be agreeable and continue to seat the rest at the table only.

When everyone is settled down, call for silence etc. and be seated ready to start. There should be a globe (crystal ball) in the center of the table. When everyone is seated, ask for the lights to dim (someone will take care of the lighting). Hopefully, the hostess will have gone over with you how the globe should be lighted . . . either by a switch hidden near you or from a central location. A rehearsal before the party with the host/hostess, you and Hugo is advisable to work out the staging. Make certain before the party just how this will work. As the lights go down, the light in the globe should be turned on. Have everyone at the table place their hands on the table splayed out so that the tips of their little fingers touch in a circle around the table. Or simply have them all hold hands and not to break the connection. Proceed to call the spirit of Frank (work this out your own way, being as dramatic as possible . . . make a show of it for this is your time to *shine*).

Frank's ghost will appear through the door behind you and have a conversation with Phyllis (a copy of this conversation is attached). Again, you will have worked out with the hostess whether to have the ghost say the words or have the ghost's conversation pre-recorded. If pre-recorded, the best one to control play would be the ghost, as your hands will be otherwise preoccupied completing the circle of hands on the table.

All lights will go out (STAY STEATED) and in the dark you will hear confusion, but do not more. When the lights come back on . . . Frank Jr. will stumble in the door, bleeding, and lunge toward you calling you. Briefly, act the hysterical mother, calling for the doctor, saying "Help, my son's hurt".

During the interrogations, you must tell the truth. All the above information must come out (with your reluctant help). Your secret out, you can now act like the *real* Angel . . . hard-assed and angry. Answer all questions honestly, as your character would based on the information given and that which you may have observed during the evening . . . all in character, of course

Be affronted when it is implied you are a fraud. Say, you give your clients what they really want.

Be startled when the Inspector reads Frank's Will and you learn Frank, Jr. (Hugo) was bequeathed $1,000,000. Later, when your past is uncovered (and you will tell the whole story including your life as a gypsy and hooking up with Phyllis etc.) demand that your son get the $1,000,000.

ACT and REACT

HUGO HANDY—PERSONAL INSTRUCTIONS

> **HUGO HANDY** is Madam Angelica's bodyguard and chauffeur. He is a disturbing presence in the shadowy background, poised for possible action from, shall we say, unbelievers.

You are Madam Angelica's son . . . she was the first wife of Frank N. Stein and you are his first born son . . . which makes you Frank N. Stein, Jr. When a freshman at Hemlock College, "Angel" (a nickname Frank gave her in lieu of her real name, Angina) met and married Frank (then a senior). She was already a little bit pregnant with you. The marriage lasted less than three years. After a bitter divorce, Angel took you away and you never saw your father again.

You grew up with a rough sort of people until your mother got into this occult racket . . . and you, naturally, became part of it. You took the persona of Hugo Handy and posed as her chauffeur and bodyguard, looming in the background as a formidable presence. When needed, you would be available for other tactical assignments . . . as in the case of this Séance, you also double as Frank's Ghost. The occult racket has done very well extorting money from rich widows using a mystic/séance scam. You love it and it's a great life.

Acting the part of the chauffeur/bodyguard, you and Angelica will drive up and make a grand entrance at a time when most, if not all, the other guests have already arrived. During the evening, before the Séance, you keep close to Angelica but inconspicuous (standing just a few steps behind her but away from the crowd, always looking stern and rarely talking except in one syllable grunts). Talk to no one . . . if people talk to you, just scowl at them or grunt trying to scare them off . . . or just turn you back to them and ignore them.

Angelica will give you a nod, indicating the Séance will soon begin, which will be your signal to disappear to a prearranged place to change into your ghost costume. Dress quickly and take your position outside the door behind her seat (this will have to be pre-rehearsed with the host/hostess beforehand) waiting to make your appearance when Madam Angelica summons the ghost of Frank N. Stein. (Use of a smoke or dry ice machine plus a backlight really makes for a spectacular appearance.)

After you hear her call for the ghost several times, open the door quietly (standing out of view) and then make your entrance (ghostily) through the door (step just inside the doorway, which should put you directly behind your mother). You will have a conversation with Phyllis (a copy of the dialogue is attached). You will either be required to memorize the words exactly or it may be decided to pre-record your side of the conversation (with gaps for Phyllis' responses) and you will control the playback. At the end of the conversation, back up slowly through the door saying "goodbye". Try practicing a "ghostly" voice . . . low . . . slow . . . and throaty.

As you are leaving, the lights will go out leaving the room in darkness. A gun will go off (cap gun) . . . the bullet (pretend) hits you! Have a packet of Ketchup in your pocket ready to smear on the shoulder of your ghost outfit . . . or you could use a red blotch of material to assimilate blood and hold it to your shoulder (it is less messy that way). When the lights come back on, stagger through the door calling "Mother, mother" and lurch toward Angelica holding your wounded shoulder, collapsing at her feet . . . you are wounded . . . NOT DEAD. Dr. Hart will probably tend to your arm (sooner or later).

During interrogations, you must tell the truth. Answer all questions honestly as your character would based on the information given and that which you may have observed during the evening . . . all in character, of course. Feel free to volunteer anything you saw or heard during the evening that you think may be important in solving the crime.

ALL the above information MUST be revealed.

ACT and REACT

TILLY TOYLER—PERSONAL INSTRUCTIONS

> **TILLY TOYLER** is Carlton's Secretary and an extremely efficient one. She is like a no-nonsense machine at work and at home as well. That could account for why she remains unmarried in her mid forties. She is also the office gossip and is never without her steno pad. She brought a steno pad tonight to take copious notes about the séance . . . or anything else that seems interesting.

You aren't much of a social conversationalist unless it is about some juicy bit of gossip . . . then you are all ears and questions. You carry your steno pad just about everywhere for the sole purpose of jotting down gossip so you won't forget the details. That is your basic assignment tonight—listen and take copious notes. They may come in handy later.

Enjoy your character and try to get into the story.

During the Séance, you will stand or sit behind Prudence and Prentice. <u>Remain where you are throughout the Séance.</u>

During interrogations, you must tell the truth. Answer all questions honestly as you feel your character would based on the information given and that which you may have observed during the evening . . . all in character, of course. Feel free to volunteer anything you saw or heard during the evening that you think may be important in solving the crime.

ACT and REACT

WALLACE WINGATE—PERSONAL INSTRUCTIONS

> **WALLACE WINGATE** is Purchasing Agent for the Stein-Brenner Company. He misses Frank and the friendship he gave everyone at the plant. Work this past year has been a real drudge, but he is in too deep to quit. He's terrified of Carl and Carl's "friends."

You got your position of Purchasing Agent at the plant because you were "assigned" to it by Mafia boss, Louis Botalinni, better known as Lobo. Louis and Carl were partners in the Stein-Brenner Company's "side business" in drugs. Mafia bosses trust as well as politicians and lawyers . . . hence, your presence at the plant. At first, you were fine with the assignment but then you met Frank and realized what a great person he was. You felt guilty and there is no room in "the business" for guilt. This makes it very difficult to do your job and you hope Carl doesn't suspect the guilt or he will suspect other things worse and you could be history. You haven't had a good night's sleep in five years.

The reason you are in this mess is your wife. She's the daughter of a Chicago mobster. You met her, fell in love, and asked her to marry you before you knew about her family. At first you thought it was bonus to be under the protection of "the family" but then you witnessed some of the things they did. Obviously, divorce is NOT an option . . . and neither is leaving "the family" for there is no place to go that they wouldn't find you.

Socialize in the group, avoiding Carl, and try not to talk about your work. Do talk about Frank and what a nice gentleman he was etc.

When the Séance is announced, stand (or sit, if there are chairs) with your wife where "Other Guests if any" is indicated on the attached *Seating Arrangement*. **REMAIN STANDING OR SEATED** during the Séance, reacting as you think your character might to the proceedings.

During interrogations, you must tell the truth. Answer all questions honestly as you feel your character would based on the information given and that which you may have observed during the evening . . . all in character, of course. Feel free to volunteer anything you saw or heard during the evening that you think may be important in solving the crime.

ACT and REACT

WINTER WINGATE—PERSONAL INSTRUCTIONS

> **WINTER WINGATE** is the daughter of a mobster in Chicago. She's "one of them" and Wallace regrets the day he met her but divorce is not an option. Winter loves parties . . . any party. She's never heard of a séance and never had her palm read.

You are the daughter of a Chicago Mafia Boss. Therefore, you were brought up feeling pretty special . . . perhaps a bit better than everyone else, because of your father's power.

You met and married Wallace and he got drawn into the family fighting and kicking . . . at least mentally. You have no clue why . . . you really don't know what it is your father does . . . he's just powerful as far as you are concerned. Get with your partner to make up stories of how you both met etc., so your facts will be straight.

What you like to do best is to PARTY. You expected a big band and dancing tonight. You never heard of a Séance so are really disappointed there will be no dancing. But you hum your own music and dance around by yourself or pull others into dancing a bit.

When the Séance is announced, stand (or sit, if there are chairs) with your husband where "Other Guests if any" is indicated on the attached *Seating Arrangement*. **REMAIN STANDING OR SEATED** during the Séance, reacting as you think your character might to the proceedings.

During interrogations, you must tell the truth. Answer all questions honestly as you feel your character would based on the information given and that which you may have observed during the evening . . . all in character, of course. Feel free to volunteer anything you saw or heard during the evening that you think may be important in solving the crime.

ACT and REACT

DANNY DINGO—PERSONAL INSTRUCTIONS

> **DANNY DINGO** serves as Company Transit Director and is Head of the local Teamsters. He has total charge of everything coming in and going out of the plant. He thinks of only two things: work and football. He doesn't know what "social" means but Carl insisted he be at the séance . . . just in case . . . despite his discomfort.

Mafia boss Louis Botalinni assigned you to this position at the plant basically to take care of his interest in the partnership with Carl in processing the drug trade. Wallace Wingate is likewise so employed. You love your job and feel pretty safe from the law. You can make up stories of how you came to be at the plant but don't mention the drugs.

You are far from a social butterfly and would rather be home in your recliner with a Budweiser in your hand watching the Baltimore Ravens. Carl wanted you here, so, you are here.

Dottie is a "trophy" wife. She's gorgeous with a body worth showing off. But when she does, you get jealous of the men ogling her. You're not so bad looking yourself and your body is still in good shape from all those years working on the docks.

Spend the evening at or near the bar talking sports or whatever you think your character would discuss. Keep an eye on Dottie and have a confrontation now and then if her flirting gets a response.

When the Séance is announced, stand (or sit, if there are chairs) with your wife where "Other Guests if any" is indicated on the attached *Seating Arrangement*. **REMAIN STANDING OR SEATED** during the Séance, reacting as you think your character might to the proceedings.

During interrogations, you must tell the truth. Answer all questions honestly as you feel your character would based on the information given and that which you may have observed during the evening . . . all in character, of course. Feel free to volunteer anything you saw or heard during the evening that you think may be important in solving the crime.

ACT and REACT

DOTTIE DINGO—PERSONAL INSTRUCTIONS

> **DOTTIE DINGO** is Danny's wife and a "real blond" but with a figure worth showing off . . . and she does. She has the license on swinging hips and low cut tops. Bonnie Booker hates her.

You're several pints short of a gallon but all you care about is showing off your body and flirting for attention. You don't dare go too far with it because Danny is jealous. But you enjoy it when he butts in to defend your honor so you're always testing it.

Get with your partner before the party and decide on a history between the two of your characters . . . like how you met etc . . . . so you get your facts straight.

Wear a blond wig (if you're not already blond), a short tight dress with a plunging neckline, lots of bangles, lots of make-up, red nail polish and chew gum.

You're on tonight. Work it girl!

When the Séance is announced, stand (or sit, if there are chairs) with your husband where "Other Guests if any" is indicated on the attached *Seating Arrangement*. **REMAIN STANDING OR SEATED** during the Séance, reacting as you think your character might to the proceedings.

During interrogations, you must tell the truth. Answer all questions honestly as you feel your character would based on the information given and that which you may have observed during the evening . . . all in character, of course. Feel free to volunteer anything you saw or heard during the evening that you think may be important in solving the crime.

ACT and REACT

MIKAL MAESTRO—PERSONAL INSTRUCTIONS

> **MIKAL MAESTRO** is the Conductor of he town Symphony. He and his wife met the Steins because Frank and Phyllis served on the Symphony Board of Directors and they became fast friends even though Mikal's head is completely full of music with room for little else. Mikal took Frank's death very hard and, although his head tells him this Séance stuff is a fake, his gut wants to believe in the possibility.

Mikal immigrated from Italy twenty years ago and met Frank by chance while Frank was in New York on business. They liked one another immediately and Frank paved the way for Mikal to eventually become the town Symphony Conductor. Mikal will be forever grateful. He hopes the séance will be successful so he can tell him in person once more.

You are a most pleasant, happy man who speaks broken English even after twenty years and eats, drinks and sleeps music Bone up on some names of symphonies and their composers you can throw out at people. Other than music, you are very naïve about the world around you.

You do know how to have children . . . you and Martha have seven and you love everyone of them. And especially Martha. She is your reason for living. She is your music.

When the Séance is announced, stand (or sit, if there are chairs) with your wife where "Other Guests if any" is indicated on the attached *Seating Arrangement*. **REMAIN STANDING OR SEATED** during the Séance, reacting as you think your character might to the proceedings.

During interrogations, you must tell the truth. Answer all questions honestly as you feel your character would based on the information given and that which you may have observed during the evening . . . all in character, of course. Feel free to volunteer anything you saw or heard during the evening that you think may be important in solving the crime.

ACT and REACT

MARTHA MAESTRO—PERSONAL INSTRUCTIONS

> **MARTHA MAESTRO** is Mikal's wife and mother of his seven children. It was Phyllis who convinced her to get help with the children so she could get out and get a life. So she joined Phyllis and Amanda in many of their social and charitable endeavors. She is terrified of the occult.

You were a booking agent in New York when a smiling happy man right off the boat from Italy came into your office looking for work as a classical musician. Your life up to then had been a drudge but Mikal brought you sunshine and you never had a dark day after.

Having seven children would be a burden for some mothers but it was your dream to have many children. They did, however, take much of your time so Phyllis and Amanda convinced you to hire a housekeeper/nannie to help a few days a week so you could have a social life. This you did and joined them in their clubs and charity work. For the past year, you have missed Phyllis's contributions to your endeavors.

Enjoy the evening mixing with folks and now and then try to convince Phyllis to come back to the group.

When the Séance is announced, stand (or sit, if there are chairs) with your husband where "Other Guests if any" is indicated on the attached *Seating Arrangement*. **REMAIN STANDING OR SEATED** during the Séance, reacting as you think your character might to the proceedings.

During interrogations, you must tell the truth. Answer all questions honestly as you feel your character would based on the information given and that which you may have observed during the evening . . . all in character, of course. Feel free to volunteer anything you saw or heard during the evening that you think may be important in solving the crime.

ACT and REACT

FELIX FARNUM—PERSONAL INSTRUCTIONS

> **FELIX FARNUM** is a long-time neighbor and close friend of he Stein family. Their children grew up with the Stein children. They are here tonight to give Phyllis their full support.

You have been neighbors of he Steins since they moved in. You consider yourselves lucky that the Steins are the finest neighbors anyone could hope for. The last owners could take the prize for the worst.

Your children were about the same ages as the Stein children so friendships were natural and they were always running back and forth from house to house.

Make yourself at home tonight. Console Phyllis and the kids.

When the Séance is announced, stand (or sit, if there are chairs) with your wife where "Other Guests if any" is indicated on the attached *Seating Arrangement*. **REMAIN STANDING OR SEATED** during the Séance, reacting as you think your character might to the proceedings.

During interrogations, you must tell the truth. Answer all questions honestly as you feel your character would based on the information given and that which you may have observed during the evening . . . all in character, of course. Feel free to volunteer anything you saw or heard during the evening that you think may be important in solving the crime.

ACT and REACT

FANNY FARNUM—PERSONAL INSTRUCTIONS

> **FANNY FARNUM** is Felix's wife and one of Phyllis' best friends. They've been bridge partners at the Marathon Duplicate Bridge Group for ten years and she's been lost without her this past year. She hopes tonight she can talk Phyllis into coming back to the group.

You have been neighbors of he Steins since they moved in. You consider yourselves lucky that the Steins are the finest neighbors anyone could hope for. The last owners could take the prize for the worst.

You and Phyllis have been bridge partners for ages and you've really missed her this past year. You make a point of trying to talk her into playing again, even if only once a month.

Your children were about the same ages as the Stein children so friendships were natural and they were always running back and forth from house to house.

Make yourself at home tonight. Console Phyllis and the kids.

When the Séance is announced, stand (or sit, if there are chairs) with your husband where "Other Guests if any" is indicated on the attached *Seating Arrangement*. **REMAIN STANDING OR SEATED** during the Séance, reacting as you think your character might to the proceedings.

During interrogations, you must tell the truth. Answer all questions honestly as you feel your character would based on the information given and that which you may have observed during the evening . . . all in character, of course. Feel free to volunteer anything you saw or heard during the evening that you think may be important in solving the crime.

ACT and REACT

CONRAD DIDDIT—PERSONAL INSTRUCTIONS

> **CONRAD DIDDIT** is the family butler and devoted servant for nearly 30 years as well as close friend and confidante to Frank.

You have been a devoted servant to the Stein family since they were married and moved into the mansion on the hill. You take your job seriously and regard yourself as a highly trained, sophisticated, educated, dignified craftsman . . . and your craft has been handed down for generations.

You respected and liked Frank Stein more than anyone you had ever met, and the news of his death was a heavy blow. But your strict training got you through with hardly an external ripple. You continue to serve Phyllis with the same enthusiasm, as was Frank's wish.

In Frank's Will, you were left $500,000, which came as a complete surprise to you and your admiration tripled for the man. You fully believed and were trained to believe that a provider of service is compensated for that service and have always felt perfectly satisfied with the generous financial arrangements of your position and had no reason, or desire, to expect any additional recompense. This was a boon. With Lance's help, you were able to find reasonably safe investments for the large sum.

In addition, Frank's Will provided a pension of $10,000 a month, in addition to your salary, paid until your death. This pension alone would secure your future in any style you wished. With the $500,000 invested well, you are totally secure and elated beyond words.

Frank also noted in his Will his desire for you to have property on Captiva Island on the death of Phyllis. Since the Will also stipulated that the fulfillment of this wish was purely discretionary on the part of Phyllis, you gave it no further regard.

The past year has been very difficult for you . . . not only because you missed the master of the house . . . not only because of Phyllis' depression and immergence in Madam Angelica's cult . . . but mostly because of Priscilla, that busybody sister of Phyllis. She has not only run you ragged physically, but her constant criticism has demoralized you emotionally. When she does so this evening, furrow your brow, grit your teeth but say "Yes, Madam" or something of the sort, bow slightly and leave, muttering to yourself.

A week ago, you received a shock equal to, if not greater than, the jolt you received at hearing of Frank's horrible death last year . . . <u>the REAL Frank showed up at the servants' entrance . . . quite alive!</u> Yes, Frank is still alive and only you and he know this fact. He confided in you the story of that evening one year ago:

He discovered Carl Brenner was trafficking in illegal drugs through the plant. He confronted Carl. They fought. Carl knocked him out. When he came to, the place was in flames. He managed to make his way to a window and when the first explosion happened, it blew him out through the window. He can't remember what he did next but he woke up in a hospital burn unit in a small mid-western town listed as a "John Doe." Apparently, he must have climbed into a company delivery truck that took off early the next day, finally getting off the truck and ultimately being discovered near a small town. For the past year he has been recovering from extensive burns, plastic surgery, and a broken jaw, arm and leg, and amnesia. His memory returned just recently so he set about returning to his home. Not knowing what reception he might expect after all this time, he thought to contact Conrad first and plan his next move.

You told Frank what has happened in the past year . . . Phyllis' depression . . . her captivation by Madam Angelica . . . Priscilla's intervention . . . Francine's participation at the plant . . . Willard's constant pursuit of Phyllis (which amused as well as angered Frank) . . . and the upcoming Séance (which interested Frank the most).

Frank told you that the Séance had given him an idea. He would make his appearance at the Séance . . . wouldn't THAT blow everyone's mind. However, he wanted a place to observe the proceedings before the Séance . . . and since his appearance had changed dramatically since the fire, what with the plastic surgery, it was decided that he would pose as a bartender, hired for the evening by Conrad to serve the large number of guests. He could mingle and observe but not really be noticed (for who notices servants!). That way he could best judge the proper timing of his resurrection. You were delighted with the plan and vowed to assist in any way directed, keeping his secret from everyone until Frank "rose from the ashes" . . . hence the chosen alias Joe Phoenix!

This evening, you are to treat Frank (Joe Phoenix) as a servant and you will mingle through the guests acting like a butler/servant, asking if there is anything they might need. Inspect (and taste) the food, etc. Respond to Priscilla as noted above.

When it is time for the Séance (at some predetermined time . . . whatever seems appropriate . . . allowing enough time for all characters to have completed their tasks), go to Madam Angelica, asking softly if she wishes you to prepare for the Séance. Then go and make sure the Séance table and chairs and surrounding area are set up as per the attached *Seating Arrangement*.

Announce to all that the Séance is about to begin, will the guests please be seated. It is very important that everyone be in their assigned places, but Priscilla will demand to chose her place . . . on the left side of Madam Angelica. Madam Angelica should request that all lights be turned down or off, leaving only the crystal ball lit.

During the Séance, Madam Angelica will call the Ghost of Frank to appear. The ghost will appear and have a dialogue with Phyllis. As the Ghost begins to go away, you or Frank (whoever is in the most convenient position to control turning off all the lights by a main switch) will turn off the main switch, causing everything in the room to go black (THIS IS VERY IMPORTANT . . . NO OUTSIDE LIGHTS CAN SHINE IN WINDOWS EITHER). You shout loudly for everyone to stay calm and stay where they are for safety sake. A gun will go off . . . someone will scream. In about 30 seconds, you or Frank will turn the main switch back on and you ask people to turn on lamps etc. to give more light. You then react to the situation presenting itself. Have everyone roughly stay where they are (allowing appropriate reactions from some). There will no doubt be some confusion . . . go around calming people and telling them to stay seated. You may need to assist Dr. Hart . . . or help others . . . all in the line of duty and your job. Then you will offer to go call the police . . . make the appearance of calling same. Announce that the Inspector is on his way.

During interrogations, you must tell the truth. Answer all questions honestly, as you feel your character would based on the information given and that which you may have observed during the evening . . . all in character, of course. All the above information must be revealed. Feel free to volunteer anything you saw or heard during the evening that you think may be important in solving the crime.

If the host plays the butler character and also the Inspector, the Inspector can claim that Conrad had already given him information on the case.

ACT and REACT

JOE PHOENIX—PERSONAL INSTRUCTIONS

> **JOE PHOENIX**—Bartender and temporary servant hired by the butler solely for this evening's event.

You are really Frank N. Stein . . . husband of Phyllis.

This is the story of the fire:

You discovered Carl's little side business in illegal drugs. You were furious he was using the business to process the raw material into illegal marketable substances like cocaine. You demanded to see him. He came to the lab late that evening and you accused him of trafficking. You got into a heated verbal fight. You went to the phone to call the police and that's when Carl picked up something heavy and beamed you with it. You were barely conscious but remember Carl smashing all the jars of chemicals. When he lit and tossed the match, you remember being so astonished at his unabashed act of cold blooded murder of not just anyone, but a lifetime best friend. He walked out without even looking back.

You came to with flames licking your feet and legs. You ripped off the bottom of your burning pants legs. The way to the door was impassable but a path to a window was negotiable. You reached the window just as the first explosion propelled you through the window, along with half the office. You were badly burned and had a broken arm and leg. You must have laid there unconscious in the rubble for only a short while as another explosion roused you. There was a delivery truck nearby. Somehow you managed to crawl to it and found the back unlocked. You pulled yourself in and wrapped yourself in old insulation quilts left on the truck floor.

You don't know how long you lay there unconscious or asleep but when you opened your eyes you couldn't remember anything about the fire or what you were doing in that truck. You tried to move but quickly discovered the injuries you couldn't account for. As your mind began processing all this new information, the truck swerved and you realized you were moving from a place you couldn't remember to a place you couldn't guess. Confused and in a state of panic, you must have passed out once again and didn't wake again until your body registered a lack of movement . . . the truck had stopped. Soon after, the driver opened the rear doors and discovered a stowaway. Somehow you ended up in a hospital somewhere in the mid-west. You had no identification and couldn't remember who you were, so was sent to the indigent ward and your injuries treated. You were very fortunate that a local church charity took up your case and provided the funds needed for the plastic surgery necessary to repair the damage from the burns. But with no photograph to use as a guide, they did the best they could; however, you ended up looking quite different from your original self. The bones healed quickly but the burns took considerably longer. But as the days passed, your memory did not recover. Then one evening you woke up coughing only to discover your room was on fire, which turned out to have been caused by faulty wiring. The fire was discovered almost immediately and quickly dealt with. The seed of shock from seeing the flames began eroding the wall of self imposed amnesia. In short . . . you started to remember and soon remembered everything.

You were out for revenge and planned hard and long how to achieve it. You made contact with Conrad a week ago and told him all that had happened (he is the only one who knows you are still alive). Conrad filled you in on what has been happening this past year: Phyllis's depression . . . her captivation with Madam Angelica (a Medium) . . . Priscilla's intervention . . . Francine's participation at the plant . . . Ruben's increased drinking and erratic behavior . . . Willard's constant pursuit of Phyllis (which amused as well as angered you) . . . and the upcoming Séance (which intrigued you).

You told Conrad that the Séance would give you the perfect opportunity to make your appearance . . . wouldn't THAT blow everyone's mind! You would "rise from the ashes"! Using the appropriate name Joe Phoenix, you arranged with Conrad to pose as a hired bartender for the evening, mingling and observing but not really being noticed, and judge the proper timing for your resurrection.

What you didn't tell Conrad was that you planned to use the Séance to take your revenge on Carl . . . you plan to kill him! This isn't at all like you . . . you are really a sweet, gentle, honest man who has gone just a little bit crazy over the pain and suffering you and your family have endured this past year because of one man . . . your best friend . . . CARL. At just the right moment, you will arrange all the lights to go out (either you or Conrad will do this). Although in darkness, you have an exact aiming point in mind to shoot Carl DEAD. No one would suspect the bartender. Beyond that, you had no other specific plans.

BACKGROUND

You were a senior at Hemlock College when you met and married a young freshman named Angina Pectoris (who you affectionately called "Angel"). She was just a little bit pregnant at the time. The marriage lasted nearly three years and ended in a bitter divorce. Angel took your money (what little you had) and your son, Frank, Jr., and disappeared. All your efforts to find your son over the years have failed.

Shortly after your divorce, you ran into Carl, your college buddy, and decided to start a chemical research and manufacturing business. Your brains and his business sense should be a successful match . . . the problem was capital. Because of the divorce you had none and Carl was estranged from his wealthy family. You just happened to be in a real estate office investigating possible properties for the plant, when you met the sweetest young thing you had ever laid eyes on . . . Phyllis. It was love at first sight for both of you and you were amazed at your good fortune to learn she had one . . . a fortune that is. With her financial backing, you and Carl were able to start your business. For the past thirty odd years, your life has turned completely around. You've had a wonderful marriage to Phyllis who has given you a son, Ruben, and a precious daughter, Francine. And your financial success has far exceeded anything you could have imagined. Then the fire.

TONIGHT

You play the bartender, so you must act like one by staying behind the bar and mixing the drinks for the guests. At times, you may mingle with the guests, asking for drink orders, etc.

When Madam Angelica and her bodyguard arrive, you recognize her as your first wife, Angel. When you serve her a drink, slip and call her "Angel" . . . she will act startled and admonish you for taking such familiar liberties etc. Apologize.

When all the guests have arrived, take a glass of wine to Phyllis (use a silver tray and serve with flair). She will look at you familiarly and ask, "Do I know you . . . have you served me before? Your eyes look so familiar." You say, "Yes, madam, I have had the pleasure of serving you in the past." She will say, "I hope you will be available to serve again in the future." (or something like that . . . and you respond favorably). Return behind the bar and serve the regular drinks.

When it is time for the Séance, Conrad will begin to ready the Séance area and then call the guests to their seats. Station yourself at the corner of the bar (as per the attached *Seating Arrangement*).

There will be an ice pick on the bar in a prominent place (it is important that it remain in view all evening up until the Séance). For the sake of the mystery party only, you should hide the ice pick under the bar or someplace out of sight during the Séance (unobserved by anyone) . . . but in reality, you did not do this act. It did NOT happen, meaning, you would not confession doing it when asked during the interrogations.

Madam Angelica will call for the lights to be turned off all but the light inside the Crystal Ball. The switch which controls the light in the Crystal Ball (and all other lights) should be previously located for ready access by you or Conrad for control later. During the Séance, a ghost will appear and have a conversation with Phyllis. At the end of their conversation, the ghost will begin to back out the door saying "Goodbye, Phyllis" (or something like that) . . . at this time, turn out the main light switch which should cause COMPLETE DARKNESS (this should have been rehearsed previously to be sure complete darkness can be achieved). You will have a cap gun hidden on you or in the bar area. quickly take the gun, step forward one step and fire toward where Carl is seated. As you are firing, you seem to stumble or bump into something. After firing, toss the gun gently (and low . . . so as not to injure anyone) toward the Séance table. Return to the light switches (you or Conrad) and turn on the lights (all that should have taken approximately 15-30 seconds). If only the Crystal Ball light goes on, call for someone to turn on some lights (lamps).

You may get some surprises when the lights illuminate the scene. React to them with surprise, confusion, bewilderment, hysteria and especially *GUILT* . . . whatever way you feel your character (Frank N. Stein . . . not Joe Phoenix) would.

During interrogations, you must tell the truth. Answer honestly as your character would based on the information given. All of the above MUST come out . . . but not until Madam Angelica tells her story. Your revelation should come last as it will come as the last big shock. You will NOT mention hiding the ice pick as that never happened in "real" time. You are to specifically state that when you aimed to shoot, you thought you bumped into the wall, a chair or a person which caused the gun to be knocked out of your hand . . . which is why it was found on the floor.

Remember . . . **ACT and REACT!**

CAMILLE LEON—PERSONAL INSTRUCTIONS

> **CAMILLE LEON**—Newspaper Reporter and Photographer for the Lightning Gazette who has been following this story since the fire a year ago. She bribed Priscilla to allow her access to this Séance. She hopes this will be the story of a lifetime…and not the end of her career. With the occult one never knows what the future holds.

This role is usually played by the hostess to record the best parts of the play and, if there is a microphone available, to interview various guests whose answers could be heard by everyone. If this is the case, choose your interviews wisely and try not to interfere with the other characters trying to achieve their piece of the puzzle.

Typical questions you might ask guests are:

> What is your name and relationship to Phyllis?
> What are your thoughts regarding this Séance?
> Do you think Frank N. Stein's ghost will appear?
> What do you know about the family?

You may keep filming during the séance but without assistance of a camera light source. Please stand out of range of the other guests so as not to interfere or be in the way. Refer to the *Seating Arrangement* and stand in the area marked "Other Guests, if any," and stay put.

During the *Interrogations,* continue filming while following the Inspector around the room focusing on the same people and things he focuses on. All things are possible in this kind of play, so, because you have been filming the events, someone among the guests, or even the Inspector, may ask to see a replay of your tape, in whole (hopefully not) or in part.

Your part is mostly utilitarian but you may participate to any degree you wish without compromising the storyline. If you, as hostess, wish to designate another person as this character, you may do so at your discretion. Also, you may wish to have this character do the interviewing while another, working in tandem, does the filming.

If you do film the party . . . you'll be so glad you did.

INSPECTOR CLOQUE JOUSEAU

> **INSPECTOR CLOQUE JOUSEAU** is the Police Homicide Detective called to the scene by the butler to solve the murder.

This character is usually played by the host of the party as the host has read the story and should have an overall picture of the flow of the storyline and murder. However, this is not a hard and fast rule and if the host has confidence in someone else playing this role, it is his choice. It should be pointed out that this character above all has the most control of the direction of the play. As this character does not enter the play until the end, it is usually the case that they play the role of a servant during the pre-séance part of the party so that they can still be a part of the party. Then change clothes and roles for the post-séance role.

The Inspector is responsible for the **INTERROGATION** following the murder. The outline for this part can be found near the end. Follow this outline to uncover as many clues as possible. It is a good idea to read the last pages of the story dealing with the interrogation and solving of the murder in order to get an idea of the information that should be extracted from the guests. Not all guests will be so cooperative, so it is your job to keep digging until you get the information out.

After uncovering the clues, take a short break and instruct the guests to try to figure out the murder and the murderer themselves, keeping in mind the three things that must be satisfied:

> ACCESS TO THE MURDER WEAPON
> OPPORTUNITY
> MOTIVE

Take about fifteen minutes to pass out ballots and have them returned. A small prize may be given those who pick correctly or perhaps just a certificate (see Chart 1 in the CHARTS Section).

The Inspector is also responsible for the **SOLUTION** via ***THE ANATOMY OF THE MURDER.*** The outline for the solution by way of the anatomy of the murder may be found in the last section.

CHARTS

Chart 1

The Certificate

THIS IS TO CERTIFY THAT

....

HAS ACHIEVED THE STATUS OF "SUPER SLEUTH"
FOR OUTSTANDING DETECTIVE WORK
IN APPREHENDING THE MURDERER
AT THE MURDER MYSTERY PARTY PLAY

MURDER in the HAUNTED HOUSE

WITNESS:

DATE:

Chart 2

THE INVITATION

MURDER in the HAUNTED HOUSE

A Murder Mystery Party Play

Mrs. Frank N. Stein

requests the honor of your presence

*on*_____

at her home _____

promptly at _____ *p.m. for a SEANCE.*

Madam Angelica anticipates making contact with the late Mr. Stein.

RSVP ASAP: YES____ NO____ ACTIVE_____ PASSIVE_____

This is a murder mystery party play where every guest gets to play a part—either an ACTIVE part critical to the plot, or a PASSIVE part which is a non-critical part. You will be provided a synopsis of all characters of the play as well as a more detailed description of your own character, sometimes with specific instructions, and you have the liberty to develop and play that character as you see fit, within the guidelines provided. Here's your chance to have an out-of-body experience. Come have fun.

Chart 3

THE NEWSPAPER
CLIPPING to accompany the Invitation

"ONE YEAR AGO TODAY, CHEMICAL MANUFACTURER FRANK N. STEIN TRAGICALLY PERISHED IN AN EXPLOSION AND INTENSE FIRE WHICH DESTROYED THE RESEARCH WING OF THE STEIN-BRENNER CHEMICAL PLANT"

Such was the headline of the *Lightning Gazette*. Phyllis Stein did not need to be reminded of the gruesome, painful details of her husband's death. A year had not been enough time for her to recover from the horrifying shock and devastating loss of her dear husband. Unable to cope, she sank deeper into depression, alienating herself from family and friends, and becoming emotionally and physically drained to a point of threatening her health. The only people she could turn to for consolation and understanding, it seemed, were her younger daughter, Francine, who was a soothing comfort to her during this tragic time, and Madam Angelica, a mystic of some note, whom Phyllis met shortly after her husband's demise. It was Madam Angelica who had given Phyllis hope . . . hope of making contact with Frank's spirit in the Other World . . . hope of speaking with him and hearing his comforting words . . . hope of sorting out the confusion of her life. HOPE in the form of a SEANCE!

*

Frank had not been her only husband nor she his only wife. Her first husband was billionaire Arnold Dumbelli of the Madison Avenue Dumbelli's Training Pants fortune, who had died suddenly in a yachting accident less than a year after they were married. Since his body was never recovered, a Memorial Service was held at the spot where Arnold's boat capsized in Long Island Sound. That marriage had made Phyllis a rich widow and had produced a healthy baby girl, Dominique. But because of Phyllis' immaturity and insecurity, neither brought her any joy.

Her second marriage to Bruce Brassiere, heir to the Itty Bitty Titty Brassiere fortune, was equally disconcerting and ended in a "hushed" annulment due to irreconcilable "likenesses" . . . both preferred the company of women in the afternoons and men in the evenings. The family managed to keep the scandal from the newspapers and made it monetarily worth her while to cooperate in this. Bruce was too wrapped up in the family business to put up much resistance. It comes as no surprise that there were no children from this marriage.

Then she met Frank! He was tall and handsome and full of enthusiasm about his future plans in the chemical research/manufacturing field. His easy charm and flashing smile just melted her heart. His first marriage to his college sweetheart had ended in a bitter, ugly divorce only a year before he met Phyllis. The legal entanglements had left him penniless, without a job and worse . . . without his young son to whom he had been devoted. His ex-wife had disappeared after the divorce taking the boy with her and all efforts to find them had failed. Frank was just getting his life together after the divorce and contemplating starting a chemical company with his college buddy, Carlton Brenner, when he met Phyllis. It was love at first "site" . . . since they both were in the Fairwinds Real Estate Office looking over property. They merged. With Phyllis' financial backing, Frank was able to join Carl in building a chemical research/manufacturing empire. Frank and Phyllis' long marriage had seemed all peaks and few valleys and produced a son, Ruben, and a daughter, Francine. It was a blissful union with staggering financial and social success.

And then the fire . . .

Chart 4

THE LIST OF ACTIVE CHARACTERS

LIST OF ACTIVE CHARACTERS
(This copy for use of the Host and Hostess only)

KEY PLAYERS

Phyllis Stein . . . Wife of Frank N. Stein and hostess of the Séance—Character is of average intelligence suffering from depression. She is very weak-willed and easily manipulated. Although from meager beginnings, she has lived in rich society long enough to actually *be* a refined lady.

Dominique Baldwin . . . Phyllis' daughter with first husband, Arnold Dumbelli, who died and left her quite wealthy—She grew up a rejected, neglected child, obsessed with achieving approval and love from her mother. In her frustration, she whine's, argues and throws temper tantrums. Ralph is capable of taming her.

Ruben Stein . . . Phyllis and Frank's son—Ruben is as much like his mother as Francine is like her father. He's not the sharpest tack in the box and has an inferiority complex topping out at zero. He is overcome with failure to come up to his father's standards and is further brow-beaten by his ambitious wife. He drinks to excess as an escape but ends up further embarrassing himself and his family. Carl has given him a chance to redeem himself, but in doing so, has added another burden . . . drugs.

Francine Stein . . . Phyllis & Frank's daughter—Beautiful, charming, witty, intelligent and confident, just like her father—women envy her and men are mesmerized by her. She has spent much time with Lance, learning the business, and has fallen in love with him. Although the flesh is weak, her conscience is troubled. She is the most adept and devoted of Phyllis' children but still has a vulnerable place in her heart for her mother.

Priscilla Penniless . . . Phyllis' younger sister—She's all things Phyllis is not—strong-willed, domineering organized, quick-minded, stern and POOR. Physically larger and stronger then Phyllis, she's had to work hard all her life, but all her hard work has been for one purpose . . . her son, Paul. She can't pamper him enough. Love for her sister is not exactly a close second to Paul, but strong just the same, and her desire to take care of Phyllis is paramount . . . but it is her way or the highway. She is jealous and suspicious of anyone or anything that might hurt her Phyllis.

Carlton Brenner . . . Frank's partner in the Stein-Brenner Plant and childhood best friend—Obsessed with money and power, Carl would do most anything to get more of it . . . and has. Outwardly, he is handsome and stylish with flash and flare. He's charming to the woman and a man's man to men. But inside there is a cruelty akin to Dorian Gray. Much of his business is in illegal drugs. He has no conscience and loves being top dog.

Willard Hemlock . . . Frank and Carl's college friend—Willard is smart like a fox. He has always leaned toward the quick, easy buck which wasn't usually gotten legally. He is an expert and successful con-man and manipulator, but can't hold a candle to Carl. He's tired of being under Carl's thumb and has put all his efforts and hopes into this séance. Think of Uriah Heap and you have Willard.

Dr. Arthur Hart . . . Family Doctor and close friend of the family—He's a most caring and devoted doctor and friend who's exceptionally concerned about Phyllis' health since Frank died. He's worried that he can't get her out of her depression and feels this séance may put her over the edge.

Lance Knight . . . Family and Business Lawyer—His life so far has been governed by fateful consequences causing him to make the wrong decisions for the right reasons. Now he's saddled with a wife he doesn't love, nor are they even compatible, and a dead-end job, although well compensated. When away from *his albatross* life, he steps into another world where he unleashes his male charisma and enjoys a life he once dreamed of. He could have that life with Francine . . . if only . . .

Madam Angelica . . . Medium Holding the Séance—Angel was married to Frank after college. Her free spirit took all the boredom it could take and they divorced rather bitterly. She left with their son, covering her tracks so well, Frank could not locate hide nor hair of her or the child. With her talent for distraction and suggestion, she excelled in the occult world as a mystic, fortune teller, card reader and eventually séance medium. Human nature fascinated her and she loved stringing along her "marks". Like Carl, she is two personalities: outwardly as a sere, she is cool, calm and completely collected, exuding trust and confidence, but inside she is ruthless. She has a soft spot—Hugo . . . Frank, Jr.—who she has brought up and indoctrinated into the *trade*.

Hugo Handy . . . The Madam's Bodyguard and Chauffeur and assistant wherever he is needed. In séances, he is usually the ghost. Hugo knows no other life except the carnie business and the life of a gypsy. He is a very quiet, unassuming young man devoted to his mother and her work. He would do anything, I repeat, anything, for his mother. One would mistake him for dimwitted but he is far from it. He has a photographic mind and can process what he sees with lightning speed and with the logic of Mr. Spock.

Conrad Diddit . . . Stein Family Butler—Conrad has learned his trade beside his father and grandfather before him. He has been breed like a champion racehorse and holds the distinction of champion in the butler hierarchy. Over the years serving as butler to the Steins, he has become not just a servant to Frank but closer than a brother. Honor, trust and loyalty is so deeply imbedded in his nature there is no possible chance of separation or breach. He will remain so until he dies.

Joe Phoenix . . . Bartender Hired for the Evening—In reality he is Frank N. Stein arisen like the phoenix from the ashes. As a bartender, he is efficient but a little playful and a bit audacious at certain times. As Frank, he is filled with hate and resentment toward both Carl, who left him to die in the fire he started, and Angelica, his lost wife now found. Transformed by cosmetic surgery, he enjoys his participation in the evening affair with unanimity and heart felt compassion for his family, but his overriding obsession and driving force is to execute Carl. And he has planned the evening, with the help of Conrad, to achieve that goal.

Inspector Cloque Jouseau . . . Police Homicide Inspector—Usually played by the Host because of the extended knowledge of the whole story picture. There are no guidelines for this character except to dig up all the pieces and lay out the facts, eventually coming to the only conclusion possible and uncovering the murderer. The personality is yours to create.

Frank's Spirit . . . Played by Hugo

SECONDARY KEY PLAYERS

Ralph Baldwin . . . Dominique's Current Husband—Ralph is a very low-keyed, quiet but confident in personality. He has simple tastes but is drawn to the bird with the broken wing . . . that is Dominique. He understands her and is devoted to easing her pain . . . with soft words or simply a gentle touch . . . almost like magic.

Helene Stein . . . Ruben's Wife—She is strong-willed, tenacious and devious. She's a woman on a mission. She is serious minded and totally focused on her objective, never wavering despite challenges and set-backs. She is determined to make Ruben head of the Company . . . not Francine.

Paul Penniless . . . Priscilla's Son and her only reason for living. Paul is spoiled and arrogant. The less effort he needs to expend to make a buck the better. He first learned the con game when he played it on his mother who believed all his stories and excuses and gave him whatever he desired. Consequently, he thinks the world is his oyster and everything is easy.

Lily Brenner . . . Carlton's Wife—She's a shell of a human being, literally terrified of everything. She shares this condition with Cassandra, and when together, they are *together*, almost like Siamese twins, with arms around each other's waist. They are a comfort to each other.

Amanda Hart . . . Arthur's Wife—A woman very comfortable in high society. She is high-energy and very caring, as the wife of a doctor should be. She misses her friend, Phyllis, sharing in all her benevolent activities and social functions and tries doggedly to re-enlist her attendance.

Florence Curtain . . . is Phyllis' personal live-in nurse. She is not happy in this job for one reason—Priscilla. They are constantly battling like lions over their territory. Florence is expert at what she does but all things considered about this assignment, she'd rather be in Brooklyn in the winter.

Holly Night . . . Lance's Wife—Holly is a woman desperately trying to hold onto to the love of her life. She is trying to reinvent herself to try to rekindle the romance of long ago. She is now in "panic mode" as she senses the situation is serious.

Chart 5

THE LIST OF PASSIVE CHARACTERS
and
THE LIST OF AUXILIARY CHARACTERS

LIST OF PASSIVE CHARACTERS
In order of suggested selection.

Calvin Booker . . . Company Controller—He's a nervous Don Knotts constantly in a state of worry, frustration and FEAR.

Bonnie Booker . . . Calvin's Wife—She's a former "exotic dancer" trying to be "My Fair Lady" but without Professor Higgins. She still dresses garishly and is loud and crass.

Prudence Pireet . . . Phyllis' Youngest Sister—She's a prim and proper school teacher usually found with her nose in a book. At present, she is in the throes of marital bliss, having just married a future U.S. Senator who shares all her interests. She's as excited as a schoolgirl on her first day of summer vacation.

Prentice Pireet . . . Prudence's Husband—Prentice is the catch of the season but considers himself the lucky one to find a partner so interesting and well read as to be the perfect marriage partner for his political aspirations. He's a Republican politician from a rich family . . . need I say more.

Cassandra Brenner . . . Carlton's Daughter & Christian's Twin Sister—Cassandra has been an abused child and is terrified of her father . . . and most anything else. You has found a kinship in Lily who is exactly like her. They are practically glued together.

Christian Brenner . . . Carlton's Son & Cassandra's Twin Brother—Christian is a playboy race car driver who relishes the adoration of his groupies. He is therefore full of audacity . . . much like his father but has no interest in what his father does.

Charity Svenson . . . Carlton's Youngest Daughter—Her mother died when she was a baby and Carl shipped her off to California to be raised by maternal grandparents; consequently, she is totally a "Valley Girl" and doesn't identify at all with her father and siblings.

Professor Sven Svenson . . . Charity's Husband—Sven is a son of a rich Swedish merchant. He believes power and influence lies in educating young minds, especially in the subject of theology.

LIST OF AUXILIARY CHARACTERS

Camille Leon . . . Phyllis' Maid or a Newspaper Reporter—Camille is a utility character usually played by the Hostess so she's in a position to control and guide the events of the play.

Tilly Toyler . . . Carlton's Secretary—The office gossip is the perfect person to have at a party where you want to keep the facts straight. She is a compulsive note taker and always carries a steno pad to take copious notes on everything.

Danny Dingo . . . Company Transit Director—Head of the local Teamsters, he thinks only of work and football. He's very uncomfortable at these socials, especially if he has to wear a "monkey suit."

Dottie Dingo . . . Danny's Wife—Dottie is a REAL BLOND with a figure worth showing off. Amazing how so little costs so much.

Wallace Wingate . . . Company Purchasing Manager—He's a good husband and a good worker . . . he has to be because he's "in it up to his chin" . . . the Mob! Winter is the daughter of a Don from Chicago and the company is a customer.

Winter Wingate . . . Wallace's Wife—Winter has been relatively sheltered from the "ugly" side of her family but the ties are still there. Mostly, she lives to party and dance. She's unhappy there will be no dancing at a séance.

Mikal Maestro . . . Symphony Conductor & Friend of the Family—His head is filled with music so not much room for other subjects. He's honest, loyal and a bit naive.

Martha Maestro . . . Mikal's Wife—A frazzled wife and mother who is now taking a little time for her own pleasures. Even after having seven children, she still has the composure of a true lady.

Felix Farnum . . . Neighbor—Typical good neighbor friends where you have seen not only the image they present to the public, but also the image on the other side of the door where your children play with their's.

Fanny Farnum . . . Neighbor's Wife—Down-to-earth lady who loves to laugh and tell jokes.

Chart 6

NEW
LAST WILL AND TESTAMENT
OF
PHYLLIS STEIN

OLD
LAST WILL AND TESTAMENT
OF
PHYLLIS STEIN

LAST WILL AND TESTAMENT
OF
FRANK N. STEIN, SR.

LAST WILL AND TESTAMENT
OF
PHYLLIS STEIN

I, PHYLLIS STEIN, residing at _____, situated in _____ County, in the State of _____, being of sound mind and memory, do make, publish and declare this to be my Last Will and Testament in manner following, that is to say:

FIRST: I direct that all my just debts and funeral expenses be paid.

SECOND: I direct that all estate, inheritance, transfer and death taxes and costs and expenses of administration of whatever kind and nature shall be paid out of my residuary estate as expenses of Administration, the laws of the State of _____ or of any other state or states to the contrary notwithstanding.

THIRD: In respect of my husband's wishes, I give, devise and bequeath to my faithful servant and butler, CONRAD DIDDIT, the property on Captiva Island consisting of a cottage on ten acres of beachfront property, absolutely and forever.

FOURTH: I give, devise and bequeath to my thoughtful sister, PRISCILLA PENNILESS, who I am deeply indebted to for her sacrifices and care she has bestowed upon me when my need was great, the sum of $500,000, absolutely and forever.

FIFTH: I give, devise and bequeath to my daughter, DOMINIQUE BALDWIN, the token sum of ONE DOLLAR, as her fortune from her father is more than sufficient to support her in style. In addition, I belatedly give her ALL MY LOVE which I failed so miserably to bestow on her over the years. For this oversight, I am deeply ashamed and honestly regret the years of love we have lost forever. I beg you to forgive me.

SIXTH: I give, devise and bequeath to my son, RUBEN STEIN, the token sum of ONE DOLLAR, in the fervent hope that having nothing will instill in him the necessary desire to make a success of himself as his father did before him. In addition, I have set up a College Trust Fund of $100,000 (to be used solely on education) in the hope he will return to school. Consider this, your parents will make no further demands of you so you are now free to be the person you chose to be. That is my legacy to you, my dear, sweet son.

SEVENTH: All the rest, residue and remainder of my property, real, personal and mixed of whatever nature and wheresoever situate, I give, devise and bequeath to my beloved daughter, FRANCINE STEIN, who has stood by me with understanding and love in my time of deepest turmoil. This bequest is absolute and irrevocable and a sign of my complete faith in her abilities to carry on the Family Empire begun by my dear departed husband, Frank.

LASTLY: I hereby appoint my lawyer, LANCE KNIGHT, as Executor of this my Last Will and Testament the requirement of bond and with full power and authority to sell and convey, lease or mortgage real estate, and hire and pay for the services of custodians and accountants, hereby revoking all former Wills by me made.

IN WITNESS WHEREOF, I have here unto subscribed by name the _____ day of _____, in the year _____.

_____
Phyllis Stein, Testatrix

AND WE WHOSE NAMES are hereto subscribed DO CERTIFY that on the _____ day of _____, _____, PHYLLIS STEIN, the Testatrix above named subscribed her name to this instrument in our presence and hearing declared the same to be her Last Will and Testament and requested us and each of us to sign our names thereto as witnesses to the execution thereof which we hereby do in the presence of the Testatrix and of each other on the day of the date of the said Will.

_____   _____

_____   _____

LAST WILL AND TESTAMENT
OF
PHYLLIS STEIN

I, PHYLLIS STEIN, residing at _____, situated in _____ County, in the State of _____, being of sound mind and memory, do make, publish and declare this to be my Last Will and Testament in manner following, that is to say:

FIRST: I direct that all my just debts and funeral expenses be paid.

SECOND: I direct that all estate, inheritance, transfer and death taxes and costs and expenses of administration of whatever kind and nature shall be paid out of my residuary estate as expenses of Administration, the laws of the State of _____ or of any other state or states to the contrary notwithstanding.

THIRD: In respect of my husband's wishes, I give, devise and bequeath to my faithful servant and butler, CONRAD DIDDIT, the property on Captiva Island consisting of a cottage on ten acres of beachfront property, absolutely and forever.

FOURTH: All the rest, residue and remainder of my property, real, personal and mixed of whatever nature and wheresoever situate, I give, devise and bequeath to my beloved husband, FRANK N. STEIN, SR., absolutely and forever.

FIFTH: And in the event that my said husband, FRANK N. STEIN, SR., should predecease me or in the event that we should die or pass away in such a manner as to render it difficult or impossible to determine which of us predeceased the other, or in the event that we should both perish away in a common catastrophe or happening, then and only in that or those events, I hereby give, devise and bequeath all of my property, real, personal and mixed of whatever nature and wheresoever situate to our children, DOMINIQUE DUMBELLI BALDWIN, RUBEN STEIN, and FRANCINE STEIN in equal shares, with representation per stirpes and not per capita.

LASTLY: I hereby appoint my lawyer, LANCE KNIGHT, as Executor of this my Last Will and Testament the requirement of bond and with full power and authority to sell and convey, lease or mortgage real estate, and hire and pay for the services of custodians and accountants, hereby revoking all former Wills by me made.

IN WITNESS WHEREOF, I have here unto subscribed by name the _____ day of _____, in the year _____.

_____
Phyllis Stein, Testatrix

AND WE WHOSE NAMES are hereto subscribed DO CERTIFY that on the _____ day of _____, _____, PHYLLIS STEIN, the Testatrix above named subscribed her name to this instrument in our presence and hearing declared the same to be her Last Will and Testament and requested us and each of us to sign our names thereto as witnesses to the execution thereof which we hereby do in the presence of the Testatrix and of each other on the day of the date of the said Will.

_____   _____

_____   _____

LAST WILL AND TESTAMENT
OF
FRANK N. STEIN, SR.

I, FRANK N. STEIN, SR., residing at _____, situated in _____ County, in the State of _____, being of sound mind and memory, do make, publish and declare this to be my Last Will and Testament in manner following, that is to say:

FIRST: I direct that all my just debts and funeral expenses be paid.

SECOND: I direct that all estate, inheritance, transfer and death taxes and costs and expenses of administration of whatever kind and nature shall be paid out of my residuary estate as expenses of Administration, the laws of the State of _____ or of any other state or states to the contrary notwithstanding.

THIRD: I give, devise and bequeath to my faithful and devoted servant and friend, my butler, CONRAD DIDDIT, the sum of $500,000 outright provided he remain and continue in the same aforementioned service of my wife, Phyllis Stein, if she has not predeceased me, following my death, that subsequently upon her death, and completely at her discretion, be given, devised and bequeathed the property on Captiva Island consisting of a cottage on ten acres of beachfront property, absolutely and forever. I also direct that he be given a pension of $10,000 a month, in addition to his normal salary, until his death.

FOURTH: It is my wish that my daughter, FRANCINE STEIN, be given control and responsibility of administering my half of the partnership in the Stein-Brenner Company in trust for my wife, PHYLLIS STEIN. I further charge that she should be recompensed for her efforts at a yearly salary of $250,000 plus a share in the year end bonuses.

FIFTH: I give devise and bequeath to FRANK N. STEIN, JR., my disunited son by my former wife, Angina Stein nee Pectoris, provided he is found and identified without a doubt, the sum of $1,000,000 absolutely and forever.

SIXTH: All the rest, residue and remainder of my property, real, personal and mixed of whatever nature and wheresoever situate, I give, devise and bequeath to my beloved wife, PHYLLIS STEIN, absolutely and forever.

SEVENTH: And in the event that my said wife, Phyllis Stein, should predecease me or in the event that we should die or pass away in such a manner as to render it difficult or impossible to determine which of us predeceased the other, or in the event that we should both perish away in a common catastrophe or happening, then and only in that or those events, I hereby give, devise and bequeath all of my property, real, personal and mixed of whatever nature and wheresoever situate to our children, DOMINIQUE DUMBELLI BALDWIN, RUBEN STEIN, and FRANCINE STEIN in equal shares, with representation per stirpes and not per capita.

LASTLY: I hereby appoint my lawyer, LANCE KNIGHT, as Executor of this my Last Will and Testament the requirement of bond and with full power and authority to sell and convey, lease or mortgage real estate, and hire and pay for the services of custodians and accountants, hereby revoking all former Wills by me made.

IN WITNESS WHEREOF, I have here unto subscribed by name the _____ day of _____, in the year _____.

_____
Frank N. Stein, Sr., Testator

AND WE WHOSE NAMES are hereto subscribed DO CERTIFY that on the _____ day of _____, _____, FRANK N. STEIN, SR., the Testator above named subscribed his name to this instrument in our presence and hearing declared the same to be his Last Will and Testament and requested us and each of us to sign our names thereto as witnesses to the execution thereof which we hereby do in the presence of the Testator and of each other on the day of the date of the said Will.

_____   _____

_____   _____

Chart 7

SEATING ARRANGEMENT FOR THE SÉANCE

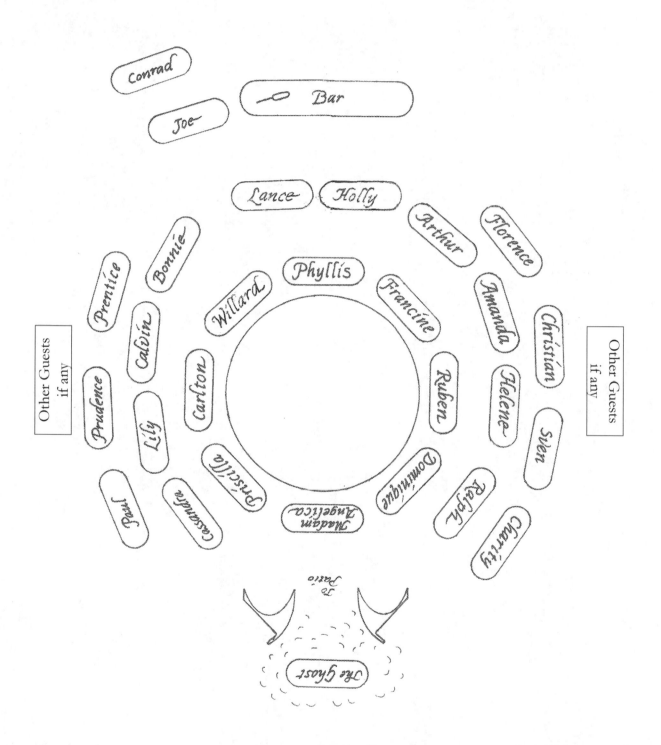

THE GHOST SPEAKS

THE GHOST SPEAKS

Madam Angelica does "her thing" to call the spirit of Frank N. Stein. At the proper signal the "ghost" should appear in a white hooded robe with a white skeletal mask (or something close . . . use your creativity). For a great effect, rent a smog machine so the ghost's entrance can be accompanied by clouds of eerie mist. A low watt backlight will enhance this effect. Try experimenting beforehand to see what works best in your environment.

Ghost should try to talk very low, slow and throaty to assimilate eeriness. It is suggested the ghost's speech be recorded with gaps for responses, and then played back during the ghost encounter. Experiment on various voice sounds to find the most eerie and ghost-like.

FRANK: Yes . . . I am Frank N. Stein . . . who calls me?

MADAM ANGELICA: Your wife, Phyllis, calls you.

FRANK: Phyllis . . . my dear beloved Phyllis . . . is that you?

PHYLLIS: Frank . . . oh, my dear Frank . . . I knew you would come to me.

FRANK: What is it you wish of me?

PHYLLIS: Frank . . . I've missed you so much . . . I'm lost without you. What shall I do? I need you to tell me what to do.

FRANK: Phyllis, my love . . . soon we shall be together . . . for eternity.

(Phyllis intakes her breath)

But first . . . I have a request of you . . .

PHYLLIS: Anything, Frank. You know I would do anything.

FRANK: Before I departed the world of the flesh . . . my dear friend, Willard, and I were on the verge of a great discovery. A discovery of monumental importance to humanity. It was my intent to invest my entire personal fortune into the development of this miracle . . . a miracle that could save millions of lives and human suffering. But alas, I left the mortal world too soon.

You, Phyllis, must fulfill my promise to mankind.

What are worldly riches when compared to eternal paradise?

PHYLLIS: Yes, Frank . . . yes?

FRANK: You ask me to tell you what you are to do?

Leave your fortunes to my dear, trusted friend, Willard Hemlock, so that he may continue our work to ease the suffering of humanity.

PHYLLIS: Yes, Frank . . . anything you say, Frank. Lance is here . . . I'll change my Will immediately . . . tonight!

FRANK: At last . . . I will rest in peace. Come to me soon, Phyllis . . . I am waiting for you . . . .

PHYLLIS: Wait . . . Frank . . . I love you . . . Frank . . . Frank . . . Wait!

Frank . . . don't go . . . Frank . . . . *start sobbing.*

FRANK: *As he leaves, backing away . . .*

Goodbye, my love . . . . goodbye . . . . g o o d b y e . . . .
fade out.

THE INTERROGATION

THE INTERROGATION

It is suggested you read the chapters in the story dealing with *The Interrogation* and the *Murderer Revealed* in order to get a sense of what information is expected to be revealed and the timing of certain revelations. Be forewarned, it is not always easy to extract information form the characters. Sometimes, they forget and other times they want to draw out their part. Or they may simply think the Inspector should work for his dollar.

The Inspector (you) enters the salon, having been called by Conrad, and introduces himself and asks to see the murder victim. You make notes, take measurements and pictures of the body, séance table and anything else you feel could be evidence, like the gun on the floor. If possible, you can have the body moved to a sofa for comfort, after you have finished taking pictures and measurements

Make sure you let everyone know you would like them to volunteer anything they saw or heard that they think may shed some light on the murder and shooting tonight.

Also, if it is the wish of the host/hostess, you might announce that there will be a chance for the guests to pick who they think did the murder.

Establish the cause of death was from a stab to the heart from an ice pick. Dr. Hart can provide that information.

Establish that the ice pick has been verified as being on the bar all evening, at least up to minutes before the seance.

Inquire of Dr. Hart the condition of the other injuries that occurred during lights out.

Establish the ice pick was on the bar all evening.

Ask everyone to take their original places at the beginning of he Séance.

Ask if someone can explain the reason for the Séance and what lead up to the Séance. This information can come from several people either voluntarily or you can ask someone you specifically choose. Try: Francine, Priscilla, Dr. Hart, Nurse Florence, Amanda Hart.

Ask someone to tell you exactly what happened during the Séance, missing nothing. If you want more information, keep asking various people the same questions to get their view point. Make certain someone mentions the lights going out, gunshot, scream, thud and scuffling sounds.

Ask about the fire at the plant last year and if Carl has replaced the position held by Frank. Question his profit margin without new products this past year.

Direct financial questions to Calvin, digging into how the profits are up with no new products on the market. Get him rattled.

Ask Willard why he quit the company and if his position has been replaced.

Ask if there was anything unusual that happened before the Séance.

> Ruben came in drunk and disrupted the party and made Phyllis angry.
> Charity introduced her new husband, Sven.
> Prudence introduced her new husband, Prentice.
> Phyllis signed an updated Will with the Harts as witnesses.

Someone might have seen some packets of "white stuff" change hands.

Ask Lance to produce the Will. He produces three Wills—Frank's Will; Phyllis' Old Will; Phyllis' Updated Will that was signed earlier this evening.

It may help to read the "guts" of each Will beginning with Frank's, then Phyllis' old Will and then her new Will. Especially the sentiments written about Dominique and Ruben.

Establish the following about the Wills:

Frank bequeathed Conrad $500,000 and $10,000 a month pension in addition to salary providing he continues to serve Phyllis and to Frank Jr. the sum of $1,000,000 if he can be found and verified. Plus, Francine is installed as caretaker of partnership with a salary of $250,000 a year plus bonuses. Rest goes to Phyllis; Phyllis' Old Will bequeaths everything to Frank and then to be divided among Dominique, Ruben and Francine if Frank predeceases her; Phyllis' New Will bequeaths Conrad property and a cottage on the beach, Priscilla gets $500,000, Dominique gets $1, Ruben gets $1 and Francine gets balance.

Question each person mentioned in the Wills - if they knew of the contents of the Wills and what are their thoughts. Especially point out Priscilla's inheritance and Paul having access to it.

Refer back to the Séance, asking specifically what the ghost said . . . the Ghost stated he wanted Phyllis to change her Will and leave all her money to Willard. How is it Angelica would ask Phyllis to do this? What is the relationship between Angelica and Willard.

This is the time to pressure them to talk and tell their stories.

Pursue Willard and Angelica to make a full confession. Willard telling his part in the fire . . . that he stole one of Frank's formulas . . . and that was the idea behind the séance. They knew each other in college. Angelica confesses to being Frank's first wife and Hugo is his son . . . and should get the $1,000,000.

Frank rises out of the ashes. Encourage his story. Now, Frank, Jr. (Hugo) doesn't get the $1,000,000 because Frank is not dead so the Will is not in play.

Ask Frank (Joe Phoenix) how he managed to escape the fire and what exactly happened that fateful night. He draws in Carl and the drug trade, and his part in the fire.

Make sure Joe/Frank uncovers his intent to shoot and kill Carl but a bump threw his aim off and the bullet hit Hugo.

Ask Calvin what his part in all this is. Surely as Controller, he knew what was going on.

Willard, Ruben and Paul are also implicated in drugs.

Make use of your notebook and appear to take copious notes.

Take one more stab (no pun intended) and ask if there is any other information that anyone has seen or heard or knows of that they would like to share.

You could go from one to the other of the guests that have said nothing so far just to get them to talk and feel involved.

After all discussions have concluded, state that you will retire to the hall and review your notes. In the meantime, all guests may fill out a ballot and write down who they think the murderer is and the motive.

Remind everyone that three things must be satisfied:

ACCESS TO THE MURDER WEAPON

OPPORTUNITY

MOTIVE

Allow about fifteen minutes before collecting the ballots and then go on to *THE MURDERER REVEALED* by following the *ANATOMY OF THE MURDER.*

MURDERER REVEALED

via

ANATOMY OF THE MURDER.

THE MURDERER REVEALED
via
THE ANATOMY OF THE MURDER

With the ballots collected, sorted and with correct answers (if any) in hand, you are ready to show the process of discovering the murderer. First, if there are any future sleuths among the guests who have selected the right answer, you might mention that at least one person has correctly deduced the murderer; or if none have done so (which I can't imagine that being the case because I expect everyone to guess correctly), then announce that if you depended on them to catch the murderer, the murderer would go free.

So, begin with the three conditions the murderer needs to commit a murder:

ACCESS TO THE MURDER WEAPON
OPPORTUNITY
MOTIVE

The murder weapon was identified as an ice pick, specifically, the ice pick that was on the bar, and used by the bartender during the evening. It was there on the bar shortly before the Séance but exactly when it was taken, it is not clear. Being there on the bar, it can be assumed that everyone had *access to the murder weapon* before the Séance.

When the room was thrown into darkness, this condition gave the killer the *opportunity* to commit the crime cloaked in anonymity. Everyone was cloaked in darkness, but does that mean everyone had the *opportunity*?

That brings us to *motive*. Let's examine who would benefit from Phyllis' death. We have read all the Wills but we need only concern ourselves with Phyllis' Wills. In the old Will, all three children would benefit equally if father Frank was dead; but, as we learned, he is not dead. However, at the time, they didn't know that. Frank would have known about the old Will because they were drawn up together. But he might not have known about the new Will in which he is not mentioned because he was thought deceased.

Conrad had inherited a great deal in Frank's Will but Frank returned two weeks ago so Conrad would have been aware his inheritance was null and void. But in Phyllis' Wills, old and new, he was to inherit expensive beach front property.

In Phyllis' new Will, Conrad still gets the property, Dominique and Ruben both get only one dollar, Priscilla gets $500,000, but Francine gets the bulk of the estate.

So that leaves the following with something to gain by one or the other Will that was in effect:

Frank
Conrad
Dominique
Ralph (indirectly)
Ruben
Helene (indirectly)
Francine
Priscilla
Paul (indirectly)

It was Willard, Angelica and Hugo's object to get Phyllis to change her Will to leave her estate to Willard but that was not allowed to happen. Someone did not want the Will changed and/or Willard to get the Stein fortune. Willard is not very well liked, a fact evident in interviews. The list below are those with some grudge against Willard:

Frank
Carlton
Ruben
Helene
Francine
Priscilla
Paul

Consider the fact that until it was made known in the Séance that Phyllis intended to change her Will in favor of Willard, there would be no reason to kill Phyllis to keep Willard from benefiting so no *motive* would exist for that reason BEFORE the Séance so there would be no reason to take the weapon before the Seance.

If someone wanted to kill Phyllis to inherit from the old or new Wills, the weapon was there to take, but only Conrad and Frank knew the lights would go out and provide the darkness for the *opportunity*.

Conrad was busy with the lights, so, although he had motive and access to the murder weapon, he did not have opportunity.

Frank, by his own admission, was discharging a gun with the intent to kill Carl, so, although he had access to the murder weapon and knew he would have opportunity, he had no real reason to kill Phyllis. If he wanted to kill Willard, he would have simply tried to shoot him as he tried to shoot Carl, after all, Willard was closer and presented an easier target.

So, since only Conrad and Frank knew the opportunity would present itself, and they were otherwise occupied, no one would have taken the ice pick off the bar UNTIL they knew there was OPPORTUNITY. Someone took the weapon AFTER the lights went out and killed Phyllis.

Since this was then a spontaneous decision, it is concluded that the murderer was someone who had no motive until the Séance, had no opportunity until the lights went out, and had no need for the murder weapon until the opportunity presented itself.

From the lists above, we can eliminate Conrad and Frank as being preoccupied, Francine, Ruben, Helene, Dominique, Ralph, Carlton, Priscilla and Paul as being too far away to negotiate the retrieval of the weapon, accomplish the murder and return to their seat in the short space of time the darkness gave opportunity.

There is only one person who knew who was to inherit Phyllis' fortune, who did not want the Will changed, had time to retrieve the weapon, but in doing so, bumped into Frank causing him to miss his target, and then plunge the weapon into Phyllis' heart and return to his seat. One person who did not want Francine to lose her fortune because his plan was to make it his fortune by marrying her.

Lance Knight . . .   YOU could take advantage of the OPPORTUNITY
YOU are close enough to acquire the MURDER WEAPON
YOU are in a position to make contact with Frank.
YOU were close enough to Phyllis to commit the deed.
YOU and only you knew the contents of the new Will
YOU had been spending excessive time with Francine, more than necessary for the purpose of indoctrinating her into the company, that would suggest a closer relationship which gives you MOTIVE

LANCE KNIGHT, I HEREBY ARREST YOU FOR THE MURDER OF PHYLLIS STEIN.

ADDENDUM

"In addition, there will be enough room in the Paddy Wagon for the following people, who need to answer some serious questions at the police station. All of you are advise to keep silent until you can contact your attorney (I suggest someone other than Lance Knight). If you do not have an attorney, one will be appointed for you."

FRANCINE STEIN – ADULTERY

RUBEN STEIN – POSSESSION & SALE OF ILLEGAL DRUGS

PAUL PENNILESS – POSSESSION OF ILLEGAL DRUGS

CARLTON BRENNER – ARSON
               INSURANCE FRAUD
               ATTEMPTED MURDER
               TRAFFICKING IN ILLEGAL DRUGS
               SPOUSAL ABUSE
               CHILD ABUSE
               RACKETEERING

CALVIN BOOKER – EMBEZZLEMENT
               MONEY LAUNDERING

WILLARD HEMLOCK – THEFT
               ATTEMPTED EXTORTION
               DRUG TRAFFICKING

MADAM ANGELICA – EXTORTION & FRAUD

HUGO HANDY – EXTORTION & FRAUD

CONRAD DIDDIT – ACCOMPLICE TO ATTEMPTED MURDER

JOE PHOENIX – ATTEMPTED MURDER
                    CARRYING A CONCEALED WEAPON

PERHAPS YOU CAN FIND MORE . . .

Hope you have FUN
with the play and everyone gives
a STAR performance!

The REAL
END